I0781044

an alpha's blood

an alpha's blood

the alpha king book 1

Tori King

WordCrafts Press

An Alpha's Blood is a work of fiction. All references to persons, places, or events are fictitious or used fictitiously.

Hardback ISBN: 978-1-962218-85-6
Paperback ISBN: 978-1-962218-86-3

An Alpha's Blood
Copyright © 2024
Tori King

All rights reserved. No part of this book may be reproduced, stored in a retrieval system, or transmitted in any form or by any means—electronic, mechanical, photocopy, recording or otherwise—without the prior written permission of the publisher. The only exception is brief quotations for review purposes.

Published by WordCrafts Press
Cody, Wyoming 82414
www.wordcrafts.net

To my husband, Damian,
my parents, Russell and Susan,
my sisters, Hayley and Kamryn,
and all my family and friends.

Thank you for all the support, encouragement, and for
believing in me when I couldn't believe in myself. I
wouldn't be here today without you.

In Loving Memory of
Van and Sandra Peterson

knight of change

The hunting party of ten left early on a bone-chilling winter's day. Angry, gray clouds hung low and heavy in the sky. A violent contrast against the snow-covered ground.

My gut told me not to go with them, but our town was slowly being terrorized. There was no other option but to leave the safety of the walls and figure out how to stop what was happening. To protect those I cared about.

"Let's move," Alaric shouted from the gate, "so we can be back before dark."

The old, but sturdy gate stood open behind Alaric, a blond-haired, blue-eyed man. He was head of the council that lead our village. He was roughly in his fifties, and fit, but not overly muscular like some of the men in our party.

Men on the watch towers looked out over the walls in a feeble attempt to provide security and prevent any incidents from happening or to protect villagers when threats got to close. Lately, they have been unsuccessful.

This is why I was going out with the party to hunt for the wolves terrorizing our village. The farms outside the wall were the first targeted. We hoped to attack the source and prevent the death toll from rising. However, we could have chosen a better time than during the start of a blizzard.

After we were through the gates, they closed with a tired

groan and crashed loudly as they fell into place. I glanced back and saw the men standing atop watching us with fear. Who knew if any of us would make it back? Or if we did, would we be alive?

I sighed and turned my gaze to sweeping the horizon, alert for any sound or movement. Squinting against the blinding landscape, I slung my bow over my shoulder as we trudged through the calf-deep snow, and my hands patted my hips to make sure my knives were in place. I wore an old set of skirts over my trousers for extra warmth, and as of right now, they were not making a difference.

I pulled my cloak tighter and fell into step next to Remus, my adoptive father and well-known mercenary. His salt-and-pepper hair, which looked more white as snow accumulated in it, was pulled back at the nape of his neck. His short black beard only accentuated his square jaw. His brown eyes were as sharp and cunning as any blade. He was fit and muscular from all of his time as an assassin.

"Are you sure you want to be out here?" he asked me.

"Someone has to help you protect this town," I replied with a smirk. "Because you know the rest of these men don't pull much weight."

He chuckled, the wind whipping his amusement away from us. "Mira Brianne, I'm more worried because your father is here than because you are going out hunting for monsters."

"I know," I replied as my eyes stopped scanning the horizon and settled on the back of the man I was related to. "I am old enough to protect myself now."

"I do not doubt that," he replied. "You had a great teacher."

I just grinned at him. He and his wife saved me from my father. He had tried to sell me to the local brothel when I turned eleven. Needless to say, I became their adopted child, and my training to become a *virago*, or warrior of the people, began.

That was fifteen years ago.

Now, I am just as well-known and sought after for my talents as Remus. Maybe even more so.

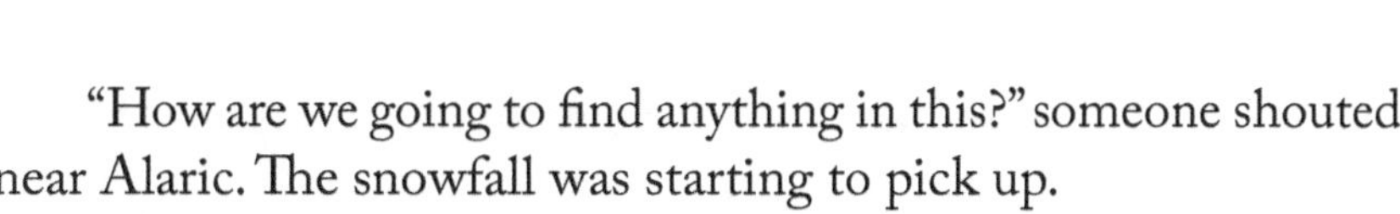

"How are we going to find anything in this?" someone shouted near Alaric. The snowfall was starting to pick up.

"We will do our best," Alaric replied.

I rolled my eyes in agitation. He was always quick to action, but not to plan.

Since Alaric was on the town council, his word was one to follow. That did not always mean it was the right or the smart choice. This would not be the first time he led a hunting party where not all returned—though it was still to be decided if he was at fault for those incidents.

Silence enveloped us as we continued our trek. We stopped briefly for lunch a few hours later, each of us snacking on dried meat and bread.

The wind whipped our cloaks around, mirroring the swirling pattern of snowflakes. I shivered as the cold pierced every inch of my being. Needlelike tendrils found their way into every crevice of warmth.

"We should head back soon," Remus told Alaric. "If these conditions get worse, we won't be able to find our way back until it calms."

Alaric seemed hesitant to agree, and upset when he did.

He knew that all of our lives were in his hands. And despite wanting to track the wolves, he knew the village stood no chance against them if none of us returned.

The sky darkened to the color of midnight as we moved on, the wind whipping around us and bringing more snow with it. Even with my senses on high alert, it was going to be difficult to find anything in this weather.

I fell back, letting my eyes drift from the horizon to the snow-covered ground. Attempting to ignore the cold dampness of my skirts and cloak.

I heard a faint howl in the distance and froze. I glanced around, my hand on my bow, ready if anything lunged at me. I could tell no one else had heard anything as they kept on.

Silence. I could barely see the rest of the group as I began forward again.

Pain lanced suddenly from my left ear and the back of my head. I stumbled and fell, turning to look at who or what might have attacked me. My father stood over me with his rifle. My eyes narrowed as I tried to fight off the wave of unconsciousness.

"You should have stayed in town," he hissed down at me. while raising his rifle in preparation to strike again.

"Morris! Mira!" The group was shouting for us.

He looked up and then just left me. I fell back into the snow. I lifted a heavy hand to the side of my head, and it came back warm and sticky. My eyelids fluttered closed as I wondered what twisted story my father would tell the group.

I was warm, but cold. Dampness clung to my body with an icy grip. I could hear the wind screaming around me and opened my eyes. I was still laying in the snow, but something large and warm was curled around me. I groaned and sat up, swaying as dizziness washed over me.

I gasped as my eyes met those of a large, black wolf. Warm golden-brown eyes stared back at me without blinking. He was curled against me, shielding me from the brunt of the wind.

A howl pierced the air, and I jumped up, bow in hand as my eyes scanned the darkness around me. The pain in my head was excruciating and pounded in time with my heart. It took all I had to keep my footing.

The wind swirled around us in strong gusts. Ice and snow blotted everything out, making the already darkening gray sky that much darker.

The wolf also stood up and pressed close to me. It was almost as if he was supporting me as I swayed. My shoulder barely reached his back. As he glanced back at me, I blinked rapidly to clear my blurring vision. His hair stood on end, but I did not feel threatened by him.

A smaller gray wolf appeared out of nowhere and attacked. I fell back into the snow as snarls whispered to me on the wind. I could barely see them—they appeared as black shadows against the blue-gray of swirling snowflakes, but I nocked an arrow and let it fly.

It found its mark in the shoulder of the gray wolf, in turn making me its next target. I dropped my bow and pulled out a knife as it lunged for me.

Claws ripped into my left side as I swung my blade up and into the wolf's neck. I cried out in pain, and with another quick move, I pulled out another knife and rammed it into the wolf's eye as it swung its head to bite me. It howled and leaped back. This gave the black wolf enough of a distraction to dive in for the kill.

I staggered toward the dead wolf and retrieved my knives and bow. I felt unconsciousness creeping back in. I felt like I was being watched. I tried to blink the blurriness and spots from my eyes as I turned to the wolf, swaying with dizziness.

"Why didn't you kill me?" I asked the black wolf as it continued to stare at me. Then it crouched down and made a gesture with its head toward its back.

"What," I asked? It gestured again more urgently. "You want me to climb on your back?"

Its head dipped in a nod.

I needed to get somewhere to patch up my wounds. My hand pressed to my side, and I hissed at the hot, stabbing pain. The black wolf stepped closer and gestured again. *I guess help from a wolf is better than none. Better than to die of bloodloss or cold.*

"Very well," I said.

I stumbled forward, and it leaped up to keep me from falling. My hands sunk into its soft fur, and I closed my eyes as I leaned against its side. I took a deep breath, trying to remain conscious long enough to gather my strength. I pulled myself into a seated position on its back. Despite my clenched jaw, I groaned against the flaming pain in my side and blinked my tears away.

Once I was settled, the wolf took off. I clung tightly to its fur as blackness settled over me.

I must have passed out from pain and blood loss, because the next thing I knew, I was lying on a pile of furs in front of a fire. My wounds were bandaged. I could feel the pain throbbing against the tightly wrapped fabric and in time with my heart. Pain pounded inside my skull like a blacksmith's mallet on a sword.

I stared at the fire in front of me. I knew I was no longer outside, which was nice, but alarming, since I had no idea where I was. I rolled onto my back and hissed at the fiery pain that lanced down my left side and added to the pounding in my head.

"Good, you're awake," a deep male voice said.

I turned slowly toward the voice and looked at the man sitting in a chair not too far from me. His chest was bare, and I could see fresh scars on his chest and shoulder.

But it was his eyes that drew me in. Golden-brown and watchful. Guarded. There was an undescribable and instant attraction to him. As if time stood still, and no one else existed.

I blinked slowly as I replayed the events and slowly absorbed what had happened.

"You're the wolf that saved me," I whispered.

He raised an eyebrow and smirked.

"How is that possible?"

"Brave and smart. But why were you out in this blizzard in the first place?"

"I was with a group," I started and sat up quickly, my head spinning from the sudden movement. "Do you know where they went?"

"Careful, you need to keep still," he said. "I saw a hunting group, but could not tell you where they went. Why were you with them?"

"We were hunting the wolves that have been attacking our town."

He seemed surprised by my statement. "If that's the case, then why were you left behind?"

I flinched as the memory came back, and I gritted my teeth with a sound somewhere between a hiss and a growl. This only made my head hurt worse, and I turned to glare into the fire. The man seemed more curious as to why I was in the blizzard than why I was not afraid of him.

"What is it?" he asked.

"My father attacked me and left me for dead," I almost growled. He startled me with a low, deep growl of his own, and I turned to him.

"Your father did this!?" he hissed in bewilderment.

"Welcome to my life," I confirmed.

I gingerly reached up and touched the welt on my head. I guess he had bandaged that too when I felt soft cloth under my fingertips. "I knew I shouldn't have gone with the hunting party." My head kept swimming, and I laid back down, my eyes on the ceiling.

"Why would he do such a thing?"

"Why would a father try to sell his daughter when she turns eleven? I do not have an answer for you, mister wolf."

"Kieran," he replied cautiously.

I turned my head slightly so I could look at him. "It's nice to meet you, Kieran. I'm Mira."

Chapter two

It felt like hours that I lay there, and he stared at me. The fire was making me too warm, and I slowly sat back up. I was never one to sit still for too long.

"You need rest, Mira."

His voice washed over me, and I paused to stare at him.

"Why did you save me?"

Our eyes met, green on golden-brown, and that magnetic attraction increased tenfold. He blinked and looked away.

"Something drew me to you. But I consider all debts paid with how you handled yourself with that other werewolf."

"Werewolf? Is that what has been attacking my village?"

He nodded. "They aren't just attacking your village."

"How is that even possible?" I pulled the blanket off and stood up slowly.

He stood and walked to me. I was only in an oversized tunic and my underwear. I could feel a blush creep across my cheeks as he held out a hand to help me. I ignored the shocks of electricity that ran up my arm. I had not realized how tall he was until now. He easily towered over my average five-foot-seven height. I would guess six-foot-three at the shortest.

"That is a long story," he said as he helped me to the chair next to his.

"By the sound of the howling wind, I'm sure we have time."

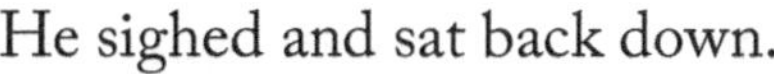

He sighed and sat back down.

"Werewolves have been around since the beginning, just as humans have. We kept ourselves a secret to prevent war and to secure our safety."

"That doesn't explain why the attacks are starting now."

He smiled despite the darkness in his eyes.

"You are different," he stated. "You don't scare easily, and you step up to challenges."

He stared at me, and I remained silent, locked in his gaze. He ran a hand through his shaggy black hair and sighed. I took in his sharp features, the way his hair fell into his eyes and his strong jaw as it clenched. He was muscular, and power radiated off him in waves.

"I don't know why wolves are going rogue and attacking. All I know is the clans are wary and have been trying to help defend the human villages in their territories."

"And *my* village is in *your* territory." It wasn't a question, but a statement.

He nodded.

"And who are you to your clan? What kind of hierarchy do wolves have?"

"As of right now, I am not willing to share where I fall in the ranks," Kieran replied.

I began to protest.

"In due time, Mira. The general hierarchy of wolves falls under a leader, or Alpha, with a second in command."

"And what is the Alpha doing to help us?" I asked. My question sounded harsher than I meant for it to, but he nodded all the same.

"He is running patrols, while his second remains at the compound. I believe he is trying to understand what is drawing rogues to attack."

I pursed my lips and stared him down. "Something tells me you are trying to hide the fact that you are someone of authority."

His eyes widened ever so slightly and I smirked.

"I am good at discerning truth from lies, or from someone who tiptoes around the truth by giving just enough information."

"Who are you then?" he shot back at me, crossing his arms over his bare chest. I must have hit a nerve.

"I am a *virago*. A sword for those who need it. I work for hire when needed and travel sometimes." I paused and looked up at him. He remained silent but kept his gaze trained on me.

"I have always been different—that's part of the reason my father wanted to sell me; that, and he is a greedy man." I shrugged. "I have no qualms sharing my history with you. But I expect some return from it."

"What kind of return?" he asked tightly.

I noticed him trembling. I stood and walked slowly to him. "Why are you angry?" I knelt next to his chair and rested a hand on his forearm. The tremors stopped under my touch, and he looked down at me.

"Because of what your father has done to you," he breathed. "It makes me want to kill him, and I don't know why."

"You can't kill him if I beat you to it," I replied softly. "I appreciate your concern though."

I stood back up, and he grabbed my hand as I turned away. Warmth and electricity radiated up my arm. I turned back to him, my gaze finding his now dark brown eyes. *I could get lost in those eyes.*

"Why haven't you before now?"

"After I left to begin training I didn't have a reason to. And at the time I was too young to even think about it. I was too afraid," I admitted.

"And you're not afraid now?" he pressed.

"Not anymore," I said shaking my head and instantly regretting it as a wave of dizziness washed over me. His hand tightened on me as I swayed.

"You need rest," he repeated softly.

"You don't by chance have anything for pain?" I laughed as I pulled away and went back to lay down. Stabs of pain radiated through my head and side—sharper now that we were no longer touching.

"Unfortunately, no. I'm not used to having someone that heals slower than me around," he said with a sad smile.

"It's alright," I hissed as I positioned myself less painfully. "I figured with the fresh-looking scars on you that you healed at a decent rate."

"You are quite observant," Kieran replied in surprise.

"I've have to be," I mumbled as I felt sleep begin to cloud my head. "It's saved me once or twice."

kieran

She laid back down, and I watched her drift quickly to sleep. She finally looked peaceful. She no longer seemed to carry the weight of the world on her shoulders.

I could tell her pale face was flushed even in the dim light, and I watched a small shiver wrack her frame. I would need to check her wounds when she woke up.

What puzzled me the most, is that she had the faintest scent of a wolf on her. And I had watched her eyes glow with a brighter green intensity. A glow that only wolves had. The first time was when she helped me fight off the gray wolf—the others were during our conversation.

Then on top of everything, this draw I had toward her.

I knew wolves had prophecy mates. And after two centuries of being king, I had yet to find mine. Yet here we sat, safe in my house, and the attraction was undeniable.

The faint metallic smell of blood mixed with her scent had drawn me to her. I had been tracking a group of rogues beforehand and got sidetracked.

Her hiss of pain brought me out of my thoughts, and I looked from the fire to her. She was still asleep. I wanted to rip everyone in that hunting party to shreds for leaving her stranded in this blizzard. Her father would pay for what he did to her. I silently vowed to make him pay.

A howl off in the distance had me on my feet and by the door. These rogues were exhausting, and they seemed to keep growing in numbers.

"This damn blizzard," I mumbled as I stared into the darkness. Mira had been asleep for an entire day, and the snow looked as though it had no intention of letting up anytime soon. I just hoped I could get her back to her village alive and well.

"Kieran…" I heard her mumble in her sleep. I turned and looked at her sleeping form.

I wondered what she dreamt about for her to say my name. Her stomach growled as well. I knew I would have to figure out what to fix for her to eat, and it looked like I needed to do that before she woke up again.

Mira

I woke to a savory scent. Inhaling deeply before opening my eyes. When I did I saw Kieran standing next to a pot over the fire. His black hair fell once more into his eyes. I watched the fire glance off the sharp angles of his facial features and highlight the planes of his muscular body.

My left side burned and ached. And I had a headache that held my head in a vice grip.

"How long have I been asleep?" I asked as my stomach growled, no longer able to stare at him in secret.

"Today is day two. You were unconscious for an entire day," he replied without looking at me.

"Therefore three days since I have been missing. No chance in me going back to my village yet then?" I felt feverish and shivered under the blankets.

"Not until the blizzard passes," Kieran replied, finally looking at me. "I'll make sure you get back safely, but until then you need to rest and regain your strength."

"You sound just like Remus," I retorted.

"Who?"

"The man who saved me from my father and trained me to be who I am. He and his wife, Selena, are the only family I will fight for."

"He is wise. You cannot continue fighting if you run yourself into the ground."

"I just want to know that he made it back safely and to let him know that I am safe." I stared at the ceiling, tracing the lines in the woodwork with my eyes. "Do you have anyone back home that you would die for?"

"I have my parents and my pack. As for anyone else, I do not."

I rolled onto my right side and looked at him. "Are you lonely?"

"Not usually," he replied as he stirred what was in the pot once more before divvying out two bowls. "Time to eat. I know you must be starving. Then I'll need to check your bandages and apply clean ones." He sat the two bowls he filled on the hearth and came over to help me sit up.

Once again, electricity shot through me as his hands hovered near for assistance. I felt feverish, and everything ached, but the worst seemed to ease when we touched. Sitting upright felt like a challenge.

Once I was seated, he retrieved the bowls, handed me one, and sat down across from me. I inhaled deeply and frowned.

"Where did you find the rabbit to make this?" I asked. Kieran paused with his spoon halfway to his mouth and looked from me to the simmering pot.

"I went hunting while you were sleeping. You need to eat so you can heal."

"But what if something had happened to you?" I demanded, my voice louder than it should have been. "You shouldn't be out there alone in this weather either."

"I'm sorry for making you worry, but I only went out with the thought of helping you get better," he replied with a small smile. He took a bite of soup, not the least bit bothered by my outburst.

"You should have at least taken me with you," I mumbled as I followed his lead and scooped a spoonful into my mouth. He shook his head and glared at me.

"You are in no condition to be out there at all right now," he hissed protectively.

"You can't keep me here forever," I joked, attempting to lighten the mood as we continued to eat.

The soup was just what I needed. It warmed me from the inside out and helped me regain some energy, though I was still tired.

"I'm not trying to keep you here forever, Mira. I'm trying to keep you alive, so I can get you back to your village in mostly one piece."

My eyes met his, and we stared at each other. Why wasn't I afraid of him? More importantly, why did being around him make me feel safe? Why did he want to protect me? And who was he?

"Why did you save me, Kieran?" I stared at him and held my bowl tightly, the wood smooth beneath my palms.

"Because I thought you were one of my wolves," he replied quietly. "I know it's not my place to ask, but do you know who your mother is or was?"

I stared at him in surprise. "My father said she died in childbirth, so I have no idea who she was. Why does that matter? And why would you think I was a wolf?"

"Because you have the scent of a wolf, so your mother must have been a wolf—or part wolf—and passed that gene onto you."

My brain reeled, and I set my empty bowl down. "How…" I fumbled for the words to ask.

It felt as though my face had paled. My head swam, and it was not only from the information he shared. Something was wrong; something that had to do with my fever. My eyes felt heavy and blurry. I felt my heart rate increase.

"Are you okay?" he asked, worried.

"I feel dizzy and disoriented," I mumbled. He was kneeling next to me almost instantly.

"You move so fast," I murmured in surprise as I reached for him to ground myself. His skin felt oddly cold under my hands. Soothing.

"You are burning up," his eyes scanned my face as he pressed the back of his hand to my cheek. "I need to check your wounds. Now."

"M'kay," I whispered as he helped me lay back down on my right side.

He gently lifted the top I was wearing up to my shoulder, being careful to keep my chest covered, attempting to maintain whatever modesty remained. His hands felt cool against my skin as I shivered in the open air. I felt gentle tugging as he pulled the bandages off, along with stabs of pain when the bandages tugged at my wounds.

The instant cold air was a relief to my wounds, but I still shivered. My eyes fluttered closed as my head spun. Nausea burned the back of my throat, and I swallowed.

"Merda!" he swore when my side was bare.

That would be my luck—surviving a wolf attack to only die from the wound.

CHAPTER FOUR

KIERAN

Her pale skin was starting to turn an angry red with infection. I thought I had cleaned it enough when I first dressed her wounds while she was passed out. The claw marks stood out in sharp contrast to her pale skin, overlapping much smaller, silvery scars.

"Why are you cursing?" she asked with a tired chuckle.

"You were hurt badly," I replied as I stood up. "And since there's a chance you have the wolf gene, I am going to try something."

I knew deep down that if I did not try to heal her with *vivifica*, she would not survive to see the end of this storm.

"What are you going to try?"

"A way to heal you. It will be painful, so I am going to apologize in advance."

"Great," she groaned as I rummaged through the cabinet next to the hearth.

My heart ached at what I was about to try. It was a two-part process. The first is used to clean the surface wound; the next is a physic to get rid of any internal infection. It was painful for a wolf. I could only imagine how it would affect Mira. I held the two bottles in my left hand as I closed the cabinet. Each bottle was labeled with the word *vivifica*, and the numbers 1 and 2 respectively.

"This won't be easy," I said as I knelt back down beside her. Her eyes fluttered open, and she glanced up at me. I could see the pain clouded in her eyes, dulling the pale green.

"So you said. Just get it over with."

I stroked her red hair, and her eyes closed. I sighed and opened the first bottle. My nostrils flared as the burning scent of mixed herbs wafted through the air.

"This will be a two-part treatment," I warned. She dipped her head in a slow nod. "The first will be to clean the external would; the second will be to drink the medicine to help clear anything internal."

"Thank you Kieran," she whispered, her hands balled into the covers in preparation.

I doused a small cloth with the contents of first bottle and began to clean the first gash on her hip. She gasped and clenched her jaw, her entire body tensing under my touch. Her hands tightened on the blankets, her knuckles popped and turned white. Her eyes squeezed shut, but not before I saw that bright green-yellow glow.

I was up to the third gash at the base her ribs when she cried out. It tore at my heart, and I wished I could take her pain. I wished I could kill her father. I wished none of this had ever happened.

"I'm almost finished," I said without pause as I doused the cloth in another round of *vivifica*.

"My skin is on fire!" Her moan turned into a shout of pain.

"That means it is working," I replied and moved to the fourth gash on her ribs, just below her armpit. Her eyes blinked open at me, and all I saw was bright green swimming behind tears.

I finished the final gash along her shoulder, cleaned the small cut on the side of her head, and began to bandage them. Her wounds were already looking better, the wolf gene seemed to be slowly kicking in to help heal her. The red already fading to pale pink as I worked.

"How do they look?" she whispered as she brushed her tears away.

"Better than they did when I first bandaged them," I replied as I wrapped up the last one on her shoulder. I could almost feel how much pain she was in.

"That's reassuring, but I'm sensing a but," she joked, wincing as I lowered her top back over her. She shivered.

"The infection took me by surprise, but hopefully it'll clear up with this."

"You said this was a two-part healing process." She slowly rolled onto her back.

"You don't have to do the second part now. You can wait for the external pain to subside some."

She was shaking her head before I finished. I hoped the movement did not give her a headache and add to her pain.

"Let me just get it over with," she said tiredly.

"It will be a long night," I warned. I only hoped this actually worked and that it did not kill her.

"It's already going to be a long night with my skin burning under these bandages."

"Very well," I said with a sigh as I reached over her for the second vial.

She grabbed my wrist as I sat back, her grip surprisingly strong for a Halfling and in her weakened state. I stared down at her as her eyes brightened in determination. Time seemed to slow as she held my worried gaze. Electricity danced along my skin underneath her palm.

Goddess, my mate was beautiful.

Mira

Kieran helped me sit up so I could drink part of whatever was in the second vial. His hand supported under my shoulders as I took the vial from him and uncorked it. The smell burned my nose as I brought it to my lips and took one mouthful and swallowed without hesitation.

I gagged but managed to get the concoction down. It felt as though I drank liquid fire. Worse than any liquor I have ever swallowed. Flames spread through my body, coursing through my veins.

Kieran grabbed the vial from me before I dropped it and helped me lay back down as pain engulfed me from the inside out.

"Whatever that is, it is disgusting," I gasped.

"I agree," he replied as he stood and returned the vials to the cabinet. "I've had to use it a couple of times, and it is never a pleasant experience. But for me it'll wear off in an hour or two. I'm not sure how long it'll take for any pain to subside for you."

"All I can do is ride it out," I mumbled.

The fire settled on the left side of my body. I clenched my jaw and closed my eyes. Even the red of my eyelids flickered in time with the pulsing fire in my veins.

I felt him smoothing back my fever-sodden hair and opened my heavy lids. Concern glowed in his eyes making them almost gold in the dim light. I reached up and put a hand on his cheek.

"You don't have to stick around," I whispered.

"I'm not going anywhere, Mira."

The corner of my mouth lifted up in a small smile. He took my hand and held it. His touch somehow made it easier to ignore the pain raging through me. "Lay here with me?"

He stretched out next to me without hesitation. His warmth washed over me, and I closed my eyes and sighed. Even breathing was painful. I shivered, and Kieran wrapped me tighter in the fur blanket. I held his hand against my stomach and could feel the trembling in my own hands.

"Once your fever breaks, you'll begin to feel better," he whispered next to my ear.

I just hummed to acknowledge his comment. I clutched his hand tightly to try and stop my shivering. It felt as though red-hot pokers were being dug into every inch of my skin, from the inside out. There would be a break in clarity and then the pain would return twice as strong as before.

I drifted in and out of fevered consciousness throughout the night. His presence was my only anchor to reality as I battled my own body.

Chapter five

Kieran

I watched Mira while she slipped in and out of restless sleep. I got up only once to get a cloth to wipe the fever sweat off her face and to keep the fire from dying. Despite her being wrapped in the blankets and me lying next to her, shivers wracked her frame.

Her fever finally broke after the sun began to rise. I smoothed her hair back and rested my head on my arm. Her breathing deepened, and it seemed her whole body relaxed. I looked at her red hair splayed across the pillow.

It was an unusual shade—one I had never seen. In certain lights it looked almost violet, in others crimson.

She still clutched at my hand as though it were a life-line. Her pale skin contrasted against my tan. Her eyes were a pale green until they began to glow with her inner wolf.

Mira turned her head toward me in her sleep, and I could see the light sprinkling of freckles on her face and neck.

As much as I would love to bring my mate back to the pack, I know that I cannot. I do not believe any of them would take kindly to their queen being human. Or even just half.

"Who cares what they think?" my wolf side asked. *"She is our mate."*

Yes, but I refuse to risk her safety. I close my eyes, wanting nothing more than to forget my duties as alpha and king and just enjoy the short time I had here with Mira.

"Don't leave me," she mumbles in her sleep.

I open my eyes to see her brow creased in anguish from whatever she dreamt. Even though she knew nothing of wolf mates, she seemed to know what I was thinking.

Even if it was only subconsciously. My heart ached at the thought.

I close my eyes and doze off.

Mira

Something was shuffling nearby, and it was not Kieran. He was fast asleep next to me. My body, sluggish from fighting off the infection and whatever potion I drank, still ached.

I opened my eyes, blinking against the brightness and heard the distinct sound of snow being crunched underfoot.

Someone was close enough for me to hear them.

It was a little ways off, but my hearing had always been sharp. I turned and gazed at Kieran's sleeping face. His sharp features relaxed and soft while he slept. He had a few days worth of black stubble, which only added to his handsomeness. I hoped his dreams were more pleasant than mine.

I dreamt he left, and though it made no sense to my waking mind, it had crushed me. Leaving me with an empty numbness that wrapped around my chest like a vice. Like a part of me that had been found was then ripped away.

I shook the dream fragments from my mind and carefully got up. There was something else to focus on. I swayed, but stayed upright.

Long rays of golden sun fell across the floor, meaning it was after midday and closer to sunset. I did not know how long I had been asleep, nor what day it was anymore. Time seemed to have no meaning here.

Footsteps crunching softly in the snow could clearly be heard now. I was surprised Kieran had not awakened. I scanned the room for my belongings and found them near the door. I padded over silently and picked up two of my knives.

"Mira," Kieran mumbled sleepily as he looked up at me.

I held a finger to my lips, and the sleep left his eyes instantly. He listened and heard two more footsteps. It was hard to tell how many were out there. I watched his eyes shift from a rich golden-brown to almost yellow.

"Are they your people?" I barely whispered.

He shook his head as he silently stood and held up three fingers. I nodded at the gesture and tiptoed behind the door.

"Mira," he began to whisper.

The door crashed open, and two wolves and a man walked in. I narrowly missed being hit by the door. Thankfully the sound of the crash masked my gasp and the soft thud of me catching the door before it smacked into my nose.

The man was completely nude, and the wolves each had various shades of brown fur. They looked mangy, as if their fur had not been washed in days. I silently pushed the door away from me as they stepped farther into the cabin. They paused about ten feet from Kieran.

They stared at him, and my blood ran cold. I lunged forward silently.

"Now, what do we have he…" the man started to ask, but never got the chance to finish.

I thrust my knife through the base of his skull and he crumpled to the ground.

"I suggest that you both leave," I hissed as I flicked the blood from my knife.

I glared at the two wolves as they turned to face me.

кieran

I watched Mira take out the one werewolf without blinking an eye. The two wolves had turned to her when she spoke and seemed to stare at her in dumbfounded awe before coming to their senses.

She stood there with a knife in each hand, framed by the white and gray expanse of the blizzard outside. Her wild hair whipped around her, dancing with snowflakes as they surged in. Her eyes were so bright they almost glowed.

Her lips were pressed into a tight, determined line as she studied the two wolves between us.

I suddenly became aware of how much space there was between us. I was fast, but since I was still in my human form, there was no guarantee I could stop one of the shifted. My chest and throat tightened, and red tinged the edges of my vision.

Time slowed as their hackles rose and growls filled the air. The one on my left lunged but fell short with a blade between his eyes.

She had thrown the knife with a speed and accuracy that only a trained warrior would have. Before the last wolf could react, Mira was on him and had dealt a killing blow. She was quicker than I thought.

I was by her side before the wolf's body hit the floor. The clatter of her knives hitting the floor sounded muffled as I caught her by the waist and pulled her away from the dead. Her body slumped against mine as the fight left her eyes. I sat her down in one of the chairs and knelt before her.

"Are you alright? Did you get injured?" I already knew the answer to the last question—she had not one drop of blood on her. Not even the rogue's blood.

"I'm fine," she replied as she grasped my fluttering hands. "How are you?"

"I guess overly worried would be a good way to put it."

She smiled tiredly and gently brushed the hair that had fallen into my eyes.

"You do not have to worry about me," she whispered softly. "My life isn't important in this world. I fight for those who cannot, and it gets me nowhere."

"You *are* important," I growled. Her eyes widened at the roughness of my tone. "Every life is."

"Every life?" she questioned slyly.

I paused. "Some more than others," I corrected myself with a shake of my head. I knew she was referring to her father.

"Mira, what you did—"

"That?" She asked motioning toward the three dead bodies on the floor. "Was nothing."

"You saved my life."

"I had too," she whispered, looking away absently. "I had an overwhelming feeling to protect you. I don't know what happened exactly."

Her eyes glazed. She stared, unseeing, lost in thought. Her hands still rested on mine in her lap. I squeezed her fingers gently and watched the color rise in her cheeks. My breath caught as she looked at me.

"I'll start cleaning, you rest."

She started to shake her head.

"You need to rest Mira. Besides, you did all the hard work."

She frowned but said nothing. I stood up and walked to the dead laying in the middle of the floor.

Mira

I watched him lift two of the wolves and trudge outside. I stared at the man still lying in a pool of his own blood, his glassy eyes stared at the ceiling in frozen shock.

Kieran came back a few minutes later and picked up the man. "Are you alright?" he asked.

"Yes," I nodded. "Glad that we are alive."

He grunted in agreement and walked back outside. I had no idea where he was taking the bodies. I stood and grabbed an empty pot from beside the fireplace, filled it with snow, and brought it back in to melt. I found a brush and started to scrub the floor.

"Mira," Kieran said from the door.

I looked up at him and sat back. "I couldn't let you do all the cleaning."

"I brought back dinner," was all he said and held up four rabbits dangling from his fist.

"How did you find them in the storm?"

"I shifted and tracked them in my wolf form."

I followed his movements as he strolled in and placed the rabbits on the table. His movements were incredibly confident and controlled. I tore my gaze from him and went back to scrubbing the last bit of stained flooring.

Once finished, I stood and dumped the water outside. By the time I returned, Kieran already had the rabbits skinned and roasting over the fire. I closed the cabin door behind me and lowered the latch. I returned the pot to its place and curled back up in the pile of furs.

"What is on your mind?" Kieran asked as he turned the spits over the fire.

"I was wondering what was going through your mind," I replied. "Wondering what would have happened if I hadn't gone with the hunting party or if you hadn't found me."

He did not answer, and I sat up. He was staring intently at the fire, his lips set in a frown.

"What is it?" I asked.

"I believe everything happens for a reason," Kieran commented, still not looking at me. "There is a reason I found you and that we are here now."

"What reason?" I asked as I stood up and walked to him.

"I don't know yet."

He finally looked me, and I could see the conflict in his warm eyes. Conflict I knew was mirrored in mine. I gave up trying to deny the attraction I felt for him.

Without overthinking it, I stood on my toes and brushed my lips softly over his. Waves of electricity shot through me, and my eyes fluttered closed, intoxicated.

"Mira," he breathed.

I opened my eyes and stared into the glowing yellow of his irises. His body was tense.

"I'm sorry, Kieran. I shouldn't have done that."

I pulled away, but he caught me by the waist, pulling me tight against him. His lips crushed against mine as a hand tangled in my hair. My hands tangled in his hair, pulling him as close as possible. But it still was not close enough. Our tongues danced together as his hands caressed my body, careful to avoid my injuries.

I had to come up for air. I gasped as his lips trailed down my throat and across my collar bone. Each touch felt like I was being branded with his heat. His hands gripped my hips as his mouth slowly made its way back to my lips. His kiss was still passionate, but slower this time. He pulled away and pressed his forehead to mine.

"Mira," he breathed again.

I opened my eyes and stared at him, feeling complete for the first time in my life.

kieran

Holding her in my arms made time stand still. Nothing else mattered, it was only her. I stared into her green eyes after our sudden passion. In that moment I knew I would do anything for her. I would die for her.

She rested her head on my shoulder, molding her body to mine as we stood there by the fire. Her finger tips traced one of the scars on my arm, and I contained the shiver that ached to course through me.

"Nothing will come of this," I heard myself say and instantly regretted it.

She stiffened in my arms and pulled away. I caught a brief glimpse of the pain in her eyes before her guarded mask went up.

"I guess not," she mumbled.

"Mira," I began.

"Don't. The storm will be gone soon, and you won't have to worry about me anymore."

She moved back to the pile of furs and curled up. I sighed and turned back to the fire. My chest ached with longing. All I wanted to do was wrap her in my arms and never let her go.

mira

I stared unseeing at the fire. The pain I now felt had nothing to do with my wounds. A small part of me hoped he had felt the same toward me as I him.

Nothing will come of this.

His words echoed through my head, stabbing me over and over again with their cold emptiness. I grasped my head and curled into a ball. This was what my dream felt like.

Kieran set a plate in front of me a while later, then went back to his chair. I kept my eyes closed and did not move. There was no point.

"Mira," he said.

I did not move nor acknowledge him. My fingers ached from grasping my hair, and my body felt tight from staying still. I heard him sigh in frustration before getting up and walking out of the cabin.

My eyes blinked open in surprise. He was gone. And with open eyes came my tears. I let silent sobs wrack my body and exhaust me into a fitful sleep.

I awoke as the sun began to rise. Pale orange light filtered in as I slowly stretched. The storm had passed overnight. I rolled onto my back before slowly sitting up. Kieran was still gone.

"I guess I was too much, and he left me here," I murmured aloud. I swallowed the lump in my throat and ignored the ache in my chest. I stood and got dressed in my own clothes.

The shirt he let me wear, I folded and placed on the pile of furs. I adjusted my pants and then pulled my torn shirt over my head, wincing as the movement pulled at my wounds.

Next came my corset. I tightened the laces as best I could and moved on to the braces for my lower arms.

I caught a glimpse of myself in the window as I pulled on my socks and boots. My shirt and corset were bloodstained and torn, my eyes looked hollow and tired, and my hair was a wild, tangled mess. I attempted to run my fingers through the curls before giving up and tying it back in a loose ponytail.

I clasped my belt around my hips and wrapped my cloak

around my shoulders. I finished by slinging my bow over my back and placing my knives into their sheaths in either boot and on my belt alongside my arrows. I sighed and took one last look around the cabin.

In the short amount of time I had been here, I felt as though I had lived a lifetime. I closed my eyes and opened the door. I paused and watched the black wolf in front of the door lift his head and look at me.

My shoulders slumped as emotion overwhelmed me. I knew I could not hide the sorrow in my eyes as I knelt in front of Kieran. His golden eyes watched me warily. I reached out and stroked the fur on the side of his face. Memorizing its softness and warmth. He leaned into my touch.

"Thank you for saving my life," I whispered.

I blinked and a tear slipped out.

"Good bye, Kieran."

Then I stood and walked away.

kieran

Mira had opened the cabin door looking like a warrior-goddess. Her bloodstained clothes only adding to the haggard look. Her pained eyes gazed upon me as she knelt before me.

And now I watched her walk away.

I sat up and howled, longingly and painfully, hoping she knew I cared for her. She paused briefly and glanced once over her shoulder, then pulled the hood of her cloak up and continue on until she was out of sight. She glance back once. That had to mean something.

Perhaps our paths would cross again one day. That thought gave me enough strength set out on my own way home.

Mira

It was easy enough to find my way back to town, although the hills of snow slowed my journey. I arrived at the gates in the late afternoon. Tired, in pain, and in need of sleep.

"Hold! What's your business here?" one of the guards shouted down at me.

"I came home," I shouted as I threw back my hood.

"Mira? Open the gates. Open them!"

The gates creaked and groaned open in front of me. Four guards on the ground greeted me with surprise.

A couple of, *Glad your backs* and *We though you were deads* followed me as I stepped through the opening in the wall.

"Did the hunting party make it back?" I asked.

"Yes! About a week ago," a young boy said.

"Thank you," I replied with a nod and continued toward my house.

The boy looked too young to be up here guarding. There must have been more attacks while I was gone. I pulled my hood back up as I neared the center square. Bustling bodies and chatter assaulted my sensitive ears. I stayed in the shadows. Everything seemed louder than normal.

"Now is the time to go and search for her!"

I recognized Remus' voice and strode over to the group of men he was arguing with.

"She is probably dead or hiding," my father replied to him.

"You said to wait until the storm cleared. Well, it has cleared. Time to gather a search party!" Remus roared at him.

"There's no need," I said and stepped forward. I dropped my hood and stared into the amazed eyes of the hunting party.

"Mira!" Remus ran to me and wrapped me in his arms. I hissed in pain as he swung me around once and quickly put me down. "What happened to you?"

"I was attacked," I said. I shifted my cloak out of the way so Remus could see the blood on my clothes. Quieter and only for his ears I added, "I'll tell you everything at home."

I watched him and the gathered men take in my appearance. My father looked less than thrilled that I was still here. His icy glare held a promise that he would succeed in the future.

"Let's get you home," Remus said as he gripped my right elbow and led me away. "Selena has been worried sick about you."

"I'm sorry," I said. "I tried to get here sooner, but there were... complications."

He nodded. "We'll talk about it after you've eaten and rested."

We strode through the streets to our home on the outskirt of town. We lived in a two bedroom home close to the north wall. Selena was in the small courtyard out front when we came into view.

"Mira!" She shouted, dropping the basket she held and running toward me.

She engulfed me in a painful hug. I hugged her back just as tightly, assuring myself I had indeed made it home alive. Assuring myself my loved ones were still safe.

"Let's get you cleaned, patched, and fed," Selena exclaimed as she pulled back and looked me up and down.

"That sounds fantastic, Ma," I replied with a small smile.

She ushered me and Remus into the house and began bustling around in the kitchen. She stirred a pot of stew over the fire and pulled a pot of water from the floor in front of the fire.

I took my cloak off and draped it over one of the chairs around the table. After removing my bow and knives I sat down, my exhaustion was finally catching up with me.

"What attacked you?" Remus asked as he sat down across from me.

Straight to the point as always. But I know he wanted to know if he needed to go after someone for me.

"Let her rest some before you start questioning the poor girl," Selena said as she turned around and gaped at the blood on me. "Off to the tub with you, we'll get you sponged off and refreshed."

"Thanks, Ma," I said. I stood and walked behind a divider wall.

The wooden tub stood there with a small cabinet and mirror on the wall. Selena brought the warm pot of water and set it on the cabinet with a cloth. Without a word she helped me out of my soiled clothes and left me to sponge myself.

A towel was thrown over the divider behind me as I tugged off my bandages and looked in the mirror above the cabinet. My wounds had closed some, but were still painful to the touch and with any quick movement. I looked as bad as I felt.

I gritted my teeth as I began to clean myself. First my wounds, then the rest of my body, before finally dunking my head into the basin to wash my hair. I wrung out my red-violet strands and wrapped myself in the towel.

Remus and Selena were both shocked to see the wounds on my shoulder.

"Wolf attack," I said as I sat down.

"Wolf?" Selena squeaked as she began to detangle my hair and braid it.

Remus watched me with a careful and worried gaze. "I was first attacked by my father," I began.

I recounted the events of the past week, leaving out the werewolf parts. I told them how Kieran had found and saved my life. And how he helped treat the infection I had gotten from the wolf attack. I finished my tale, then sat there and stared back at Remus and Selena.

"I am going to kill your father," Selena said. "And I want to find and thank this Kieran for keeping you safe."

"My father will get what's coming to him, sooner or later."

"I prefer sooner," Remus said. "We're just glad you are safe and back home."

"I'm thankful to be back home too," I replied. I was not going to mention that *safe* was a loose term with all of the werewolves attacking the village.

I had a feeling it was only going to get worse.

The next few months were a blur. Selena would not let me leave the house for the first week. I could barely talk her into letting me get out of bed while I continued to heal. I chaffed at my enforced convalescence. It was difficult coming up with defense tactics from my spot in bed.

Even after I was allowed to leave the house, Remus kept a close eye on me. It felt as though they were afraid I would disappear before their eyes. I started doing my patrols again, finally feeling a little freedom in the cold dusk air.

Within month after being back on patrol I had already killed two rogue wolves. It seemed that each month the attacks doubled, and the wolves got stronger.

But I was getting stronger too. Something had awakened when Kieran found me. Now, almost four months after meeting him, I could feel myself changing. My eyesight and hearing sharpened. Wounds healed faster than before. Reflexes quickened, and my strength increased.

I felt like a stranger to my own body.

I walked around the perimeter of the gate, allowing my eyes to sweep over the landscape; keeping my ears sharp for any noise.

Nightfall was the most common time for attack.

I was nearing the gate when the alarm rang out. I drew my bow and scanned the landscape. Movement caught my eye. It was coming in fast. Three more wolves, their focus on the front gate.

I nocked an arrow and prepared to fire. The lead wolf was closing in quickly, and I loosed my arrow. It found its mark in the wolf's neck. Its howl pierced the night sky as I lunged forward, quickly closing the distance, to deal the killing blow.

The remaining two wolves skidded to a halt in surprise. I stood in front of the gate as the men inside tried to open it. Blood dripped onto the snow with a hiss as it made contact. My heart beat was steady as I gazed from one to the other, their glowing eyes meeting mine.

Growls muted the screeching gate behind me as the wolves changed their attack from the gate to me. I drew my blades, and the wolves pounced.

"Mira!"

I heard shouting as men rushed out of the gate. I ducked under the first wolf and slashed across the other's shoulder. It howled in rage and barreled toward me. I barred my teeth at him and met his attack head on.

The first wolf turned it's attention to the gathered mob of fighters. Remus headed that group, and I knew they would be able to hold off the wolf until I finished the other.

The wolf I fought snapped its jaws at me, and I danced back. He lunged for me, and I sidestepped. It tried to regain it's momentum, but I took a quick jab to it's throat and tore it open. It's death howl died in a gurgle. I jerked my blade free and turned my attention to the last wolf who was still focused on the men. I jumped on its back, plunging both blades through its skull.

I caught Remus' eye, and his slack-jawed expression told me he saw my glowing eyes. I quickly looked down and dismounted as the dead wolf collapsed beneath me.

I took a deep breath—first to calm my racing heart and second in preparation for the questions I knew Remus would have.

"Your eyes…" Remus whispered when he stood next to me. "You didn't tell us the whole story did you?"

"No, but I did it to protect Kieran," I whispered back.

"We'll talk at home. Meet me in the tavern after you get these cleaned up. Alaric wants to speak with us about more tactics."

"He needs to stop thinking strategy and start reaching out to other villages for support," I hissed. "But I'll see you two shortly."

Remus nodded, and I turned back to the dead wolves. Three men came forward, two with torches.

"Alright, let's get them piled up and light the pyre," I ordered.

kieran

Since the weather had calmed some in the months following my meeting Mira, I began to travel to different villages in my territory and see what was happening with my own eyes.

I sat in the back corner of a tavern, by back against the wall. My Beta, Gage, sat beside me, his eyes scanning the room. It had been a long couple of weeks traveling, and Montvale was our last stop. We would only be here for a day or two. Shorter if I found out the information I needed on how the attacks were taking a toll on the people here.

There was a man named Alaric talking with a group of men at the bar. He appeared to be the leader, his short blond hair shone in the candlelight around us. All looked rough and tired, a common sight among the villages I had visited.

I lifted my cup as another man walked in. He had a black beard, long black and gray hair, and a sharp expression. He looked as though he did not want to be here. He might be a good person to question about the attacks.

"Is everything alright, Remus?" Alaric asked.

Remus? I knew that name, but couldn't remember from where.

"Three wolves, all dead now," the man named Remus replied heavily.

I was surprised to hear that although three wolves had just attacked, no further alarm in the village had taken place. Perhaps this one was shaping up to be the best for standing against the rogues. Which meant they would not need as much help as some of the others.

"Anyone hurt?" Alaric asked, suddenly much more concerned.

"No, not since…" he paused as the door burst open, cold air once more winding through the room.

My heart skipped a beat. Mira strode through the door and directly to the gathering of men. Her hair was pulled back from her pale face, and I could smell the blood still on her.

My eyes scanned every inch of her, trying to see if she had any injuries. She wore the same look Remus had when he walked in— a look of determination and disagreement despite the exhaustion in her eyes.

Now I understood.

"Not since Mira was doing her patrol on the outside. She took all three down."

"Mira, you know you should not be taking chances with the wolves," Alaric began.

She shot a sharp green gaze at him. I could see where she learned that glare from as Remus also mirrored it. I was now not as surprised that they were still staying strong in their defense. Especially since I now knew Mira was here and fighting.

"I was out there doing your job," she retorted. "There would have been more damage if I wasn't outside the gate."

Outside the gate? Gage whispered through our mind link. *Who is this woman?*

She's the one I rescued, I replied quickly. I sensed Gage cut a quick glance at me, but my eyes never left Mira.

"You need to be more careful," Alaric said quickly.

"Are they taken care of?" Remus asked, ignoring Alaric's comment completely.

"Yes," she said tightly and looked up suddenly.

Our eyes met, and she visibly tensed up. I could hear her heart race as we stared at each other. She tore her gaze from mine and looked back at Remus. Her hand gripping the back of his chair tight enough for her knuckles to turn white. A wave of frustration and longing washed over me. I blinked. I should not be able to feel her emotions like this. I glanced at Gage and tried to refocus on the conversation.

I remember Mira telling me that Remus was the man who had adopted her. It was all starting to make sense now.

Alpha, are you alright? Gage asked.

Yes. I was not expecting this on our journey.

He nodded. I had known that Mira's village was somewhere on my territory. I hadn't realized which one it was until now, despite how close my safe house was from here. I was relieved to see she was still safe.

"I am going to head home," Mira said. "Let me know if you two come to any conclusion that actually makes sense."

I saw that last part was directed at Alaric. She had her arms crossed and was staring at him pointedly. She turned and bumped into a drunk at the bar.

"Watch it whore!" The man slurred at her with angry eyes, almost pouring his drink on himself.

My vision turned red at the edges as I watched her glare at the man and then stride out. *No one talks to my mate like that.*

I could feel Gage's gaze on me. He knew who she was. He was the only one I had told after I returned home.

"I have to talk to her," I whispered.

"Do you think that's wise?" Gage asked.

We both knew the answer. *Probably not.*

Mira

It felt like my heart was in my throat as I left the tavern. Why was he here? I had felt someone watching me when I had entered the tavern, but he was the last person I expected to see there.

I strode a couple of buildings away before cutting down an alley and stopping. Pain and anxiety had me leaning against the wall for support. I had kept telling myself I would never see him again. That I meant nothing to him. And now he was here, making it difficult. Making me feel everything I was trying so desperately to forget.

"Mira?"

My heart raced as I raised my head and looked at Kieran. He stood with another man almost as big as him. My guess was another wolf from his pack.

"Why are you here, Kieran?" I breathed, my chest tight with anxiety and my heart thundering.

"I wanted to see the villages for myself and assess what should be done," he replied.

"Well, I'm sure you can see that we are surviving to the best of our abilities."

He nodded and stepped forward. I froze in place as he moved to stand in front of me.

"Why are you patrolling outside the gates?"

"Because she's a worthless rat that deserves to die," someone shouted.

I clenched my jaw and turned toward my birth father. He stumbled in the alley entrance, glaring at me.

"And I knew that you'd end up consorting in an alley, even if Remus hadn't stepped in and taken you."

"Morris," I warned, my knuckles popping as I clenched them into fists. I itched to throw one of my blades into his throat.

"Don't mind me, *dear daughter*. I just wanted to make sure you ended up where you belong," he sneered with a satisfied laugh.

"This is the man who first tried to sell you and then tried to kill you?" Kieran snarled, placing himself between me and my father.

"The one and only," I whispered, feeling his protectiveness wash over me.

"Gage, take him back to the inn. I'll deal with him later."

Kieran's partner stepped forward with a nod and took my father away by the elbow as he rattled off curses at us. Gage threw

me an odd look over his shoulder before disappearing around the corner.

"Kieran," I began.

But in truth I had no idea what to say to him. I turned and started to walk further into the alley. I just wanted to go home and forget he was here. To wallow in the daily numbness I had grown accustomed too.

"Mira, wait," he said as he caught my hand, turning me back to him.

We stood frozen as electricity danced from his hand to mine. The next thing I knew, my back was against the wall, and his lips were on mine. One hand gripped my waist pulling me closer, the other caressed my jaw. My hands tangled in his hair, clutching him to me.

His chest rumbled with a deep growl as I pulled away, and he ran his lips down my neck.

"You said we can't," I whispered hoarsely.

His teeth grazed a sensitive spot between my neck and shoulder. I shuddered with a small moan, pulling him closer. His hands gripped my hips tighter at my response to his touch. I pulled his mouth back to mine for a soft kiss.

"And I can't seem to resist you," he whispered when he pulled away.

He stared deep into my eyes for a few moments longer, before sighing and stepping away from me.

"Please don't leave me," I pleaded, feeling all the pain from our first parting flood over me.

He pressed his forehead to mine. "You know I won't be able to stay here. I have to go back to my kind."

"At least join me and my family for dinner before you leave. So I can have a proper farewell."

"We are leaving the day after," he began. "But I guess I could join you tomorrow evening."

"I will see you tomorrow evening, then."

"Until tomorrow," he agreed, placing a light kiss on my lips.

I smiled sadly, turned, and walked away before I lost my last shred of composure. I knew he was going to do something to Morris before he left, and knowing that he cared enough to do that had me in tears before I made it back home.

Chapter ten

Kieran

I watched Mira walk away, struggling to calm my racing heart. Once she was out of sight, I trekked back to the inn.

I had her father to deal with.

The wind picked up as I strode through the gradually quieting streets. Based on the moon, it had to be late into the night now. I entered the inn and went up to our room.

"Alpha," Gage greeted as I opened the door.

"Please, while we are here, call me by my name." I closed the door and shook off my cloak.

I eyed the drunk man sitting in the middle of the room. Gage had tied him to a chair and gagged him. I raised an eyebrow in amusement. This human must have truly annoyed my Beta.

I crossed to him and pulled the gag from his mouth.

"Who the hell are you, and why am I here?" Morris demanded with a slur.

I stepped back, wrinkling my nose in disgust as the stench of alcohol permeated the air. The scent practically seeped from the man.

"I have a few questions concerning Mira," I replied.

"And what makes her so damn important that you have to drag me here?"

"I want to know—who was Mira's mother?"

"No one from around here," he spat. "She just showed up one

43

day, and we fell in love. After Mira was born, she left. I never saw her again."

"Mira said you told her that she died in child birth."

"It was the only way to shut the brat up."

"What was her name?" Gage asked. He was getting just as impatient with this man as I was.

"Lillia," Morris slurred. "I never knew her last name. She never said and I didn't ask. I didn't care. All I cared about was her and having a family. But she took all of that away when she left."

"You're the one who destroyed your family," I snarled. "You had a daughter who would have loved you for you, yet you punished her for Lillia leaving you."

"It was her fault Lillia left. If Mira had never been born, she never would have left me!"

Disgusted with the sot, I shoved the gag back in his mouth and sat down. *So he blames Mira for her mother leaving. Understandable, I suppose, but still no excuse for how he treated his own flesh and blood. I will make him pay for what he did.*

At that thought I felt a stab of sadness. I knew it was not my own emotion. My mate was dwelling on something painful, I could feel it. I put a hand to my heart. We were unmated, yet I could feel her emotions. The thought that our connection was strong enough for that already scared me. My inner wolf felt antsy as well.

Gage looked at me curiously.

"Mira," I whispered.

Mira

When I arrived home, Selena and Remus waiting for me around the table.

"We were wondering where you were," Selena said with relief.

"I'm right here. Got stuck in a conversation after I left the tavern."

"Are you up for talking tonight?" Remus asked.

"I'd rather not," I replied, closing my eyes and pinching the bridge of my nose. "It's been a long and taxing day. And on top of it, I have invited Kieran for dinner tomorrow."

"Kieran is here?!" Selena replied excitedly.

"Yes, he was sitting in the tavern listening to our conversation."

"I can see why it took you longer than usual to get home," she said with a smirk, her eyes twinkling in the firelight.

I could feel the heat rise to my cheeks. "We just talked."

"Alright, if you say so," she replied.

"Well," Remus said after clearing his throat. "We will talk tomorrow. Get some rest."

"I will, Pa," I replied. "You two should get some rest as well."

I went over and hugged each of them before climbing into the loft. I stripped out of my bloody clothes and changed into a clean pair of trousers and shirt. I had learned over the last few months to be prepared for late night alarms. I unbraided my hair and let the waves fall around my shoulders.

I laid down on my bed and blew out the candle. A soft glow from the fire illuminated the ceiling as I laid there lost in thought. Kieran was actually here. I knew he was not here for me, but part of me wished that were the case.

He was only here on duty to his people. Despite what he had said in the alley, I was still trying to convince myself that he did not care. My chest ached with longing, and I curled into a ball. I laid there listening to the howling wind and nursing the empty longing in my chest. Who knows how long it took for me to fall asleep with the turmoil in my head.

Morning dawned without any interruption. I had slept fitfully, consumed by nightmares of Kieran leaving once again. I still could not pinpoint why it hurt so much to not have him.

There was still a dull ache in my chest as I sat up. I sighed and prepared myself for the day ahead.

I pulled on my corset and boots before heading down the ladder. Selena sat at the table chopping vegetables.

"Good morning," I said as I grabbed some dried meat and a piece of bread.

"Good morning, sweetheart!" Selena said brightly. "I'm glad you were able to sleep in some."

"I don't feel like I slept much at all," I replied as I sat across from her.

Her silvery-black hair was pulled back into a bun, and her round face was bright and cheerful.

She frowned at me. "I'll have to see what I can concoct to help you sleep," she said thoughtfully.

"You don't have to worry about it," I said as I took a bite of bread. "With everything going on, it will be difficult to sleep anyway."

"I still worry." She paused. "What do you have planned for today before dinner?"

"Just some training and anything you need help with."

"I might have you run to the market for me and pick up a couple of things for dinner. Remus has gone out hunting and should hopefully be back soon."

"Of course. I don't mind at all."

She stood up from the table and crossed her small writing desk by the couch. She scribbled something on a slip of paper before she returned.

"Here is what I need to finish dinner preparations," she said as she handed me the paper.

I read through the ingredients and nodded as I finished my last swallow. "I will go and gather these now."

She smiled at me as I stood and kissed her cheek. I wrapped my cloak around my shoulders and grabbed one of the small money purses. With Selena's basket in hand, I headed to the market.

The snow was still ankle deep as I trudged into the town center. Wind whipped around me, cutting through the fabric and chilling me to the bone. My hair floated around me in brilliant tendrils, cutting through the monochromatic setting of my village.

"Mira! What can we get for you today?" An elderly woman asked from the first stall.

Her grey hair was hidden beneath the hood of her cloak as she tried to stay warm. Alena had always been kind to me. She used to feed me when I was a child—before I was taken in by Remus and Selena. She ran a bakery with her husband and also sold various ingredients during the morning market.

"Hi, Alena." I handed her the list Selena had given me. "Here's what I'm looking for today."

"Yes ma'am! I'll get these ready for you. How are Selena and Remus doing?"

"They are doing great," I replied as I watched her check the list and forage for the ingredients around her. "How are you, Declan, and the kids doing?"

"We are surviving," she replied as she wrapped a bundle of herbs and placed it in my basket. "The bakery is busy, as always, and we have two grandchildren on the way."

"That's fantastic!"

She beamed. "We are all very excited, but also wary about how everything plays out with these wolf attacks."

"I will do my best to make sure nothing happens to them," I told her as she handed my basket back to me, full with all the items on the list.

"You need to be careful as well, child. You cannot protect everyone here if you are not able to protect yourself first."

"Thank you, Alena. For everything."

"Any time, Mira. You know I always thought of you as one of my own." She smiled warmly at me.

I smiled back and handed her more than the amount I knew the herbs cost. She shook her head.

"Please, it's the least I can do," I said when she refused to take the coin at first.

"You are too kind," she said with a sigh and small smile as she took the payment from me. "Take care now. And don't wait too long between visits."

"Yes, ma'am!" I waved and trekked back home.

I kept my eyes peeled for Kieran, but he was nowhere to be seen. They were probably staying in for the day. I hoped he had not left already.

Selena was gathering more fire wood when I neared home. I quickly went up to her and took the bundle from her.

"That was quick. Thank you," she exclaimed.

"You should be relaxing too," I replied. "Take it easy while things are calm."

She waved her hands at me and held open the door. "You know we don't have very many guests, let alone one that saved our baby girl."

I smiled, and she took the basket of ingredients from me so I could set the firewood down. "Is there anything else I can help with?"

"Nope, I've got it all covered," she said while rifling through the herbs and separating them onto the table.

I grabbed my blades, put them in their sheaths, and headed outside. I decided to take a quick patrol around the village and made my way to the outer wall. Since we were farther in, there was no need to travel all the way back to the gates.

I scaled the wall and fell to the other side. I landed lithely and glanced around. Snow piled up to my mid calf out here. I straightened my clothes and started to walk the perimeter.

Being on the outside allowed me to check for weaknesses in the wall and make sure nothing could easily scale up and over.

My eyes scanned over the few farms that resided outside the wall, all abandoned now. They had taken the brunt of the first attacks, but now with the farmers inside the walls, the wolves concentrated on attacking the village gates.

I finished my trek around midday and was let in through the gate.

"You know Alaric doesn't like you being out there," one of the guards said as they closed the gate behind me.

"He also doesn't like standing up in a fight, but who's to make him?" I questioned sharply.

I turned and walked away as the guard murmured flustered apologies. The market was bustling with people at this time of day, so I wove around the buildings and went home through the alleyway.

One positive of being who I am, was that people knew not to challenge me. And now, since most of the guards had watched me take down more than one wolf, I knew that they were afraid of me. But loyal as well.

I undid the clasp of my cloak as I neared home and threw it over the fence. My blades felt cold in my hands as I pulled them out and practiced my training techniques.

My hair flew wildly around me as I cut and slashed the air—an elegant dance that would leave my opponent, if I had one, in shreds.

mira

I lost track of time as I trained, and before I knew it, I spotted Remus in the distance.

"Look who I found," he said as he opened the gate and held it open.

I spun to face him with my knives raised. Kieran stood behind him with a large stag over his shoulder. He carried it as if it weighed nothing.

"I was about to come searching for you if you didn't show up soon," I told Remus as I lowered my weapons.

Remus waved a hand at me. "Nonsense. Finding a stag like this took a little more time. Then I ran into Kieran on my way back through the gate."

"Do you need a sparring partner, Mira?" Kieran asked after he set the stag down where Remus gestured.

"That would be fantastic," Remus said as he prepared to skin and butcher the animal. "It's been difficult finding a partner that can challenge her."

"I guess that answers that," I replied. I slipped my blades into their sheaths and then leaned them against the fence.

"I want to see how good you really are," Kieran said playfully. He took off his cloak and placed it with mine.

I huffed at him as he prepared his stance. I moved into my own. Left foot forward, right back. Hands raised to my chin, right

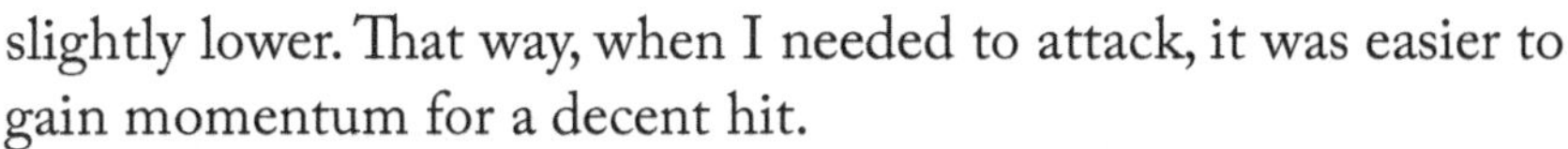

slightly lower. That way, when I needed to attack, it was easier to gain momentum for a decent hit.

"Ready?" I asked.

He nodded and moved to my right. I countered his movement, stepping half a foot closer as I did. His eyebrow raised at my slight advance, and he lunged. I spun out of the way as his fingertips grazed my waist. I went to jab his shoulder with my elbow, but he twisted at the last moment.

He caught my attempt and pulled me to the ground with him. I rolled away and leapt up, prepared for the next move. This time, I advanced. I swung out with my fist, but pulled back before he could block and spun my leg under his.

Down he went.

"That was a good one," he said with a grunt. He stood back up.

It was his turn. He came at me with a high attack. I ducked the first two shots, but the third found my ribs. I gasped and locked my left leg around his. This kept him too close to do any heavy punches.

Our eyes met, and he smirked. His shoulder was behind mine. He bent at the hips, wrapped his left arm around my waist, and rolled. I got loose before I could be pinned down.

We stood, and I launched forward using my momentum to swing around his shoulders and cling to his back. With my legs wrapped tightly around his waist, I bent backwards, placed my hands in the snow and swung Kieran backwards.

Kieran

Mira's strength and agility surprised me. Her movements confident, precise, and effortless. She seemed stronger than when I first found her. As if her wolf had awakened. I laid in the snow for a moment after she had thrown me backwards.

"Does that prove to you how *good* I am?" she asked as she stood over me.

I laughed. "You definitely have talent."

"Talent?" she asked with a frown.

"Of the people I have fought, you are the best. And a challenge, even for me."

She raised an eyebrow and watched me as I regained my feet, her arms folded across her chest. She seemed overly guarded toward me today. I wondered if it had to do with the pain I felt her experience last night.

"Alright you two," Remus called from the doorway. "Dinner's almost ready."

Mira looked surprised and glanced up at the darkening sky. "Have we really been dueling that long?" she asked.

"I guess so," I replied and turned to get my cloak.

"I need to talk to you," she said quietly.

I turned toward her. "About?"

"Remus saw my eyes change."

"He hasn't ever seen that before?" I asked in surprise.

She shook her head. "I don't think it happened much, if at all, before I met you."

I looked at her for a moment. It was possible that her wolf never came to the surface until another wolf was around. She fidgeted in the snow before me.

"I can't tell Remus the full story without telling your secret," she continued in a whisper. "And he isn't one to not get answers. I can only put off telling him about my eyes for so long."

She was concerned about me.

"I will tell him."

"What?"

"I will tell him the whole story," I repeated without hesitation. "But…"

"Mira, if you trust them, I trust them." I had no idea what would come of this. "I will tell them about how I was able to find you, what I am, and what I think you are."

"Kieran, I don't want to cause any trouble or consequences for you or your people," she insisted.

"You won't be."

She studied me. I could feel the bubbling conflict of her emotions. I stepped forward and wrapped my arms around her. She relaxed almost instantly.

"Why does it hurt when you leave?" she mumbled.

"That is a story for another day," I replied with a quick kiss to her forehead.

"Dinner!" Selena called from the door. "I'm sure you're both hungry after dueling."

"Be right there," Mira called out. She collected her things and turned back to me.

"I'm looking forward to a nice home-cooked meal. It's been a couple of weeks since I've had one."

"Thank you," she said. "For being here. I thought you might have left already and wouldn't show up."

I stared at her. I had almost considered doing just that, but thought better of it. She smiled sadly at me, as if she knew what I was thinking, and turned to the door.

"I wouldn't miss being here," I called after her.

She turned with the door partially open. "Good. Come eat."

Mira

Having Kieran in our home was a treat. He doted on Selena and her cooking, and talked up hunting and fighting with Remus.

While we ate, he told them the full story. Remus and Selena watched him intently, only breaking their stare to glance at me or each other.

Silence ensued when Kieran finished talking. I could hear the wind picking up outside.

"So, you're a wolf shifter, and you think Mira is as well?" Remus asked.

"At least a half-shifter. I think her mother is, or was, a shifter— or at least a half one herself," Kieran confirmed.

"I should be surprised, but it makes sense," Selena said.

"Ma?" I asked.

"You were a different child," Remus began. "You adapted very quickly to fighting and tracking. Quicker than most people; quicker even than me."

"But you said her eyes glowed," Selena said.

"Everyone seems to forget I'm here," I snapped in annoyance. They all turned to me in surprise. "Are my eyes glowing now?"

"Yes," Kieran said. "Seems that your eyes glow with intense emotion and when in combat."

He reached over and gripped my jaw to get a closer look at my eyes. Sparks danced along my skin where he touched—my heart raced in my chest.

"That is incredible," Selena whispered.

We both turned to her in unison. "What is?" I asked.

"How you two interact. I can't quite put my finger on it," she replied thoughtfully.

I glanced at Kieran and caught his eye. He shrugged.

"I guess when you're stuck with someone for a week, you learn a lot about them," I said.

"And she talks in her sleep," Kieran said with a chuckle.

"I do not," I exclaimed with a playful punch to his shoulder. Kieran cut me a look and smirked. I knew I talked in my sleep. I also knew that I had not done that since I was younger.

Kieran cocked his head to the side. I wondered if he was listening to the wind picking up even more and the icy rain hitting the roof.

"I should probably head back to the inn soon," he said, "before the weather gets too severe."

"You are more than welcome to wait out the storm here," Selena said. "We have plenty of room."

"I could not do that to you," Kieran began.

"Nonsense!" Remus said as he stood up. "You will stay until the storm passes."

Kieran nodded and leaned over. "I see what you said about Remus being overprotective," his voice was loud enough just for me to hear.

I chuckled and nodded.

Selena wandered into their bedroom and brought out a couple of extra blankets. She set them on the sofa and came back to the table to start clearing dishes. I stood and helped her.

Remus and Selena went to bed a little while later. The wind had picked up to almost blizzard force and sleet hammered against the house. Kieran was getting the blankets ready on the sofa.

"You and Gage are leaving in the morning?" I asked, going over to help him.

"Yes," he replied, pausing. "We'll be leaving pretty early, so I'll try not to wake you and your family when I leave."

"You can't leave without saying goodbye."

He stared at me for a moment. "Mira," he began.

"Please, Kieran."

Without saying a word he pulled me into his arms and buried his face in my hair. He held me tightly, and I felt my fears and worries wash away. His presence was intoxicating. I did not realize I was crying until Kieran pulled away slightly and wiped the tears with his thumbs.

"It's going to be alright," he murmured.

"No it won't," I whispered back. "We both know the rogues will only get stronger and more determined. They seem to be after something, and if they are, they won't stop until they find it."

"I'm not going to let anything happen," he said as he traced my bottom lip with his thumb.

"You won't be here. You have your people to take care of."

kieran

Her words stabbed at me. I knew she only meant that I would not be able to be here for her, but the way she said it troubled me. Like she had already given up. As if she had already resolved that she would never see me again. That she would die fighting...alone.

"You know I won't let anything happen," I replied. "Whether I am here or not."

She stared up at me warily. I could see the conflict raging inside. I could feel it mixing with my own emotions.

Defeat. Determination. Protectiveness. And underlying it all was rage.

"We'll hold them off as long as we can," she sighed.

I could see the depth of her exhaustion at that moment. She felt as though all the fighting fell on her shoulders.

"You don't have to do it alone," I whispered as I pulled her tighter to my chest.

"If only that were true."

I pulled her down to the sofa with me and held her tightly. I knew that no matter what I said, she would not believe me. Her mind was made up. I also knew that if the end came, she would die protecting those she loves.

It was quiet moments like this that made me wish I could bring her with me. I could feel her heart beating against mine, our breath in sync.

I lost track of time as we sat there. Her breathing deepened. She slowly relaxed and fell asleep.

You know it wouldn't take much to convince everyone that she's worthy, Gage's voice growled in my mind.

I can't risk putting her in more harm's way by marking her.

In the end it is up to you. But from my perspective, she is already your queen.

My eyes closed at his words. I knew he was right. No one else would make me feel whole.

I'll be headed that way shortly. It's time to head back home, I sent through the link.

I lifted Mira up and carried her to her loft. I set her on the bed and pulled the quilt over her.

I kissed her forehead and smoothed down her hair.

"Good-bye Mira," I whispered and left without a backward look.

Mira

Screams penetrated my subconscious and I bolted upright. I was out of my bed and out the door without a thought, knife in hand as I ran through the streets following the screaming.

I skidded to a stop on the edge of a crowd. Slipping on ice and powdered snow.

"Move," I shouted, weaving my way through the bodies.

The scent of blood was strong in the air as I neared the center. The metallic tang sharp to my heightened sense of smell. I stopped short when I broke through the crowd.

There in the center of town was the beheaded body of a man—his head was on his stomach. A large stain under him.

This was not just any man either. My knife fell from my hand.

A large paw print, still visible to sharp eyes, was imprinted in the snow beside my dead father.

"Kieran," I murmured as I fell to my knees, my hands framing another large print.

My chest tightened as my hands fisted the snow before me. *Dammit Kieran!*

"What's going on here?" someone demanded.

I looked up through my windblown hair as Alaric and Remus pushed through the throng of people. I shivered as my eyes met Remus'.

"Clear out!" Alaric yelled. "We will get to the bottom of this."

"Mira," Remus whispered as he stepped closer. "Do you know what happened?"

"Wolves breached the walls," I said flatly, pointing to the faded print in between where my hands had just been.

"Wolves?" Alaric squeaked. "How did they get in?"

"I'll have to scout the perimeter and see," I replied.

I needed to get away from everyone. I could tell by the sympathetic looks people shot me that they thought my reaction was due to the loss of my father. All I could think about was how Kieran snuck out without saying goodbye.

"Go get your cloak and gear," Remus said. "You should have at least grabbed your cloak before you ran out."

"I was a little distracted by the screaming," I seethed as I turned toward home. I jogged back, knowing there was no point in checking the inn for Kieran. He and Gage would be long gone by now.

I armed myself properly and threw on my cloak before scaling the wall. My mind raced, wondering why Kieran would do this, wondering why he would kill to protect me. Why do such an act only to leave without a word?

The rest of the day passed without incident. Nothing outside the walls could tell me what I wanted to know. It also did nothing to answer Alaric's questions.

I spun a false story, but I knew Remus saw right through me. Alaric and the rest of the council only had more questions as they placed the town on high alert.

Days passed in a blur. Spring arrived. The snow melted. Wolf attacks increased.

Farmers refused to leave the safety of the town walls. No one could blame them, but everyone knew food would have to come from somewhere. Townspeople tried to grow crops anywhere there was room. In alleys, on rooftops of homes and shops, in makeshift flowerbeds that lined the streets.

Wolf attacks were near constant, and sleep was near non-existent. I patrolled the walls at dusk everyday. In between patrols and attacks, I attempted to train what little fighting power we had left. We seemed to lose more fighters every week. Some were wounded, some were sick, some simply refused to fight.

As our defences grew weaker, the wolves grew bolder.

I sat down with Remus and Alaric in the tavern after a rough attack. Six wolves tried to get past the gate. Two men were killed, more injured.

"We can't keep doing this," Remus said, fixing me with a stare. "*You* can't keep doing this."

"I don't know what else we can do," I replied, rubbing my temples. My body ached with exhaustion and minor wounds. "The alternative is for everyone to die." I could not remember the last time I had a full night's sleep, let alone not been covered in bruises, scrapes, scratches, and bites. It appeared Kieran had forgotten all about us. We were on our own. Or at least I was.

"I can send some of the better fighters to nearby villages and see if we can join forces," Alaric suggested.

I ignored him and tightened the knot on my bandaged right arm. A wolf had bitten me during an earlier attack. It was deep, but I was glad the pressure had not broken the bones. Thankfully, I was quick enough to get away before my arm was ripped off.

"That might be our only chance," Remus said to give Alaric an answer.

Alaric nodded and left the table.

I looked up at Remus when he sighed. "Mira, maybe we should try and find—" Remus began.

"No," I interrupted, knowing exactly what he was going to say. "He left and won't bother helping us."

"He might know someone who could."

"I doubt it," I replied. My jaw twitched as I attempted to contain my emotions.

"I think you should find Kieran. You haven't slept more than an hour or two a night in months."

I rubbed my temples again and locked gazes with Remus. "Alright," I said, defeated. "I'll start out in the morning."

"Want me to go with you?"

"Not a chance, old man," I said with a humorless chuckle. "Who else is going to protect this place while I'm gone?"

He laughed. "I guess you're right. Head home to prepare, and try to get some rest. I'll send for you if we get attacked again."

I nodded, stood, and walked outside. Clouds crowded the sky as I walked home, threatening to drench us for the rest of the day.

I walked through the streets. Villagers gave me a wide berth, and very few bothered to look me in the eye. Or at me at all.

After these last few months, they were terrified of me. They had all seen what I could do. I was now more than just a *virago*. I was the last defense these people had against the rogue wolves.

"Mira?" Selena asked.

I blinked and looked up at her. I stood outside the gate, and she stood in her small garden watching me. I had tuned out most of my walk home, ignoring the stares and whispers. I had no idea how long I had stood there lost in thought.

"Everything alright, dear?"

"Nothing out of the ordinary," I replied and opened the gate. "Remus sent me home to prepare for my trip."

"Trip?" she asked, fear immediately clouding her features.

"He wants me to attempt to find Kieran, so I'll be leaving in the morning."

"Are you sure? Even after…" She trailed off, and silence reigned for a moment.

"Yes," I sighed. "Remus thinks he might be our last hope. And as much as I hate it, he's right. I don't know how much longer I can do this."

And if I fall, if won't be long before everyone else does too. Those unspoken words hung heavy between us. I pressed my lips into a hard line as my eyes burned with tears.

She set her basket down and wrapped her arms tightly around me. I melted into her hug, wanting to feel like a kid again. To not have all this weight on my shoulders. To feel some semblance of normal.

"Let me finish here, and I'll come in and help you prepare," she murmured into my hair.

I nodded as she wiped away a couple of the tears that had managed to escape. She went back to harvesting her early crops while I went inside.

I pulled my pack from the storage space under the loft and set it on the table. I opened it and examined my bed roll, blanket, coin purse, and water skin.

Everything was in good condition. I pulled out a smaller roll and opened it. Five knives of different sizes glinted up at me. I rolled them back up and set them to the side.

After filling my water skin and replacing all the items into my pack, I went to my bow and continued my examination. I set a quiver full of pristine arrows on the table, then climbed into the loft.

I put my hands on my hips and looked around. My small bed was pushed against the far wall under the window. A side table placed next to the head was covered with candle stubs and various other items, and to my right was a small chest of drawers that contained my clothing.

Shelves above the drawers held a couple of books, journals,

and small knick-knacks from my travels and souvenirs Remus had brought me when I was younger.

My eyes landed on the white stone pendant that sat among those treasures. I had found it in my father's belongings after he was killed. I figured it was probably something my mother had left behind. I was surprised he had not bothered to sell it. I guess it had meant more to him than I had.

I picked up the pendant by the chain and let it dangle before me. The stone was no bigger than a cherry in size, but flattened, and intricately encased by fine filigree details that resembled the phases of the moon. A symbol that appeared to be an intricate 'M' with a third point was etched into the stone itself.

Without thinking I clasped it about my neck, then gathered a change of clothes to put in my bag. I grabbed my notebook and some charcoal. *I will have a little more free time and can do some sketching while I search,* I thought. I opened to the last sketch I had made.

It was a rough portrayal of Kieran, in both human and wolf form. I had written his name with the images. At least I would have something of him to prove he was real.

I snapped the book closed and gathered up my items. I descended the ladder as Selena opened the door and came in. Remus followed her.

"What time will you head out?" Selena asked.

"If I can sleep any, it will be at dawn," I replied. I looked out the window at the overcast sky. "Or I might just go ahead and start."

"You should try to rest," Remus said.

"There is no time for rest. Or else you wouldn't have asked me to go find Kieran," I said sadly. I placed my items in my bag and sat down at the table.

"She's right, Remus. The sooner she leaves, the sooner she'll be able to find him," Selena said as she started braiding my hair.

Remus nodded. "All of your stuff packed?"

"All but rations," I replied.

"I'll start gathering some. Ma, could you rebandage her arm when you're finished?"

"Of course," she replied with one final tug on my hair.

I watched them bustle around for various items. Remus stepped outside while Selena sat down beside me with a fresh bandage, her homemade healing salve, and a bowl. I lifted my arm, and she began to unwrap it.

I winced. The pull on the bandage tugged at the bite

She gasped at the wound. "Was this from today?"

"Yeah, six wolves attacked. One thought he was clever enough to try and get a piece of me."

"Are you sure you are ready to go on a trip?" she asked as she cleaned my wound.

"I have no choice," I replied.

My arm was irritated and a little swollen from the bite, but it was only painful when bumped or touched.

Selena finished cleaning the bite then covered it with her special salve before wrapping it back up. I kept my left hand clenched under the table to distract myself from the pain.

"I'll put a couple of extra bandages and some salve into your bag," she said. "Don't forget to change it every so often."

"I won't. Thank you."

Remus came back inside with a small bag. "I've pulled a week's worth of rations for you. Enough to hold you over if you have any issues hunting."

"Thank you," I replied. I took the bag of food from him and packed it into my bag.

Selena followed by handing me a small batch of bandages and a tin of her salve. I quickly double and triple checked the contents of my pack, then stood. It was time.

"Whatever happens, come back to us," Selena said as she wrapped me in another tight hug.

"I will try," I said, squeezing her back.

"You'll find him," Remus assured. "I've no doubt of that."

I gave him a small smile before hugging him. He squeezed me just as tightly as Selena. I could almost taste their fear and worry.

"I will be back as soon as I can," I said as I pulled away.

I threw my light-weight cloak over my shoulders and picked up my gear. All of my weapons were in place, and my pack sat comfortably on my back.

"Be safe," Selena said.

"I always am," I said.

They snickered, and Selena wiped a stray tear. I turned my back and strode out the door.

part two
as the gauntlet falls

CHAPTER THIRTEEN

MIRA

So many whispers followed me to the gate. Alaric was nowhere to be seen thankfully. I had no desire to tell him where I was going nor what I was trying to do. He would not understand.

Remus would talk him down from sending anyone else out, spinning a story that I was searching for reinforcements.

The gate opened as I neared, and no one said anything to me. At this point, if I wanted through the gate, I was getting through one way or another. I pulled my hood up as the gate slammed closed behind me and rain began to fall.

I had roughly three hours before the sun began to set. My eyes scanned the horizon, taking just a moment to decide which direction to take first.

I started down the dirt road, letting my instincts lead. I knew there was a kingdom to the north, I had been outside the wall once for a job there. I decided heading there would be the best way to find Kieran. I did not remember how many villages were between me and the kingdom, but I was going to turn everything upside down in my search for him.

I was a great distance from the gate when I saw my first wolf. It attacked without hesitation. I responded with a head on attack, swinging my blade up and down quickly.

The body hit the ground before its head. I flung the blood off my blade without a pause in my step.

It seems the wolf had been patrolling, because not long after I killed it, I heard at least three more running up ahead. I detoured off the path and stepped into the shadowed tree line.

I watched the wolves run past my spot in the shadows. I crept silently along after they were out of sight, making sure to keep the road visible in the dwindling light.

Howls pierced the air. *Sounds like they found their dead comrade,* I thought, a rue smile creasing my lips.

My eyes adjusted to the dimming light, and I hurried silently forward keeping to the trees as much as possible and moving as silently as the foliage allowed.

It was late into the night before I decided to take a break. I estimated I had been traveling for six or seven hours. I could see lights from the next village off in the distance.

Another two-hour trek, at least. They looked to be in the same boat we were. Torches lined their walls, and I could just make out the movement of the men patrolling on top.

I would be safer waiting until morning to go there. But it would also be easier for me to scale the wall while it was dark. Now to choose which option I wanted to partake of.

Something shifted behind me. I spun, pulling my knife and peered into the darkness.

A pair of glowing green eyes peered at me. The man stepped forward, his chest bare. I could tell he was a wolf by his size and the air he radiated.

"You shouldn't be out here," he said. "The others aren't as cordial as I am."

"Others?" I asked.

He just smirked. "You don't seem to be afraid of me."

I watched his slow movements. Even in the dark, I could tell he was probably in his late thirties. Dark hair and covered in scars. He paused and looked at me as I shifted to follow his moves. His eyes flashed down, and I realized he had caught sight of the pendant around my neck.

"Why haven't you attacked me?"

"I don't usually attack if unprovoked. But answer me this, where did you get that stone?"

"I found it with my father's goods after he was killed," I replied, tucking the pendant under my shirt.

"Interesting," he replied while sniffing the air. "You aren't one of us, yet you aren't human either."

He stood there, staring at me. Analyzing me.

"What do you want?" I demanded.

"If you are going into the town, I suggest you make haste and don't wait till morning."

"Why?"

He smirked again, as if I had said something amusing. "You're *slightly* safer inside the walls. And there will be an attack closer to dawn."

"And you are telling me this because?"

"Rogues have no place here. And they are looking for someone. Good luck, little halfling," he said as he turned and melted back into the trees. "Until we meet again."

I was too shocked to say anything as I watched him dissolve into the darkness.

There was going to be an attack—if the wolf told the truth. There was no way to know, but my instincts told me I needed to get to that village before they did. My eyes scanned around me, trying to see a path that would be quick and safe. My options were limited, and I would not be able to rely on the cover of the forest anymore. Better to make a straight path, and quickly.

I pulled my weapons out and stepped out of the tree line. I started out in a brisk, silent walk, my eyes peeled for any signs of movement. My ears atuned for the slightest sound.

In thirty minutes I found the main road leading to the gate. Small farms and cottages littered the landscape, within easy access of the road. Howls started somewhere off in the distance, and I ducked into an abandoned home. The single room was covered in dust, and I could smell the lingering metallic scent of blood in the air.

I looked out the window as a howl sounded closer. From the shadows down the street a wolf stepped out. It scanned the area and turned toward the town wall.

Getting to the wall was going to be tricky now. If there was one wolf here, there were definitely more close by. I stepped silently out of the house and crept up the road.

The wolf turned as I neared, its eyes narrowing as it spotted me. I lunged, my blades plunging into its eyes before it could react. I lowered the wolf to the ground and pulled my knives out, creeping forward without pause.

I avoided two more wolves on my dance to the wall, but my luck ran out as I pressed myself against a home facing the gate. A howl pierced the air, followed by another, then another. My blood ran cold at the sound. I knew what that howl meant.

The attack had commenced.

At least ten wolves entered my line of sight, barreling toward the gate. An alarm sounded in harmony with the shouts and screams from inside the walls.

Townsfolk shot at the oncoming pack. Some arrows found their marks, but to little effect. None were deadly and only frustrated the wolves.

I took off running after them. I caught up as the first few wolves slammed into the gate, trying to force their way in. The wolves in the back glanced at me in surprise, causing them to slow just enough.

I sliced through the neck of the one on my right, then I leapt onto the back of the one on my left.

The wolves growled as the ones far enough from the gate turned to me. I leapt forward, using the momentum to bring myself closer to the wall.

More shouts from inside the walls. They were going to open the gate.

With a burst of energy, I jumped onto the back of one more wolf before launching myself at the gate itself.

My knives burrowed into the wood, giving me an easy hold to scale to the top.

Wolves launched themselves at me, but I was already out of their reach.

Up and over the gate, I slipped onto the guard post.

Five guards pointed their bows at me. Fear and exhaustion rolled off them from behind their helmets.

"If you want to survive until sunrise, I suggest you lower your weapons," I demanded as I dropped my pack to the floor.

"Who are you? And why are you traveling at night?" one guard asked.

"My name is Mira, and I come from the next town over. We don't have time to waste. Do you have men below?"

"We have about twenty men that are ready," another said as he lowered his bow. The others followed suit. "But it won't be enough against what's out there."

"It'll be plenty," I replied, as I shrugged out of my cloak and dropped it onto my bag. "They will follow my lead, you keep firing from here. The shots you do make will aggravate the wolves, which will lead them to make mistakes."

"You heard her!" a voice shouted from down the post. "I watched her as she ascended the wall. She knows what she's doing. Let's move!"

The guards reacted by moving back to the wall and sending down a volley of shots. The gate began to creak and moan from the assault.

I launched myself over the railing and landed before a group of stunned men. "Let's go. Stay close to each other. Aim for lethal spots—eyes and throats. We don't have the luxury of mistakes gentlemen," I said. "They will target me first."

I turned to the gate and looked up at the guards. They nodded to me and began to open the gates.

The howls grew louder as the gates opened before me. I leapt through when there was an opening wide enough.

Two wolves were pressed against the opening as I passed. They turned to follow my movement. A wolf lunged. I jumped at the last moment and brought my blades down and through his skull.

Silence.

I tugged my blades out and flicked the blood off. "Who's next?" I challenged.

Growls sounded and hackles rose. Three charged me at once.

CHAPTER FOURTEEN

Mira

Of the three, only one had been shot with arrows. I went for that one first. I rolled out of the way from the first, made a slice across the second's chest, and as I came up from my roll, I stabbed up through the third's jaw. My blade broke through the top of the skull with a sickening crunch.

I placed my foot on its chest and tugged my weapon free as the other two confronted me. Two more wolves took the place of the one I felled.

My eyes darted from wolf to wolf as a battle cry from within the walls soared through the air. The distraction was enough for me to lash out and kill two of the pack around me. Another lunged at me. I dodged, but his claws raked across my already injured arm, and I growled in pain.

I sheathed my weapons and went after him. I saw the fear in his eyes as I caught his jaws and pried them apart with my bare hands. His whimpers grated on my sensitive ears, followed by silence as I ripped his jaws open, and he went limp.

A howl sounded and I turned toward the men as they sliced and stabbed at the three wolves circling them. I ran up behind them, tugging a knife free as I leapt and landed on the back of the wolf closest to me.

It yipped in surprise and tried to buck me off. I dug my knife into its shoulder, then leaned forward and sliced its throat.

Another howl. This one longer, mournful, and angry.

The last few wolves glared at me and took off running. I followed them with my eyes.

As I turned, I caught site of the wolf I had met in the tree line. He was propped up against a house in the shadows; his green eyes glowing at me from the darkness. I could just make out a slight smirk on his lips as he tilted his head in acknowledgment, then he turned and disappeared.

Cheers behind me broke my concentration. I turned as men gathered around me and lifted me into the air. I was ushered back into the safety of the gates, and an older man approached me.

"That was some fighting," he said as he tugged on his beard in thought.

"I've learned to adapt during these attacks," I replied.

He nodded, watching me cautiously. "Let's get you to the infirmary and have your arm looked at. Then I'll buy you a hot meal, and we can talk."

"I appreciate it," I replied as a guard handed me my belongings from the post. "Don't let your guard down, they might be back."

"We've already switched teams to allow those who fought to eat and rest," the older man said. "This way."

I followed him from the gates, past a few buildings, to a small cottage. The house was overrun with vines, and the flower beds were just beginning to awaken from their winter slumber. This house would be beautiful in full bloom. Definitely a healer's domain.

The man knocked on the door, and a woman with pale hair answered. She pulled her robe tightly around her.

"What is it?" she asked.

"Our guest here just saved our lives and is in need of bandages," he told her.

She looked over his shoulder at me and nodded. "Come on in, and I'll take a look at you."

"Thank you," I said as I moved past her. She looked young for a healer, perhaps around my age.

Another woman sat by the fire, her gray hair woven into a loose braid.

"Ma," the woman said. "We have one injured."

"Only one?" The older woman asked in surprise as she stood and walked over to me.

"I took the brunt of the fight," I replied. "I was passing through and saw them start their attack."

"Bless you," the pale-haired woman said. "I am Loraine, and this is my mother, Elise."

"I'm Mira."

"Loraine, set her belongings down and put some water on the fire. Let me see what we've got here."

As Loraine did what she was told, Elise rolled up my sleeve and unbandaged my arm.

"My goodness, child. A scratch over one you already had. How old is the first one?"

"It's from yesterday. I've lost count of how many attacks and which wound is from when," I replied.

She clicked her tongue.

Loraine came back with a bowl of boiling water and some rags that she sat on a nearby table. "Let's get you cleaned up, and then we can see if you need stitches. Would you take a seat?"

I sat down, and the women went to work.

The older man kept his gaze fixed on me the whole time. "Where are you headed?" he asked while they examined my arm.

"Nowhere in particular," I replied. "I wanted to see how the rest of the towns were and see if I can find a solution."

I hissed as Elise poured alcohol over my arm.

"Looks like you will need a couple of stitches. Especially where the scratches cross the punctures. We don't want anymore separation in those areas," Elise said as she set my arm on the table. "Loraine has steadier hands than I do now. She'll get you stitched up."

"Thank you for your hospitality," I said.

Loraine sat next to me and started stitching me up.

"You saved this town from it's biggest attack yet," the man replied.

I tightened my left hand into a fist as the stitches stung and pulled. I was beginning to feel the weight of my exhaustion creeping back in.

"Make sure you eat and get some sleep," Loraine told me as she tied off the last stitch and began to bandage my arm. "I would normally tell you no hard work that would irritate your stitches, but I suppose that would be difficult to do."

"The unfortunate truth of the time," I replied.

Loraine smiled. "If you find a solution to this mess, let us know. We will do our best to help."

I nodded. "Thank you. I will do my best."

She rolled my sleeve back down. "It was a pleasure to meet you Mira. I hope our paths cross again."

Elise handed me a small sachet. "Mix a pinch of this with hot water. It will help fight off infection. And since you're traveling, find a doctor or healer to remove your stitches in seven days."

I nodded.

"Good luck, Mira. Stories will be written about this day and what you have done for us," Elise said with a smile.

I smiled as the man led me from the house and even further down the street.

"The Inn is still open. We'll get you a room after we eat," he said.

"What is you name?" I asked.

"Thom," he replied. "I am head of the militia here."

"You seem to be running it better than my town. At least until my father and I took over."

"You and your father run the guards?"

"Yes, our town leader has no battle sense. And with the attacks, it was up to us to properly train and defend."

"Not many women would do what you are doing," Thom said as he opened the door to the Inn and motioned me inside.

"Not many had the upbringing I did either," I replied.

The Keeper greeted us. "What can I do for you this evening Captain?"

The Keeper was a middle aged man with a receding hairline. His large body told me he had never suffered a food shortage. But his eyes were kind enough that he looked helpful.

"Dinner for the lady and then a room for her as well," Thom said. "I'll take care of the expense."

"Is this who the men are talking about?" The Keeper asked. "They came in for drinks a little while ago chatting about a woman who saved us."

"I don't know about saved," I began. "I just helped scare off the wolves."

He laughed. "You are modest. I am Aldor. My wife, Greta, will bring you food and something to drink shortly. When you're full, swing by, and I'll show you to your room."

"Thank you, Aldor," I replied with a smile.

We turned to the left and entered a small dining hall. There was a bar along the back wall and various tables scattered about.

I picked one closest to the door and sat down with a sigh.

"When was the last time you had a decent night's sleep?"

I rubbed my face and shrugged. "Months probably," I replied. "I get woken up every couple of hours with alarms. Both false and actual."

"How is Remus doing?"

"How do you know Remus?" I asked, suddenly cautious and on edge. My left hand crept toward the knife in my boot under the table.

"He did a job for me a few years back. He's an old family friend. After his reputation grew, he moved to where he is now because it's quieter. Towns get more chaotic the closer you get to the kingdom," Thom said. "He told me, last I saw him, that he and his wife had adopted a young girl and that she was shaping up to be a better fighter than himself."

"How did you know that was me?"

"I watched some of your techniques from the wall, and the underlying movements reminded me of Remus. He and I would train together. He was always quicker—and more ruthless."

"I call it determination," I replied as I relaxed and placed both hands on the table. "I will have to let him know I visited with you if I make it back home."

"If?" he asked with a raised eyebrow. "I saw you. If anyone else were out there, there would be an *if*. Not you. I saw your eyes change for a brief second."

I opened my mouth to say something, and he held up a hand.

"I don't want to know details. Right now, the less I know is probably for the better."

"Remus would be grilling me for details," I chuckled. "He wants to know everything."

"That's what makes him great at what he does. He analyzes every little thing before making any decisions."

A woman came over and set two cups on the table. "Aldor said you were the one who saved us," she said looking down at me.

"I wouldn't use the word *saved*," I said.

Thom huffed and took a long pull from his drink. The woman smiled brightly.

"That's how everyone here is saying it, sweetheart."

"News travels fast here as well," I mumbled.

"I have some stew, I'll bring you both a bowl."

"Thank you Greta," Thom said.

"I doubt you wanted to just ask me about Remus," I said after she left.

"You're right. I wanted to ask what kind of *solution* you are looking for?"

I shrugged. "I met someone months ago that is a better fighter than me, and I want to see if I can get his help."

"I hope you can find him," Thom said. "We all need a miracle at this point."

Greta came back with our meals, and we ate and drank in silence. When we finished Thom sat back and eyed me. "How long will you be in town?"

"Not long. I'll wander through tomorrow and see if I spot who I'm looking for. But I don't think he's here. He would have joined the fight if he was. I'll most likely be gone by noon," I replied, taking another drink of the ale Greta had brought.

The warmth of the alcohol settled in my stomach, and I hoped that one drink would help calm me enough so I could get some sleep.

"Do you need any supplies? I see you didn't bring much with you," Thom asked with a note of concern in his voice.

"No, I packed the bare minimum on purpose so I can move faster. And if I have any encounters on the road, a light pack makes it easier."

He laughed. "I understand. Well, if you need anything or pass back through here, our gates are always open."

"Thank you, I really appreciate it."

"I'm going to check on the guards and then get some rest. Make sure you rest as well," Thom said as he stood up. "I bid you safe travels, young Mira."

"I will do my best," I sighed.

He smiled down at me, squeezed my shoulder, and left. I put a couple coins on the table and then made my way back to Aldor.

"How was dinner?" he asked.

"It was delicious. I can't remember the last time I could sit and eat," I replied.

"Fantastic!" he boomed. "Let's get you settled in for the night, and don't hesitate to let me or my wife know if you need anything."

"Thank you," I replied with a tired smile.

He led me up the stairs and to a door about halfway down the hall.

"Here's the key to the room. We will see you in the morning."

I smiled and took the key. He left, and I walked into my room. I placed my pack on the small table inside the door. I made sure the door was locked before changing into a clean top and pants. I used the small basin to wash what I was wearing and hung them by the fire to dry while I rested.

I warmed a small cup of water over the fire and mixed in a pinch of herbs. I held the warmth between my hands before drinking it in one long gulp. The concoction joined the alcohol in my belly, and I could feel sleep tugging at me.

I sank down on the bed, and sleep pulled me under.

I awoke with a start when a door slammed somewhere in the Inn. I sat up and rubbed my eyes. It was bright out, which meant I had slept much longer than I expected. It looked like a late morning sun.

I stood and stretched, going through my morning routine of exercises. When I was finished, I packed my now dry clothes and slipped into my boots. I put my weapons in their places and wrapped my cloak around my shoulders.

I picked up my bag, unlocked the door, and made my way downstairs.

Laughter floated from the dining area as I placed my key on the front counter along with a couple of coins.

"I hope you're not leaving that for us," Aldor said as he stepped from a back room.

"Of course I am, it's the least I can do."

"Stay safe out there—and good luck."

I nodded back and asked, "Aldor, what is this town called?"

"Spinehold," he replied with a nod as he scooped the coins up.

I put my hood up, and stepped outside to resume my search. My suspicions were right. Kieran was not here. I did not expect him to be. Spinehold was too close to me for him. I tried to ignore the ache in my chest that accompanied that thought.

I left the safety of the walls behind. Time to continue onward. The next town was a couple of days from this one. I set off without looking back.

Kieran

I sat with Gage in my office. Spring was usually a welcome sight to us. But not this year. As the temperature increased, so did the casualties.

"The attacks have gotten worse," Gage said flatly. "There was a large pack that attacked Spinehold yesterday."

"How bad was the damage?" I asked as I got up to look out the window.

"At least twenty wolves, so our source says."

I pinched the bridge of my nose. "How many casualties?"

"None," Gage said.

I spun back to him in surprise. "None? How can that be with an attack that size?"

"Our source said he saw a woman outside the gates and that she alone slaughtered almost half the party."

"Mira?!" I growled.

"He didn't describe her, but it's possible that she would help out her sister town. Spinehold is only half a day trek from Montvale."

I looked down at the map sprawled out on my desk. Those two towns were the very southern tip of the land we tried to protect. My wolf twitched in anticipation and worry.

"I have no doubt it was her," I murmured.

"Can you still feel her emotions?"

"Sometimes. I felt a surge of rage early yesterday morning that woke me up."

"Maybe you should send for her?" Gage suggested.

"No. You know my stance on that."

"Alpha, you and I both know that with her by your side, both of you will be stronger."

"I am not willing to risk her life on the slim chance that our people will accept a halfling as my mate."

"There is one more thing our source said about the woman he saw," Gage began.

"And what did he say?"

"She had a Tala stone around her neck."

I looked at Gage, and then down at my own Tala in the ring on my right hand. I'd had mine broken and put into a couple pieces of jewelry. It was the stone of the Alphas.

"So we are dealing with another alpha then, not Mira?" I asked.

"Perhaps. But the Tala he saw used to belong to a particular alpha's daughter."

"And which alpha would that be?" I asked, getting annoyed.

Gage sometimes enjoyed dragging out information. "Alpha Lycus."

My blood ran cold, and I stared at him.

"We have a descendant of the Rogue Alpha on the loose?" I whispered. "And she is attacking her own people? Or is it another wolf that killed an alpha and is wearing their stone?"

"I'm just sharing what was shared with me. I don't have anymore details."

I turned back to the window, trying to control my thoughts and keep my anger in check. Having another rogue alpha did not make my job any easier. It made me want to take back everything I had said about keeping Mira away.

My wolf bristled.

"See if we can keep eyes on this woman. I want to know where she is at all times and what her motive might be."

Mira

The next town was worse off than the last. Homes outside the walls had been burned down, and the gates barely worked.

I sat in the tavern with three other people, the barkeep being one of them.

"Where you from?" the Keep asked as he set a cup of water and a bowl of stew in front of me.

His light brown hair was pulled back at the nape of his neck, skin pale and drawn. I could almost taste the fear and exhaustion rolling off him. "Montvale," I replied.

"That is a long way for a woman to be traveling alone," he replied, worry drawing deeper lines into his features.

"I am capable of defending myself. Your town doesn't look to be doing too well."

He sighed. "We made the mistake of sending out too many hunting parties. Now there are maybe only thirty men left to fight. Some of the women who are able try to join, but it's a loosing proposition."

"I'm sorry to hear that. Is anyone able to do repairs on your gate and walls?"

"We've tried, but the wolves just keep coming. It's like they know we are all dying in here."

"How frequent are the attacks?" I asked.

"Nightly, right at dusk. Usually three to five attack. I believe they think they don't need more than that."

"Maybe I can help deter them."

He raised an eyebrow at me and looked me up and down.

"You seem like you know a lot, but I would not put you out to face a single wolf, let alone a group."

"Has news spread about Spinehold yet?" I asked.

"Yes, a woman helped them against their last big attack," he trailed off and his eyes widened. "No. There's no way."

83

"Like I said, maybe I can help." I moved my cloak out of the way so he could take in my weapon assortment.

"If you survive," he said as he reassessed me, "I'll pay your dues to stay a night at the Inn."

I raised my cup to him. Sometimes it paid to be helpful, and not just with coin. "You've got a deal."

I ignored the few stares I got as I paced along the guard post, my eyes sweeping the darkening horizon.

"So you're the one that saved Spinehold?" a giant man holding a spear asked. He had paced from his spot further down.

"Yes," I replied, giving him a brief glance before turning back to watching for any movement.

"I have a hard time believing that," he continued. "A woman isn't capable of fighting off a wolf."

My entire body tightened at his words. Before I could make a remark, movement caught my attention. Just as the barkeep said. At least they were punctual.

"I guess you'll just have to watch as I save your sorry ass," I retorted.

I drew my blades. The guard stepped back in surprise at my sudden movement. Quicker than a normal human.

"I'll be the one digging your grave," he declared.

I snorted and leaped over the wall. The wolves paused as I landed in their path. I looked at them from my crouch, analyzing how the six would attack me. I stood, keeping my knives hidden behind me.

"If you're lucky," I said. "One of you will leave here alive. And the one who is that lucky little wolf, will be the one to spread the word that this town is no longer to be tormented. If attacks do not stop, I will hunt down whoever is ordering these attacks and put their head on a pike."

The blond wolf to my left growled. *He must be the head of this group*, I decided. I turned to him slightly and cocked my head to the side.

"Why, you're awfully chatty. Are you going to be the lucky one?" I taunted. "No? Very well."

I did not want to waste anymore time. I lunged toward the right as the blond wolf lunged toward me. I nicked one of his hind legs as I spun out of his way. The other wolves growled and yipped in surprise with my attack.

The leader was back on the attack again, growling at the others as a means to keep them at bay. I lunged as they all paused momentarily at his actions. My blade sliced through his neck before my feet hit the ground.

"Four to go," I said as his head dropped to the ground with a thud.

The wolves stared at me in surprise. Time slowed as they processed what happened and then launched themselves at me. I made sure my movements were quick and precise. I wanted to behead them, but leave their heads uninjured.

I remained rooted in place as they closed in. I crouched as they closed the final few feet. When I stood again, two more heads fell to the ground. A paw had swiped lightly across my shoulder in the process, and I could feel the warmth of my blood spreading over my top. But I did not let my eyes stray.

I spun to the three remaining wolves. "Two more," I hissed. They began to retreat. I bounded after them, leaping onto the closest one. I plunged my blades into his neck and twisted. The wolf went down, his momentum sending me tumbling forward. I used that to go after the next.

The last two wolves turned on me at the last second, but I was ready. With a quick slice across one shoulder and the throat of the other, I was done.

"Tell your leader what happened here," I ordered the last wolf. He cowered, his head bowing to his paws. "Tell them, this is what will happen to them if they continue attacking anywhere."

The wolf whimpered as if to say he got the message. "Now go," I said flatly.

He took off in the direction they came from. I turned to the last two wolves and promptly removed their heads. I lugged the enormous masses closer to the wall, and the gates opened.

"How?" the stupified guard asked.

It was the same one who berated me on the post right before the fight. I leveled my gaze at him. "I need five pikes. Put their heads on them, and put them near the gate. They shouldn't bother you for awhile now."

The four other guards scrambled to follow my orders. The last one just stood there gawking at me.

"How?" he asked again.

I stepped up to him, and he flinched. "By training from a very young age and not letting men like you stand in my way," I hissed. "I suggest you help your people get these heads on pikes before the sun sets completely."

The guard shook visibly as I stepped around him and made my way back to the tavern.

Women stepped out of their ramshackle homes and buildings on my way. I would have to find a way to get them to a different town. But that was a problem for another day.

"Miss?" a woman asked.

I paused and looked over at her. Her red hair was pulled back into a bun, and she held a little girl's hand—she was probably about six. A boy about ten stood nearby. Both children had her brilliant hair.

"Yes?" I replied.

"I can tend your wounds if you'd like," she began softly. "I don't want to over step, but I noticed your shoulder and the blood spreading."

"I would greatly appreciate it if you would," I replied with a soft smile. "I was on my way to the tavern to see if the barkeep knew of anyone who could help."

"Herald would have brought you back to me," she said with a smile. "Please, come on in."

I followed her and the children into the small home. The boy went to tend the fire while the girl stayed glued to her mother's side.

"I'm Imelda," the woman said as she motioned for me to take a seat on a stool by the small table. "And this is Josie and Jon."

"It's a pleasure to meet you. I'm Mira."

"You are a better warrior than my father was," Jon said, his back still to me.

"What makes you say that?" I asked him.

He turned and looked at me sadly. "You're still alive."

"Jon," Imelda began.

I held up my hand. "I'm sorry about your father, Jon," I began. "My real father was also killed by wolves."

His eyes lit up when I said that. He stared at me for the longest moment before stepping away from the fire and wrapping his arms around my neck. Small sobs shook his body. I ignored the fiery ache in my shoulder as I wrapped my arms around him. Imelda looked on with tears in her eyes.

There was no need to tell them my father deserved his fate.

"You know what we have to do now?" I asked him. He shook his head against my neck. "We have to keep living. Keep fighting. It is up to us to protect the ones we love."

"But how can I do that?" he asked, pulling back so he could look at me.

"By staying strong no matter what happens."

He set his jaw and thought about it for a moment. "I want to be a fighter like you," he determined.

"And so you shall," I said with a small smile. "Me too!" Josie squeaked.

"The more the better," I exclaimed. "But first, let's let your mom patch me up so we can keep on fighting, yes?"

"Yes!" the children shouted in excitement.

Jon gave me one more squeeze before heading back to the

fire. Josie sat across the table from me, watching her mother's every move.

"Thank you," Imelda said as she set her tools on the table. "For what?"

"For giving them hope."

"We all need it," I replied as she rolled the collar of my top out of the way.

Josie hissed. "Does it hurt?"

"Only a little," I said. "I have much worse ones on my arm."

"I'll go ahead and take a look at those too while you're here," Imelda said. "If you're traveling from town to town fighting like this, it's best to keep a watchful eye on any wounds."

"Spoken like a true healer."

She blushed at my compliment. Jon and Josie started chatting as Imelda fell silent. She cleaned my shoulder and wrapped it.

"Thankfully these are shallow and don't need stitches. You got lucky."

"Tell that to my lower arm," I joked as I rolled up my sleeve for her.

She unwound the bandage and gasped. "Oh my." She looked up at me.

"Is it infected?" I asked. I would not be surprised if it were.

"No," she shook her head. "I just wasn't expecting such a criss-cross of slashing and puncture wounds."

"That's a warrior's mark," Jon proclaimed. "That one has to hurt," Josie said.

"Yes, it does. It's better than a couple of days ago, but still tender." I winced as Imelda probed at it with a cloth doused in alcohol.

"So far it seems to be healing well. How long ago did this happen?"

"Almost three days ago. Why?"

"The healing is farther along than what I would expect for so little time. Did the healer who stitched you say how long to leave the stitches in?"

"Seven days," I replied as I took a look at my arm.

The older scratches looked like angry red scars while the most recent ones were angry open wounds. My arm looked like I had an odd hatching pattern from my elbow to wrist with a sprinkling of dots where teeth had punctured my skin.

"I'm going to remove them early. I don't want you to have any complications in a couple of days if that's the case. Especially if you are healing a little faster. Then I'll just wrap them with a little extra padding."

"Sounds like a plan."

She opened a small cupboard and rummage around, then came back with a small knife and a pair of tweezers. She cut the stitches and pulled them free. My jaw popped as I clenched it shut. I guess being part wolf had sped up my healing, and I had already started healing around the stitches.

"Oww," I hissed.

Imelda pulled one from the top center of my arm, and white hot pain electrified my veins. I blinked the spots from my vision and focused on Josie. She watched me with concerned eyes.

"I'm sorry, Mira. Only a couple more. You have healed faster than the other healer thought."

I put my head down and clench my eyes closed as she pulled out the last few stitches. Josie came around and put her hands over mine. I looked up at her, and she smiled at me.

"You are going to be a great healer, just like your momma," I said.

Her smile widened. I looked back down as more alcohol was poured over my arm, my breath coming out as a sharp exhale. My jaw hurt from clenching it shut.

"And...done," Imelda said as she began to wrap it back up.

"Thank you," I breathed with relief. The intense pain began to fade to a dull, throbbing sting.

"I'll give you a clean shirt before you go. Just don't forget about us here."

"You've done more than enough already. I will send help as soon as I find it."

Chapter sixteen

Mira

"Well, I'll be damned," Herald said as I strolled into the tavern.

"Your town shouldn't be bothered for a little while," I said as I sat down heavily on a stool at the bar.

He passed me my belongings along with a cup of ale. "How many where there this evening?" he asked.

"Six." I paused and took a long swig. "Five heads are on pikes at your front gates. I sent one to his master with a warning."

"You think they will listen?"

"They better, or I will be the one hunting them down."

"After you finish your drink, I'll hold up my end of the deal. Thank you."

"It's my job," I replied and raised my cup to him.

And this time, instead of being paid to kill people, I was killing wolves to save what remained of humanity.

When I finished my drink, Herald gave me a couple of coins and directed me to the Inn. He told me to find a woman named Abigail. I thanked him once more and went to settle down for the evening.

Abigail welcomed me with open arms and even included a hot meal with my room. She sent me up to get clean with the promise of food to follow.

I placed my belongings on the floor and used the basin to

wash my hands, face, and hair. Before I finished a knock sounded at the door. I answered, and Abigail stood there with a tray of food.

"It's not much, but it's warm," she said, her brown eyes twinkling.

She reminded me of Selena. "Thank you very much," I replied and took the tray.

"Give me a shout if you need anything," she said. She smoothed her hands over her graying hair, then turned to go.

I nodded and closed the door behind her. I set the tray on the table and looked at what she had brought. A small cut of meat, some steamed vegetables, and two slices of fresh bread with butter. I warmed more water and mixed in a pinch of herbs. Then I dug in.

Once I was finished, I stripped down and sponged myself off. I redressed in the clean top Imelda had given me and the spare trousers from my bag. I rinsed my dirty clothes in the basin and hung them by the fire.

I sat on the edge of the bed, brushed my hair, and braided it loosely. Exhaustion tugged at every fiber of my body, but my mind was too alert. I rummaged through my pack, pulling out my notebook and charcoals. I sat back down at the table and set to work.

Flipping to a new page, I began to sketch my journey. The town gates, the people who helped me, the wolves I killed. All of it flowed from me and onto the pages of my book. I took note of my wounds and recorded a rough timeline of them.

There had to be a way to get the people of this town to Spinehold. That would be their best option until a better solution could be found.

I flipped back through the faces of all the people I had met already. They were the heart of humanity. They were the ones who needed to be saved. I flipped one more page.

Kieran stared back at me. I slammed my book closed, hoping I would not die trying to find him.

Rhudi

I had watched the woman kill five wolves and let the sixth go before nightfall. After her show at Spinehold, I had followed her here, curious as to what she was up to.

She was strong and determined, I'd give her that.

A wolf came up behind me, and I turned. It was one of the Alpha's.

"Yes?" I whispered.

He shifted and nodded. "The Alpha ordered for her to be watched. He wants to know her movement and motive. Anything else to report?"

I looked back at the quiet town.

"Nothing yet," I replied. "I'm not sure why she is traveling, or where she is going. But she just killed five more rogues and sent a message to Lycus."

"What kind of message?"

"I'm not sure, but she made the sole survivor cower as if he were under an alpha's command."

"I'll pass on the information, Rhudi," the wolf said. "How are things on your side?"

"Rogues are rogues. But this woman has caused a stir, and my father isn't pleased. It'll be interesting how he receives this message from her. How is your Alpha, Lyell?"

"He is upset over this new player and worried that we have another Rogue Alpha on our hands," he replied.

"I don't think she's rogue," I replied. "But an alpha?"

"She has my sister's Tala. I hadn't seen that pendant in over forty years. Yet I walked right up to it in the woods less than a week ago. And after watching her fight and what she did yesterday, there is no doubt that she has alpha blood."

"Do you think she killed your sister?"

"No, not at all. But she's the spitting image of her. Which means that my niece is in danger, and has to be protected."

Mira

I awoke when the sky was still purple and orange. I was through the gates before the sun had even made it halfway over the horizon. Fog settled low over the ground, swirling around my legs as I trekked onward.

My pack weighed on my shoulder, irritating yesterday's wound. I knew most of the trip to the next town would be wooded—at least until I got closer.

Winboro was near the ocean. They had the advantage of having the water to their backs, just like Montvale had the mountains.

I kept a steady pace all day and did not stop until nightfall. I built a small fire and sat down to rest. My body ached. I was exhausted. My wounds pestered me with needles of stabbing pain.

I took a swig from my water skin. As I put the top back on, a rabbit carcass was thrown out of the tree line and next to the fire.

"Why are you following me?" I called out, not bothering to look in that direction.

The wolf I had met stepped out of the trees and crouched across from me. He watched me intently. Green eyes glowing with curiosity and amusement.

"How did you know I was following you?" he asked.

I raised an eyebrow. "I know when I am being tailed, and if you were concerned, you wouldn't have thrown that out here." I motioned to the rabbit.

I had sensed him following me starting around mid-morning. He was persistent, I'd give him that.

"I thought you could use something other than old bread to eat," he replied as he sat back and got comfortable. "I'm Rhudi."

"Mira," I replied. "You still haven't answered my question."

I leaned forward, picked up the rabbit and began cleaning it.

"You intrigue me, Mira. It's not everyday that I meet a halfling, especially one with your talent."

"I've heard that before," I mumbled. I kept my eyes on my hands as I worked.

"Why are you traveling?" he asked, ignoring my comment.

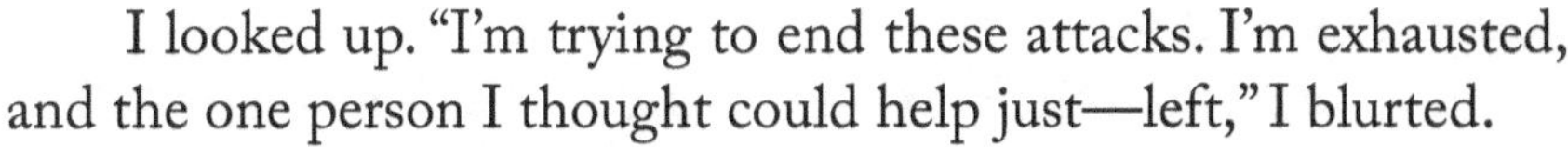

I looked up. "I'm trying to end these attacks. I'm exhausted, and the one person I thought could help just—left," I blurted.

"And who might that be?"

"Kieran."

I watched surprise flash across his features then disappear as if I had not said anything. He rubbed his chin in thought. I narrowed my eyes.

"You really think this...Kieran...can help you?" he asked.

"I hope so," I said while I finished cleaning the rabbit. "He's like you, so who better to help."

"Ah," Rhudi said

I stood and found a branch long enough to use as a spit, then returned to the fire and set the rabbit to cook.

"Do you know where to find this Kieran?"

"No. That's why I'm traveling. I'll find him eventually."

"And if you don't?"

"Then I will either figure out a solution to getting rid of the rogues myself, or die trying." I growled in annoyance as I turned the spit. "Why does it interest you so much that I am doing this? Other than I *intrigue* you."

"I have seen success fall to the rogues too many times to still be in their corner," Rhudi began. "The Alpha of the rogues wants full control. He wants to eliminate anyone and anything that is not a shifter. He believes only the pure can shift and the tainted were punished and confined to one form."

"No wonder he's been attacking all of the villages," I said absently as I stared into the flames. "That also paints me as a much larger target."

"But in his attacks, he's been searching for someone."

"So you mentioned when we first met." I looked up at him. "I'm guessing you know who this alpha is looking for?"

"He is looking for the daughter he banished years ago."

"If he banished her, why look for her now?"

"There was a prophecy told to him that only the child of his daughter would be strong enough to defeat him. My guess is he wants to make sure she never had a child, or if she did—to kill it."

"And what happens if he never finds her? He's just going to keep killing everything in his path? For what?" I asked.

"For control and power. As of right now, he is the most feared rogue," Rhudi said. "And he wants to keep it that way."

"Not if I can help it," I mumbled.

I caught the small smirk on Rhudi's face at my comment. I plucked the rabbit off the fire and tore a piece off.

"Eat and get some rest. I'll make sure nothing bothers you tonight."

"How do I know I can trust you?"

"If you didn't, you would have killed me the second I stepped out of the trees."

He had a point. I tore off a leg and tossed it to him. We ate in silence then threw the skin and bones into the fire.

"I have one more question for you, Rhudi," I said.

"And what would that be Mira?"

"How did you know that I was a halfling?"

He smiled. "Your scent. You smell mostly human, but you have an underlying wolf smell. And your eyes. They shift color with your emotions."

"They seem to do that more since I met Kieran," I said. I rolled onto my side and faced the fire.

He nodded. "If you hadn't grown up among wolves, being around one would awaken that side of you, and certain characteristics would start to show."

"Makes sense, I guess."

"Get some rest. I'll try to warn you when I can of any attacks."

I nodded at him and closed my eyes. Sleep came easier than I thought.

Rustling branches awakened me. I sat upright and looked around.

The morning was gray. The fire was out. Rhudi was nowhere to be seen. I could not sense him anywhere nearby. *Wolves. They never want to stay around.* I packed up my belongings and set off into the day.

I came across a pack of three rogues a couple of hours later. I was just going to keep walking, but they decided to target me for entertainment. Their mistake.

I killed one with an arrow through the eye, the second with a blade through its skull, and the third with a slit throat. I retrieved my arrow and went back on my way. I hoped Winboro was close, but it was after dark when I finally saw the flickering flames of the village in the distance.

Once the sun had set, I caught the movement of Rhudi following me again. He stayed far enough away that a human would not be able to sense him. Perhaps he thought I was not able too either, since he was being silent and slow.

Screams echoed in the distance followed by howling. I cursed and pushed away my pain and exhaustion. I broke into a sprint, quickly covering the remaining distance between me and the town walls within a matter of minutes.

Another pack of wolves, another town, another siege. They all began to blur together. But I had to keep going. Something kept pulling my forward. Kept drawing me closer to some kind of solution. To some end.

I launched myself into the fray. Two heads fell at my hands, and I stood before the wolves. They stared back at me. It was hard to tell if it was awe or fear I saw in their eyes.

One stepped forward and shifted. He had a similar build as Kieran, but he was blond, a few years older, and his wolf form was smaller.

"Who are you?" the wolf asked. He stared down at me as if I were beneath him. As if he could control me.

"Your worst nightmare if you continue these attacks," I hissed, ignoring the shouts from inside the gate.

He smirked. "You think you can best us?"

"Spinehold," I spat and watched the wolves behind him exchange glances and fidget while he took a half step back. "Do you know it?"

"I heard the stories, and comrades did not make it back."

It was my turn to smirk. "Yes, well, they did fight bravely. Do you want to send your pack to the same fate?"

"I will challenge you," the man said. "No weapons."

"Very well." I sheathed my blades and took off my pack. I set it and all my weapons on the ground.

"You are not afraid?" The man taunted.

"Fear only makes the weak cower. It awakens the strong," I threw back. "Since I can't have weapons, you can't shift. You have to fight me in your human form."

His jaw tightened in frustration. "Agreed."

"And none of your men are allowed to help," I ordered. I watched a shudder course through them.

"If you die," the wolf said through gritted teeth. "My men will tear this town and every other town to shreds."

"And if *you* die, they will leave with yet another message to your leader. But this one won't be a warning."

"What is going on here?!" someone shouted.

The wolf glanced over my shoulder and grinned. "Good, an audience. We are about to duel, and the fate of your town depends on who lives and who dies."

I heard the shuffling behind me and estimated about ten guards had made their way out of the town.

"You all should return to the safety of the walls," I called over my shoulder, never taking my eyes off the wolf.

"We aren't leaving you by yourself."

I rolled my eyes. "Suit yourself, but if I die, they will kill all of you."

Their frantic whispers carried over to me, and I was relieved when they scurried back to the wall.

"Why do you try to save them?"

I shrugged. "I got caught in a war that has nothing to do with me. But I will defend those who cannot defend themselves."

"How noble."

He charged me. I sidestepped into a spin and planted my foot in the center of his back. He sprawled on the ground a few feet away. I swayed where I was, balancing from one foot to the other, waiting. A variety of small growls and whines sounded from the pack as he leapt to his feet and faced me again.

He moved forward cautiously this time, hands up to block his face. But that left other areas of his naked body exposed. He aimed a punch at me. I dodged, stepped closer, jabbing my fist into his stomach and my knee into his groin. Down he went again.

"You bitch!" he gasped.

"Are you just going to play? Or are you actually going to fight?" I crossed my arms and stared down at him.

"Why not just end me now? It'd be the perfect opportunity."

"Because I'm not you, and I was taught to never kick someone when they were down."

He growled in response as he tried to get up. More whining from the wolves. I circled him, making sure to stay just out of arms reach. He reached his knees and glared at me. Then lunged. I let him have a quick moment of victory as his arms wrapped around my waist and he threw me to the ground.

I brought my head up right before it made contact. He pinned me down, straddling my stomach.

"You've lost," he hissed down at me, raising his hands to strike.

I laughed. I lifted my legs and wrapped them around his torso. "You are really making this too easy."

I squeezed his arms by his sides and pulled him down with my legs so I can sit up. I wrapped my arms around his thighs and twisted. My legs go left, my shoulders right, and he screams, drowning out the sharp cracks of his breaking spine.

"I'm done playing, and you're wasting my time," I said.

He remained limp on the ground, glaring up at me. "You won't win," he hissed.

"Maybe not. But with each wolf felled, I get closer to the one who started all this. I am sorry that you had to end up on the wrong side, perhaps the rest of your people will choose differently in the future."

"They won't listen to a halfling like you," he spat, grimacing from the pain.

"One way or another they will." I knelt by his head. "I am sorry."

With one quick move I broke his neck. I looked up at his pack. There were six. Two had their heads bowed, their eyes never leaving me. The other four whimpered in defiance.

"You know your part now," I said as I stood and walked over to them. "Tell your leader that the attacks stop, or I target them next. Take him back as proof."

I returned to the dead wolf and lifted his carcass off the ground. I gritted my teeth against his weight and went up to the closest wolf that had shown defiance. His eyes narrowed.

"Either you take him, or I cut him up and burn him," I sighed.

The wolf huffed at me but stretched out so that I could drape the man across his back. I placed a hand on the side of his neck before stepping away. He turned to me in surprise, brown eyes meeting green.

I smiled sadly at him and let my hand drop. He continued to stare at me as I stepped back. Something flickered in his gaze.

"Good luck," I said.

The wolf nodded and led the others away. My body sagged as I watched them go. I gathered my belongings and turned to the opening gate.

There was one long, mournful howl as I stood in the entrance. I turned and looked out over the land.

"Are you coming in or not?" an annoyed guard asked.

I turned and glared at him. "I just saved your ass. You really want to pick a fight with me?"

"N-n-no," he cowered. "I just want to get the gates closed before they come back."

"They won't be coming back. At least not tonight," I replied and I strode past him.

"I have some questions for you before you find your business here," a rough voice demanded.

I turned and looked at the older man. He had a scar under one eye, gray hair was pulled back from his face, and a sword hung at his hip. He watched me quizzically, one hand resting on the hilt of his weapon. Alert.

"What kind of questions?" I asked. "This way," the man said.

He turned without another word and followed along the wall. I clenched my jaw but followed behind him. He led me to a building farther back, up the stairs, and inside.

Cells lined the right side of the interior. "You're locking me up?" I demanded.

"Until I know if you are friend or foe, yes. I will have someone bring you something to eat, and I will question you in the morning."

"I just put my life on the line to keep them from attacking you, and this is how you treat me?"

"Like I said," the man said through gritted teeth. "Until I know who you are, you will stay here."

He opened the cell door, motioning for me to go inside.

I complied.

Chapter seventeen

Mira

I paced along the front of my cell, my anger growing with each step until the edges of my vision were tinged red. The guard let me keep all of my belongings, but that did not soften the fact they locked me up. No one brought me food, and I ended up snacking on some of my rations. I did not shout. I did not make a noise. I simply paced.

The darkness faded to gray and then orange as the sun rose outside. Still no one came.

The day shone warm and bright, and as I fumed, night began to settle. Still no one came.

I stopped pacing when the walls turned pink. I unbraided my hair and sat down in an attempt to reign in my anger. I rifled through my pack, pulled out clean bandages and Selena's salve, and went about rebandaging my arm and shoulder.

Might as well be productive.

"Mira."

I jumped and looked at the bars. I had been so focused on my arm that I had not been paying attention to my surroundings.

"Rhudi," I whispered. "What are you doing here?"

"I watched you enter the walls last night, but your town to town routine was interrupted, and I wanted to see why."

I sighed, set the clean bandages on the bed and walked over to the bars.

"I have news for you," Rhudi said before I could say anything.

"What kind of news? Unless it's a way to get me out of here, I'm not sure I want to hear it."

His eyes glanced down at my arm, and he frowned. "What happened there?"

"Old injuries," I said with a wave of my hand. "I've had them the entire time I've been traveling. What's this news? I don't want you to get caught here."

He grinned. "You have allies."

I looked at him in confusion. "What's that supposed to mean?"

"The wolves from last night. Three of them came back. They've been waiting outside the walls with me."

"But why are they *my* allies?" I asked using his term.

"Because they want to make you their alpha. They admired how you handled last night. No one has ever won a challenge that way."

"I think you and I have a different definition of *challenge*," I began.

"Yes," Rhudi said, cutting me off. "When a wolf challenges you, it's usually to take your position and show their strength. With humans it's more of something that needs to be overcome and doesn't have to result in death."

"So, because I accepted the challenge and that wolf was a leader, I won his spot?" I asked.

"Simply put, yes."

I shook my head. "I can't be a leader or *alpha*, as you call it, I'm not a wolf."

My head hurt, and I rubbed my temples. There was more to all this than I ever thought possible.

"Not a full one," Rhudi said. "Think about it. We'll think of a way to get you out of here if you aren't released in the morning."

"Don't kill anyone," I warned. Rhudi froze. "As much as I want to tear myself out of here, no more deaths."

"We are on your side Mira. I don't want to see any more human deaths than you do."

rhudi

"What is going on?" Cal asked.

"They have her locked up," I replied.

I watched the tension rise in them. Even if she would not admit it, she was already their alpha, and they were ready to save her.

"Then we have to get her," Cal said as he ran a hand through his shaggy brown hair.

"We will. She was surprised that you three are here."

Cal sighed. "I'm more surprised I'm here than she is."

"You were defiant in wanting to carry Les," Knox said, his boyish features bright with a grin.

Cal punched him in the arm. An alpha can command to be followed, but the loyalty that these three had was rare. It was a deeper pull to follow an alpha that ran deep in the soul. I had felt it when she told me not to kill anyone. That pull to follow her. To die for her. I shook my head.

"And you're sure she's the granddaughter of Lycus?" Ivan asked.

"Yes," I replied. "She is my niece. And if my father finds out, he will destroy her."

All three of their gazes harden. I knew after her display last night, that it would not take her long to start creating her own backing of wolves.

Word was spreading fast of a traveling warrior strong enough to fight off the wolves. And no one could tell who or what was fighting back.

"Does she know that you are reporting her movements to Alpha Kieran?" Cal asked, his arms crossed over his bare chest.

"No, and, for now, I don't want her to know. Only you three will know so that you can protect her accordingly," I replied. "I have a meeting with the rogue council that I need to attend in a few days and won't be able to keep an eye on Mira."

"We'll keep her safe," Knox said.

"You better," I challenged. "There's some reason she's searching for Kieran."

Kieran

"Winboro? Why the hell is she in Winboro of all places?" I growled.

"Currently—imprisoned," Gage said as he reviewed his notes.

"For doing what?"

"Apparently winning a challenge to save them against an attack. Apparently the townsfolk could not determine if she were friend or foe."

"She's getting stronger and moving north, but making sure to hit every town as she travels. Do we know of her motive yet?"

"I think you might find that part very interesting, Alpha."

"My patience is wearing thin, Gage. Spit it out"

"It's Mira," he said with a grin.

"What does Mira have to do with this?" I growled, not liking the way he smiled at me.

"Mira is the Rogue Alpha's granddaughter," Gage said slowly and clearly. "And she is looking for you."

"Merda!" I hissed.

That makes things much more difficult. But it also explained a few things.

She was an Alpha Heir. And a strong one at that.

Mira

Rhudi showed up again the next evening after I had still not been released.

"I have to run an errand," he said.

I eyed him. "Well, I'm not going anywhere, but thanks for letting me know."

He laughed. "Like I said last night, three wolves are ready to follow you. They will help protect you until I can make it back, and they will be breaking you out in a couple of hours, so be prepared."

"How are they going to do that?" I asked.

"Just wait for the signal and stay safe. I'll see you soon, Mira."

With that he vanished. I cursed. I had only been visited once and that was for a guard to bring me a moldy piece of bread and a jug of water. Sleep had avoided me as well.

I quickly packed up my things and started pacing. Heavy footfalls sounded on the stairs outside. A guard came in and stood before my cell. It was the old man who had locked me in here two nights ago. I glared at him.

"What happened to food and questioning in the morning?" I demanded.

"We had some town emergencies," the guard said with a smug smile.

"Well I know it wasn't wolves."

"And how would you know that?"

"No alarms. No howls. I have very good hearing. So what took you so long?"

"I was questioning the other men who witnessed the attack."

"And?"

"They kept saying that there were nine wolves that attacked, you beheaded two. But you killed a man and sent the body back with six. What happened to the last wolf?"

I started laughing. "You already know the answer. You want to see if I will play along and either say that there were only eight and the man was with them. But no. There were nine. These aren't your normal wolves."

"My other question is why weren't you as surprised as the rest of us when one changed from animal to man?"

"I've been traveling quite a bit, and you couldn't imagine what I've seen."

"That may be. Or you're one of them," the old man said.

"Ahh," I replied. "If I were one of them, you would never have gotten me in this cage. And if you had, this entire town would be leveled to the ground for trying to keep me prisoner."

His face paled at my words. "And if you keep locking up people who are trying to help you, you will never survive this."

"Either way, your trial is tomorrow. We'll let the people decide." He turned to leave.

"What's your name?" I asked.

"Grady."

"Grady. Make sure you sleep with one eye open, because I'll be coming for you."

As if on cue, a howl sounded. I grinned as Grady scrambled out the door and the alarm bell echoed through the town. Time to go.

I put my weapons in place and waited. I heard light footsteps from the other end of the hall.

"Mira?" a man asked.

I went up to the bars and grabbed his chin. His brown eyes met my green. His tan skin warm under my fingertips.

Shaggy brown hair fell into his eyes. He looked scared for a moment.

"You carried your fallen leader away. Why are you here?" I whispered.

I let go of his chin and stepped back. I eyed him up and down. His chest and feet were bare, and he had on a pair of simple trousers.

"Because it was the right thing to do," he replied. "We can talk after we get you out of here."

He grabbed the bars of the door and easily pulled it from the wall. I grabbed my pack, and we raced back the way he had come.

We ran out of the building and to an unguarded spot in the wall. The wolf paused as if to help me up. I jumped without breaking stride, pulling out two knives and climbed up the wall. He was right behind me.

We were up and almost over before anyone noticed.

"You!"

I looked down and saw Grady glaring at me. I motioned for

the wolf to go on over, and he did. I looked back at Grady.

"I'll be back for you," I shouted.

I let go of the wall and was surprised when the man caught me before I landed.

"It will be faster if we run, but it is up to you," he said.

"Okay, so long as we keep heading north."

He nodded and in one fluid motion shifted as his pants hit the ground. Without thinking, I picked them up and hoisted myself onto his back. He howled and took off.

Soon after, two more wolves flanked us. We ran for a few hours before stopping in a clearing. I slid off and collapsed from exhaustion. All three hovered over me instantly.

"I'm fine, just exhausted," I said. "Thank you." They all shifted and slipped into pants.

"Of course," the man who had pulled me from my cell said.

"It's still early, I'll set a perimeter, and we'll take shifts. Get some rest Mira," a younger looking wolf said with a small smile.

"What are your names?" I asked as I sat up to look at the three of them through blurry eyes.

"Cal is the one who helped you out of the cell. I am Knox," the younger of the three said. "And that is Ivan."

Ivan had dark skin and black hair. His pale brown eyes stood out against his complexion. My lack of sleep and food the last two days was catching up.

"It's a pleasure to officially meet you all," I replied. "I hate to keep conversation short, but I really need to sleep now."

"Get your rest, Alpha," Ivan said. "We won't let anything happen to you."

I mumbled unintelligibly as I took my pack off and laid back down. Sleep pulling me under immediately.

Darkness surrounded me. Pressed against me. Cold.
I looked around in an attempt to see anything. I turned, and there

he was. Seeming to appear before me as if he were made of fog. I caught the glint of silver.

I moved too slow. He, too fast.

My hands wrapped around his. His hands were just as cold as the knife handle he held.

But the pain. White. Hot. Radiating from the blade in my chest. I looked up into his cold, angry eyes.

"Kieran," I whispered.

His response was to twist the blade deeper.

I awoke with pain radiating from my chest. I sat up gasping, hands fluttering. Eyes blinded by the midday sun.

"Mira," Cal said kneeling beside me. "Mira!"

I froze as he caught my wrists and forced me to be still.

I could still feel the knife in my chest, my heart beating against it. I stared into his eyes, blinking a couple of times to focus.

"Cal?" I whispered.

"We're all here. It was a dream. You are safe."

My gaze found Knox sitting by a fire and Ivan stepping from the tree line. Concern etched into their every feature. I took a deep breath, and Cal let go of my wrists. I absently touched where the blade had been in my dream.

"We are here if you want to talk about it," Ivan said. He dropped a large buck down by Knox.

"It just felt so real. I woke up still feeling the pain," I said.

"We can spend the rest of the day and night here and set out in the morning," Cal said. "Give you some more time to recoup from the last few days."

I thought about it, watching Ivan and Knox preparing to cook the buck. I nodded.

"A day without fighting sounds too good to pass up," I replied.

"We'll set out first thing in the morning," Cal confirmed.

kieran

Pain. White. Hot. Burning through my veins. I bolted upright, gasping.

Mira.

My hand went to my chest. The intense pain was fading. I closed my eyes and concentrated. If I focused hard enough, I could sometimes make out other emotions.

Fear. Betrayal. Loss.

"Alpha!" Gage burst into my room.

"I'm fine," I replied. "Close the door and sit."

He complied and sat in front of the dying fire. I got up, threw a couple of logs on the flames, and sat down across from Gage.

"What happened? It felt like you were being killed."

"Can mates feel the other's physical wounds if they are bad enough?"

"I don't believe so. Pain is a physical experience. Unless," he paused in thought.

I stayed silent, my fingertips massaging my temples.

"It would have to by the psychological way. It could be a memory or a dream even."

"I don't think Mira has ever been stabbed in the heart," I replied. "But a dream might make sense with all the fighting she's doing."

"It would," he agreed.

We sat in silence for a moment longer. "Go back to bed, Gage. I'm sorry I woke you."

"Never apologize for waking me up. Danger is danger no matter the form. Get some rest, I'll see you in the morning."

Chapter Eighteen

Mira

"Let's see what you're made of," I said to Knox.

I stood from my spot next to the fire. We had all enjoyed a hearty lunch.

"What do you mean?" he asked.

"If you three are going to be traveling with me, I have to make sure you know what you're doing in a fight."

"I know what I'm doing," Knox said with a pout.

"Then come prove it," I taunted. "I'll even throw in some pointers if you need them."

"This ought to be good," Ivan laughed as he stretched out lazily.

Knox stood and approached me, making sure to keep a little distance between us.

"And no shifting," I said. "I want to see how you fight as a human first. That way I know if you can come into any of the towns we pass through with me."

"Sounds fair," Knox said. He took his stance.

I motioned for him to make his move. He started by circling to the left. I countered, keeping my movements slow and smooth. He barreled forward, taking a swing at me. I ducked with a quick upper cut to his side. He swept a leg out, and I jumped over it. I crouched. Waiting. Knox lunged. I rolled.

My only goal was to gauge his strengths and weaknesses; his speed and accuracy of attack. Though Knox was obviously stronger than I, brute force would not win him this fight. I was quicker and more agile.

On his next attack, I let him wrap his arms around my waist, to trap my arms under his, to bring me close enough that I could feel his heartbeat against my back.

"I got you," he proclaimed.

"She wasn't trying to avoid you," Cal said.

I widened my stance during their banter. Knox squeezed as if to confirm to himself that he had indeed *gotten* me.

"One thing to note," I said. "Never get too cocky. It makes you think the fight is over when it's not."

With one abrupt move I raised my arms, ducked, and swept my leg out. Knox collapsed. Ivan and Cal cheered.

"Not bad, but you've got some learning to do," I said as I offered Knox my hand.

He huffed at me as he stood. I patted him on the shoulder and grinned.

"Ivan, your turn."

Cal was the more skilled warrior of the three. More observant and patient. We sat around the fire after our mock fight, breathing heavy. The sun was about to begin its evening light show.

"It might be safer if we stay outside town walls while you go in," Ivan said. "That way on the off chance we have to break you out again, we will have a strategic advantage instead of all being trapped together."

"That makes sense," I agreed.

I took a sip from my canteen and leaned back against my pack.

"If you don't mind my asking," Knox began. "How did you learn to fight the way you do?"

"That's a long story, and it doesn't start out well," I replied with a sad smile.

"I was just curious. You don't have to share if you don't want too."

"My birth father tried to sell me to the pleasure house when I was young," I began with a sigh. "He tried to do this after I started to fight against his mental and physical abuse. I was eleven. It was as he was trying to strike a deal with the Madam that Remus and his wife found me. They took pity on me after they saw the bruises, cuts and scrapes."

I paused, reached up and traced the pale scar under my right eye. My father had backhanded me, and his ring had cut deep. Sooner or later my story would come out.

"They threw a small coin bag on the ground for my father and led me away. Once I was healed, Remus began training me to defend myself and follow in his footsteps. I got my first assassination job when I was sixteen. Jobs were regular and normal up until the attacks started. At that point it took everyone in the village to defend what we had left."

"You are an assassin?" Ivan asked.

I nodded. "More or less, they called me a *virago*, sword of the people. I was trained by an assassin to help those who are unable to help themselve. Sometimes it involved rescuing a girl from an abusive relative. But when it came to my own father…" I trailed off.

"So he's still alive?" Cal growled.

"No. Kieran made sure of that the last time I saw him."

"That's how you met Kieran?" Knox looked confused.

I shook my head. "Kieran saved my life when my father left me for dead in the middle of a blizzard outside the town wall. He thought I was one of his wolves. Needless to say, he was shocked to find out I'm just a human."

"You're not *just a human*," Cal interjected. "You are a halfling. Wolves haven't seen one in hundreds of years."

"That's because they killed them all," Ivan said. "They usually could not shift and were seen as a weakness in the pack."

"I would have liked to see them take on Mira." Knox laughed.

"Hard to say what would have happened back then," Ivan nodded.

"It's nice to know that even wolves don't like their own blood," I replied sadly.

The three of them stopped laughing and looked at me. "That's not what we meant—" Ivan began.

"I know you didn't," I cut him off. "It's just one of those things. No matter how strong you or your people are, one difference and they turn on you. I see it everywhere. Humans don't have the pack mentality that wolves do. I noticed that in the brief time I saw Kieran and one of his pack members. And the way you three move. It's as if you are all connected somehow."

"Did Kieran mention the pack link to you?" Cal asked.

"Pack link?" I asked with a shake of my head.

"We can hear each other," Knox said as he tapped his temple.

"We can choose what everyone hears, and it helps with communication. Especially in our wolf forms when words aren't possible," Cal said.

"That makes sense. Do halflings have that ability?"

Cal shrugged.

"No one knows. It was never documented what characteristics halflings grew into," Ivan continued. "Most never lived long enough."

"Having you as an alpha is new for everyone," Knox added.

"I guess we will learn together," I replied with a yawn.

"Try and get some rest. We will start out early," Ivan said.

"Wake me up for watch," I said as I stretched out on the ground.

None of them woke me up for watch. My eyes fluttered open at the first signs of light, and I bolted upright. Ivan and Knox were passed out on the other side of the ashes of last night's fire.

Crack.

I was up with an arrow nocked, eyes scanning the tree line. A wolf peered at me. Cal.

"Cal, you should be more careful or you'll get an arrow through the eye," I called.

"What are you talking about?" Cal asked as he stepped out of the trees behind me. The other two stirred.

A fourth wolf stared at us. Ivan was up and shifted before I could blink, growling. "Not someone you know?" I asked, as I leveled my arrow back at the newcomer. My gaze unwavering.

"No," Cal whispered. "He is alone at least."

"From what you told me last night, that doesn't mean anything," I said sharply.

The wolf took a small step forward and shifted.

"I apologize for the alarm," he said with his hands held up in surrender.

I glared at him. His gray-blond hair was cut short, a few days worth of stubble across his chin. Definitely a cleaner wolf. Older too. Perhaps in his mid-fifties.

"Who are you?" I demanded.

"I am Pascal. Rhudi sent me to warn you. There's a problem."

CHAPTER NINETEEN

MIRA

"What do you mean by *problem*?" I asked, my bow still aimed at him.

"The rogues are moving up their timeframe," Pascal said.

I caught the glances between the three around me and narrowed my eyes. "What timeframe? What is going on? What the hell do you know that I should also know?" I demanded after no one said anything.

Pascal seemed unfazed, but I watched his jaw tighten. "The Rogue King has ordered a large scaled attack on Rivermont. He has not taken kindly to your threats."

"Your Rogue King has ordered this attack, but he still refuses to show himself?" I asked.

Pascal nodded.

I lowered my bow and pinched the bridge of my nose. "Then I guess we better get moving," I sighed. "How long before the attack? And do you know how many rogues we should expect?"

"Dusk. Last headcount I heard was fifty to a hundred."

"Inform Rhudi that you gave us the message," I directed at Pascal. "Let's go, we don't have much time."

Knox created a makeshift saddle for my bags and put them on Ivan's back.

"Safe travels to you. You may yet be the end to all of this," Pascal said as his form blurred into the shadows.

I ignored him as I rolled up my blanket and donned my gear. Anxiety and adrenaline coursed through my veins.

"We will have to run," Knox said. "If we are to get there in time. And we will have to skip searching a town."

"That's fine," I said tightly. "The people being attacked are the priority."

Cal shifted and Knox followed suit. I gathered up their trousers, tucked them into my bag and jumped onto Cal's back without a word.

The forest blurred by as they ran. I gripped Cal's fur with both hands, keeping low over his shoulders.

Midday, they came to a panting halt outside the town we had to skip. Silence greeted us—an unnerving, haunting silence.

"Wait here and catch your breath, I'll be right back," I said as I swung down and sprinted toward the wall, a blade in my right hand.

An open gate greeted me. It was a splintered and charred mess. I ran through and stopped short. Bodies littered the street before me; the buildings were in various stages of burned ruins; the ground stained with blood—some spots were black with the amount. My heart thundered in my ears. I stood transfixed, stunned by the carnage.

I went up to the closest group of bodies and knelt. I could just make out the teeth and claw marks that had shredded the bodies. I stood, suddenly feeling sick.

"Mira?" Cal asked.

He stood a few yards away, his eyes sweeping over the remains just as mine had.

"Why would they kill an entire town?" I asked him. "What is the point of it all?"

Tears stung my eyes, and I turned away. My hands clenched and unclenched, joints popping at the movement. I heard the soft pad of Ivan and Knox behind me. I did not need a wolf link to feel their shock at the carnage before us.

"Is this a message?" I asked as a tear escaped and rolled down my cheek. I turned to my companions. "Is this all my fault for fighting back?"

"Wolves aren't particularly fond of fire. They prefer to use their teeth and claws to make their point, so it is possible they did this to show you that they won't back down," Cal confirmed.

I closed my eyes, took a deep breath and steadied myself. "I am not backing down either. If this is how they want to play, then I will show them who they are playing with. Let's go. I don't want to see another town suffer for my actions."

"What is your plan?" Cal asked as I turned my back on the town and stepped over to them.

"We give them a taste of their own medicine at Rivermont. Then we find Kieran and figure out a way to stop all of this."

"Rivermont it is," Cal said with a thoughtful smile.

I nodded, and he shifted. Ivan and Knox each dipped their heads toward me as I climbed onto Cal's back. Something in me snapped. Red tinged the edges of my vision, and my muscles vibrated with rage.

"Let's show them they have no claim to anything," I growled as we took off.

The time for games was over.

Kieran

"So Ironvale is gone?" I asked.

"Completely wiped out. And apparently set on fire," Pascal said. "That was the Rogue King's message to Mira."

"Why would he be sending her messages?" I demanded.

"Because she's been sending him messages."

I stared at Pascal with narrow eyes, trying to disguise the fear that was beginning to rise in me.

"I am tired of not having all of the information about the situation," I seethed.

"What kind of messages is she sending?" Gage asked.

"Threats to try and get him to stop the attacks."

"Well it doesn't seem to be working," I replied as I ran a hand through my hair, "because we now have the biggest attack yet headed toward Rivermont. And I'm guessing she's also headed there in an attempt to stop it?"

Stress and worry flowed through my body. Mira was still trying to play hero. And I feared it would get her killed.

"She and her pack are on their way there," Pascal confirmed. "Rhudi sent me to tell them the attack news before heading here."

"Her pack?" I asked.

"The challenge she won resulted in three of those wolves naming her their alpha."

"And why didn't we know of this sooner?"

"The information had not been confirmed until after she escaped Winboro," Pascal replied.

I sat down at my desk. "Do you know who has named her their Alpha?"

"Ivan, a younger wolf named Knox, and..." he trailed off as he eyed me.

"And?" I growled.

"Cal."

Pascal cowered at the growl that erupted from me, and Gage's eyes widened in surprise.

"Cal?" I hissed. "The notorious head of the Rogue King's guard?"

"The very one," Pascal said in a hushed voice. "And from what I saw, he is the most protective of her."

"It is in his blood to protect the blood of Lycus," Gage mused.

"That doesn't matter. He's killed more alphas than any other wolf out there," I growled. "Some he even turned on."

"He won't turn on Mira," Pascal said abruptly.

I turned my gaze to him, and he stared at me with more defiance than I thought possible. "And why do you say that?"

"She has an air about her. She demands loyalty without even

trying. The pull to follow her..." Pascal paused, searching for words. "I have never felt a pull toward an alpha like that or the need to kneel at every word she said. It took all my power to stay upright when I told her the news about the upcoming attack."

"What about the pull toward me?" I asked curiously. "How does that compare to the pull you felt toward Mira?"

"I don't mean any disrespect toward you," Pascal said nervously.

"I'm not taking it that way. I'm just curious. How you would compare two alphas."

"She has a strength about her that is much different from a normal alpha. It's hard to describe. And I have only been around her once."

"That means she's getting stronger," Gage said.

I could feel his eyes on me as I processed the new information. *Why would I be mated to the granddaughter of my enemy? One who has no knowledge of her lineage? And a Halfling at that.*

"Alpha?" Gage asked.

I shook my head and stared back at him. "Send twenty warriors to Rivermont. Hopefully it isn't too late to save them."

To save Mira.

Those words hung unspoken between the three of us. Heavier than their spoken counterparts.

Pascal bowed and exited the chamber.

"What are you doing?" Gage asked. "If she wants to die trying to protect the towns that can't defend themselves, let her."

I glared at him. "My mate is the only one trying to make a difference here. Her actions are what have sped up the attacks and made them more violent. If anything, she will be the one to end this while I die trying to find a solution behind these damned walls."

"I am only trying to protect the future of our race," Gage said cautiously. "I meant no disrespect."

"I understand. It is your job as Beta to do that. But you of all people should know better than to say a wolf's mate should die."

He flinched at my words, then posed a question.

"What happens if she survives the battle at Rivermont?"

"Then she will be only a few days travel from here. We will have to be on the look out at the gates for when her pack arrives. I don't care what Pascal said about Cal. He's the one I am most worried about turning on her."

Mira

Time moved too fast. Despite how fast we ran, we were going to be late to Rivermont. I knew it. My muscles felt as though they would snap with the tension rising in me. Dread caused my heart to thunder in my chest. The sky darkened not only with the waning day, but as a storm rolled in.

Cal came skidding to a halt, almost throwing me over his shoulders.

"Hey!" I exclaimed, my knuckles cracking as I unclenched his fur.

He looked back at me.

I frowned. "What is it now? We don't have time to be stopping like this."

He grunted and rolled his eyes at me.

"Cal," I warned as I jumped down. "What is going on?" He shifted and pointed. I looked where he gestured. "What—" I froze and listened.

Screams floated to us, and smoke filled the air. I looked at the sky. It was still an hour or so until dusk. The sun made the bottom of the black clouds look as though they were dipped in blood.

"It's not dusk yet. Pascal lied."

CHAPTER TWENTY

Mira

"We need to move. Now!" I shouted.

Cal shifted as Knox and Ivan took off. I jumped on to Cal's back and once again we were full speed, this time downhill. I hovered low over Cal's back, my eyes scanning the terrain ahead of us.

Knox and Ivan led the way, and I could tell Cal was pacing himself with them. We did not have time to waste. Thunder rolled in the distance, the rain-heavy sky darkening even more. My vision sharpened with the darkness.

"Cal, I know you can go faster," I murmured. "Let them catch up to us."

He huffed, but sped up. He quickly overtook the others.

"We'll see you there," I shouted over my shoulder.

My heartbeat thundered in my ears, joining the screams and shouts in a horrific cacophony. We broke through the tree line and we saw at least a hundred attacking Rogues. "Merda," I growled.

Cal bolted forward as I pulled a blade from its sheath. And as he neared the fringes, I launched myself off his back and into the fray.

My blade plunged up to the hilt through a Rogue's skull.

The man that had been the Rogue's opponent stared at me in horror and awe.

"Get your people behind the wall," I growled as I jerked my weapon free.

Electricity charged the rage-filled air as the storm loomed

overhead. I turned without another word and beheaded the next wolf without blinking. More soldiers stared at me, mouths agape. Three more wolves barreled toward me.

I drew my second blade and leapt into the air. I came down onto the back of one wolf, thrust a blade through its skull, spun off its falling corpse, and sliced through the second Rogue's throat.

The third leapt, and I stabbed both blades through it's chest and stomach. I guided the body to the ground and yanked my weapons free. I turned and stared at the guards who were watching me in fascination.

"Go! Focus on putting the fires out and get behind the wall," I ordered as I sliced through two more wolves. There was no point in saying the walls were safe any longer.

They scrambled away as fast as they could, stumbling over wolf and human corpses on their way.

I turned to face a wolf that had set its mark on me. It snarled and lunged. I crouched in preparation, but Cal blurred past me, slamming into the Rogue's side and driving him into the ground. Cal spared one glance at me before tearing out the Rogue's throat.

I nodded, then turned and shoved a blade through the jaw of another as it lunged for me. There were so many. Fur, teeth, and metal pressed in from all sides. Just then the downpour joined the fray from above.

I heard howls behind me. Ivan and Knox were joining us even as more Rogues began to turn to see who was interfering with their attack.

A wave surged toward us. My companions attacked those on either side and made sure my back was covered. The humans that had stayed to fight followed our example and joined together in groups of threes and fours.

I lunged, taking on three at once. One lunged, and I spun with a quick slash across its stomach. The other two watched, suddenly more cautious. They advanced as lightning lit up the sky behind me.

I stalked forward. "Where is your leader?" I growled. "Why

is your Alpha not here?" I lunged—blade through one heart and a slash across the other's throat.

A heavy weight slammed into my right side and pinned me into the mud. Snapping teeth were inches from my throat. Paws pressed heavily into my chest, and claws ripped at my shoulder. Angry howls echoed around me. I tried to push the wolf away... but then he was gone. I watched Ivan rip the Rogue's throat out.

I gasped, trying to regain my breath. There were too many... no way to defeat them all. I knew what I had to do to save my pack and my people.

I stood up and quickly scanned the area. Fires were out at least, and the gates were closed.

Two wolves lunged for me.

I dodged one while the other swung a paw and caught my thigh. I hissed and promptly stabbed it through the eye.

The second turned back and lunged again. I kicked out, my foot connected with his head, and he collapsed in surprise. Thunder growled overhead.

He stared back at me as another group started to close in. "I challenge your Alpha!" I roared.

Rhudi

The Rogue King decided to send more than one hundred wolves to Rivermont. Thankfully he did not want me to lead them into battle. That would have been hard to explain to Mira.

I suggested I scout ahead and see if there were any problems with the attack. My father agreed.

The first thing I did was send Pascal to find Mira and tell her about the attack before telling Kieran the news. Then I ran a quick route to Rivermont and then back to my father's castle.

"Rhudi," my father said as he stared at me from across the table. "Anything new to report from your travels?"

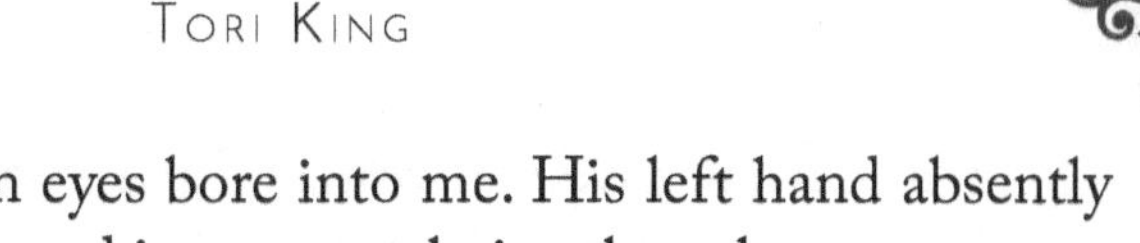

His yellow-green eyes bore into me. His left hand absently stroked his ash grey beard in contemplative thought.

Despite his age and hair color, he did not look a day over fifty. His gold crown, tarnished with age and stained in some places with old blood, glowed softly in the firelight.

"I have been watching the wolf that is sending you these messages," I replied.

"And? Anything of note?"

"She is strong and determined. And from what I've seen, an incredibly skilled fighter."

"She?" he asked before bursting into laughter.

"Yes," I replied watching his fit of laughter warily.

"There is no way a she-wolf is causing this much havoc."

"I assure you, that she is the one causing all of it."

He eyed me thoughtfully, then his eyes glazed over. The whites and irises turned to a silvery-white glow. *He must be getting a message from the Rivermont attack.* The hand stroking his beard now wrapped around it and tightened. He frowned.

"What news? Have they taken Rivermont?"

"That bitch just demanded a challenge," he growled.

"Which leader did she challenge?"

"She directly challenged the Alpha."

My blood went cold. Despite the initial fear, I was in awe of Mira's bravery. She knew the quickest way to stop a fight was to challenge a leader. But Mira hadn't just challenged any leader. She challenged the Alpha—my father.

Her grandfather.

Mira

Time seemed to slow as every wolf in the battle froze. Some stared at me in horrified awe, while others turned and fled. My feet sank into the mud. I attempted to push soaked strands of hair out of my eyes.

"Mira, what have you done?" Cal asked, his eyes wide.

"This needs to end. And the quickest way is to challenge the Alpha."

"You do realize that you are challenging *the* Rogue King himself," Cal said tightly.

"If that's what it takes," I replied. "I will play their games and by their rules."

The wolf I had kicked in the head shifted. He stared at me with fearful blue eyes. Blood was splattered across his tan skin; black hair fell into his eyes in shaggy curls. The left side of his face was bruised, his eye almost swollen shut.

"The Alpha accepts your challenge," he declared.

Cal placed a hand on my shoulder while the wolf conversed silently with his Alpha. Cal's hand tightened as we waited. It took all of my resolve to not say anything as he applied pressure against the needle-like pain from the wounds that marred my shoulder.

"He said the challenge will take place in exactly one month at the Hall of Alphas," the wolf said. "The duel will happen at midday. If you are late, the King automatically wins, the attacks continue, and there will be a bounty on your head."

Cal's hand tightened even further on my shoulder. I let out a breathy hiss and cut a look at him.

"That means we have one month of zero attacks?" I confirmed.

The wolf nodded.

"I accept the terms," I said. "I will duel the Rogue King in one month."

"I have relayed your acceptance. I wish you luck, Challenger."

As one, all of the rogues began to filter away from Rivermont. When the field was clear, Cal turned me to face him and released my shoulder.

"Mira, I know it is not my place, but I feel like you made a mistake by challenging him outright."

"Why?" I asked him.

"Just a gut feeling," he replied. "Something doesn't feel right."

Before I could reply, the wolf that had relayed my challenge to the Rogue King locked his blue eyes onto me with a thoughtful gaze. "You're different," he said. "You are not a wolf, yet you smell of one."

"Go back to your master," Cal growled as he stepped between me and the wolf.

"I mean her no harm," he said. "You know the rules as well as I that a challenger must not be harmed, for the penalty is death to the dealer."

"It's more for your protection than hers," Cal replied coolly.

The wolf shrugged. "May we meet again in the Hall of Alphas." Without another word, he changed and sprinted away.

Cal wiped a hand down his face with a sigh. "There is much we need to teach you."

"It's about time somebody taught me something." I replied. "Everything I know now has been gleened in bits and pieces of information. It seems no one wants to tell me the whole story."

Cal sighed and glanced at Ivan and Knox. I threw my hands up in the air with exasperation.

"My Lady?"

I turned with my weapon raised toward the five soldiers that approached.

"I am no lady," I replied and sheathed my blade.

The man bowed his head, not at all perturbed by the wolves still nearby.

"As thanks for your help, we offer you and your companions a warm meal, and a chance for our healer to look over your wounds. We unfortunately are unable to allow you to stay the night at this time."

"That is fair. We have more business to attend and need to keep going," I replied.

"Have them tend your wounds," Cal said. "We can eat on the road."

I nodded. "Very well," I said tightly. "Take me to your healer."

CHAPTER TWENTY-ONE

Kieran

"**A**lpha! *"Your Majesty!"*

Voices shouted at me through the pack link as I paced in my study. The barrage of voices was enough to give me a headache. My vision swam as my wolf blocked all visual relays for a moment.

Gage burst in before I could reply. I took one look at him, and my heart sank. An icy coldness crept into my veins.

"She's dead," I didn't say it like a question, because I did not want to know the answer.

"Worse," Gage replied tightly.

I planted my hands on my desk and stared at him. I breathed in deeply, trying to calm the tremors as my wolf attempted to surface. My nails turned to claws, and I dug them into my desk in order to ground myself.

"What can be worse than my mate's death?" I whispered.

"She has challenged the Rogue King."

Whatever color I had left drained from my face. My heart skipped a beat, and my breath caught in my throat. There was no way she would do that. Not this early. But Gage was here with the news, and I could see the replay of events in my mind from the warriors we had sent.

"Do we know of the terms yet?" I stammered.

Gage shook his head. "I'm afraid not. I will keep digging for more information."

I nodded at him numbly. Her bloodstained face, set in determination, floated behind my eyelids. Her eyes glowing bright green out of the storm's darkness. Even though I had not witnessed the declaration, I knew the fight for the royal throne was on the line.

My wolf broke free as my emotions overtook my sanity.

Mira

The healer at Rivermont was a stern old man. His white hair puffed out around his head like a cloud no matter how many times he smoothed his hands over it. His weathered face was lightly lined. His blue eyes seemed to cut deeper than any blade I have ever faced. He did not say much as he set to work cleaning and bandaging my wounds under the scrutiny of the five men that accompanied Cal and me through the gate.

"You all need to leave," the healer said after he patched my shoulders. He was not looking at me, but at the entourage that watched us closely.

"Orders Fen," the eldest of the group said.

He looked to be in his mid-thirties. However, he seemed overly cautious of Fen.

"I need to stitch her thigh, and will not have the lot of you gawking while I do so," the healer's gravely voice demanded. "Now leave, before I have her... *companion*... escort you out."

They all cut a glance at Cal and hurried out the door. Cal gave me a quick nod and ducked out after them.

"Finally some peace," he said more to himself than to me.

"Let me have a look at that thigh," he continued a little louder.

I pulled my pants off and sat on the exam table with my undergarment and top still on.

"Damn werewolves," he muttered after a glance.

"You know about them?" I asked in surprise.

He looked up at me with a sly smile that told me all I needed to know.

"My dear," he began as he started stitching. "These are not the first attack we have endured. Nor are you the first halfling."

"But this is the first I've ever heard of such stories and attacks."

"Those of us a little closer to the kingdom know of their secrets. Some chose whether or not to believe them. Then you have those of us, that are neither Rogue nor a part of the pack."

"You are a shifter."

His smirk widened into a grin as his sharp eyes softened and brightened. Looking at him now, I could see more. He was slightly taller than other men and still very muscular for his age.

"I am a very old shifter," he said, as if reading my mind. "A healer then and a healer now."

"How have you stayed away from one side or the other?" I asked.

"The King knows I am here, but he won't bother me if I don't bother him. There are a couple of us here that way. The Rogue King on the other hand, would stop at nothing to have all of us bowing down to him."

"I've noticed that much," I replied with a sigh. "Everyone I have come across only tells me scraps of information. I can't get a full story from anyone."

"My guess is that they are trying to protect you," he said as he finished bandaging my leg. "You have become a source of hope for those against the Rogue King. Especially now that you have challenged him outright."

"Cal thinks I shouldn't have," I said as I slipped back into my pants and boots.

"He is wise. But he is also looking out for his Alpha. He wants to make sure you make the decisions that will benefit you *and* your pack."

"Thank you for your insight," I said with a small bow.

He chuckled. "There is no need to bow to me, Halfling. It is I that should bow to you. You remind me of a young healer I apprenticed long ago. She was just as spirited as you. Came from a well-known line and chose healing over her birthright."

"Birthright or not, few can determine how one lives their own life."

"True emough. You will be highly regarded here. The savior of Rivermont."

"I'm no savior. At this point I am just a *virago* helping those who cannot help themselves."

He grinned. "Like I said, a savior. Now, I won't keep you any longer. I am sure the King is wanting to know who is causing an uproar. Your pack will help you get there safely."

"Thank you, Fen."

I turned to leave, limping slightly with my wounded leg. "Halfling," Fen called.

I turned and looked at him.

"For hundreds of years, I have not followed an alpha. But if you were to call on me, I will gladly follow you."

I smiled sadly at him. "My path might not be one you want to follow."

I strode out of the cabin without another word. Cal lifted an amused brow at me, and I shook my head. We were escorted back out the gate.

Ivan and Knox lounged by my gear. The rain had let up to a steady drizzle while I was being patched up.

"That was interesting," I said as I donned my weapons. "Did you know that there were wolves outside of the Rogues and whatever the King's pack is?"

Cal nodded. "We come across a few every now and then. They tend to live much more peaceful lives than we do."

"I can see how they would by blending in with humans," I replied. "How far are we from the kingdom?"

"Two to three days," Cal replied. "At least now we don't have to worry about any attacks on the way."

"That doesn't make a difference in urgency. Remember, I have one month before I fight the Rogue King."

Cal sighed. "I know."

"We'll go as far as we can before sundown, then stop to sleep."

"Very well," Cal conceded. "Let's move out."

rhudi

Mira's challenge visibly shook my father. It had been decades, perhaps centuries, since he had been challenged. The wolf who had relayed her message had played back the memory of her fighting.

My father had accepted, though, and now had to keep his word.

Mira had bought a month of peace with her challenge. That would give Lycus plenty of time to prepare, and her time to recover from her encounters with his men.

He stared at me now with a puzzling expression. It was difficult to tell if he was trying to place whether he had seen her before, or if he was thinking back on his own daughter's banishment.

"Tell me," my father began. "Do we know anything else of this she-wolf?"

"Nothing more than what I have shared already, Father."

I was happy that he still called her a she-wolf. If he found out that she was a Halfling, complications could arise. But also the prophecy his first Beta had told could also arise again—a prophecy that foretold the end of his reign by his own blood and brought forth the rightful King of all shifters. And so far, Mira was living up to that prophecy. Showing strength and determination to protect what she loved.

She was the opposite of my father. She had no need of followers, yet there were wolves coming out of the shadows to join her. Even some holding high ranked positions in my father's court had left.

"I noticed that Cal is with her," my father began. "It seems he has left our side and joined hers."

"I believe that has to do with when she won her first challenge, which he was a part of," I replied.

"Perhaps," he said.

His eyes were unfocused in thought as he continued to absently stroke his beard.

"Is there something in particular that you are wanting to know? I can go out and do some digging," I offered, trying to find a way out of the castle.

"There is something about her... something that makes me wonder," he mumbled. "But yes. Go out and see what you can dig up on this girl. I will summon you in a week or two to hear what you have discovered."

"Yes, Father," I said with a bow of my head as I left his study.

I wasted no time striding through the halls and out of the castle. Once I was free, I shifted and ran. If I could find Kieran before she got to him, maybe there was a chance that we could still save Mira.

Mira

We stopped at the edge of the road for the night. I was not sure exactly where we were, but I knew we were not as close to the kingdom as I wanted to be.

All three shifted back and sat down in the growing darkness. I could feel their eyes on me as I stared down the road, straining my ears for any noise of Rogues nearby.

"There aren't any near," Ivan said after a moment. "All fighters are required to return after a challenge declaration."

I sighed and sat down. "I guess I am still on edge then."

"Rightly so," Knox said. He rose and began to gather wood for a fire.

I rubbed at the exhaustion on my face. When I lowered my hands, Cal was moving toward the tree line.

"Food," Ivan said absently as he cleared a spot on the ground for the pile of wood Knox had gathered.

"We'll get something cooked up and then we can all rest before setting out in the morning," Knox replied.

"Can you tell me about the rules of a challenge?" I asked. "I only know about the potential power and position gain from it."

"In the old days, challenges were used by those of pack rank. Such as the alpha, beta, gamma, but the ranking is a whole other story," Ivan began. "It was used as a way to show strength."

"Alphas used challenges to gain more territory," Cal interjected as he stepped out of the trees with a buck over his shoulders.

"Or it was a chance for those of lower rank to step up into a higher position," Ivan continued as if he had not been interrupted.

"Did it always end in death?" I asked.

"Yes," all three of them said at once.

"That was the only way to assure that power had been gained by the challenger who won the higher rank, or to protect from future harm if the lower rank lost," Ivan said solemnly.

"It also helps weed out weaknesses," Knox interjected. "Only the strong prevail."

"You said it used to be just between positions of rank, but now anyone can declare a challenge?" I stood up to help Cal clean the buck for dinner.

"Anyone can declare a challenge, but the terms have to be agreed upon by both members while in public. For example, I could not challenge you if it were just the two of us walking through the woods. There has to be at least one other person present to witness the terms exchanged and the actual challenge itself."

I broke off the antlers and held them as Cal quickly skinned the animal. I rubbed my thumbs over the velvety surface in an attempt to calm my nerves.

"What about location? Does it matter where the challenge is held?" I asked.

"In the old days, challenges were required to be fought in the Hall of Alphas. Now, they can be fought anywhere and at anytime."

"The Hall of Alphas is where I fight the Rogue King," I mumbled as I sat down.

"A challenge has not been held there in centuries," Ivan

declared. "Nor has there been a month long wait for a challenge either. Those terms were used among alphas to come to a brief peace agreement before one or the other took over."

Shock numbed my body as I absorbed what he had shared. My hands still stroked the velveteen antler as the scent of cooking meat began to fill the air.

There was no way the Rogue Alpha knew who or what I was. Yet he was bringing back old traditions as if this were a fight between two alphas.

I would be a fool to say I was not afraid. But I also knew I was a fool for jumping into a challenge against the Rogue King without more information. My heart pounded. I took a deep breath.

"We believe in you Mira," Knox said.

"There's one other thing to note about a challenge," Cal said as he turned the spit over the fire.

I shifted my gaze from Knox to Cal. "And that is?" I asked as strongly as I could.

"If either of the challengers is injured by another, whoever is responsible for the injury, whether intentional or not, is to be executed. No questions. No trial. For they interfered with a challenge."

"Dueling for training doesn't count," Ivan threw in. "You are allowed to train, but most injuries resulting from sparring consist of only a black eye or random bruises."

"Would it be just the person committing the act, or all parties involved?" I asked with a nod of understanding to Ivan.

"Everyone involved. Sometimes a family member or jealous lover will act to try and save their loved one."

"Good thing my family is not here," I replied quietly.

"And a challenge can only be completed at full health. That is the only way a challenge can be postponed and rescheduled."

"Okay, so don't get sick or injured in the next twenty-nine days. Got it," I said sarcastically.

Knox chuckled. "I guess that means no more training until after the challenge."

"I can train you without getting seriously injured," I said with a laugh. "So don't get your hopes up."

"Damn," he pouted.

We all burst into laughter. Despite the events leading up to now and everything that was going to happen, we laughed.

We laughed until we were all either bent double or splayed out on the ground. Tears welled up in my eyes and my stomach hurt, but I could not stop.

"Whyyy," Knox moaned in between fits.

Slowly our laughter quieted, blending in the with night sounds.

I stared up at the stars. "I think we needed that."

"Definitely," Cal said.

We sat in silence for a while, each of us lost in our own thoughts.

At the sound of a knife tearing through flesh, we all sat up to see Cal carving the buck over the fire. Time to eat and then try to sleep.

I took a bite of venison and couldn't help the momentary glimpse of hope. Despite my impending death, I knew that I would see Kieran in two days.

Rhudi

It felt as though my paws barely touched the ground as I flew across the land. I did not bother tracking Mira in my hurry to get to Kieran. There was not enough time.

Ideas on how to protect Mira floated through my head as I ran, but nothing solidified. I almost plowed into a sentry while lost in my thoughts. He growled at me as two more came sprinting over.

I stayed still, panting. Then I shifted and held my hands up. "I have news for King Kieran," I said in between breaths.

The wolves exchanged a glance before motioning me to follow them. I let my wolf surge forward as we ran the rest of the way through forest and came upon a stone wall.

We followed it a little ways to a bridge. Once we crossed over, I shifted again. Clothes were laid out for me, and I donned them quickly.

"He is waiting for you in the throne room," the closest guard announced.

"Thank you," I replied, then sprinted through the streets toward the castle. I'd made up my mind.

There did not seem to be anything we could do. Not now that she had declared a challenge. We would just have to prepare her the best we could. Train her the way a full- blooded shifter trained.

It was time for Mira to know her birthright. And to claim it.

Mira

"So tell me about this castle?" I asked when we stopped outside the walls.

We were far enough away that no scouts or sentries would spot us. We had an hour or so before sunset.

"How are the streets mapped?" I continued my barrage of questions as they shifted from wolf to human.

"The castle is at the center," Cal said, slipping into his pants. "I don't remember anything about the streets. It has been years since I was last here."

I frowned. "Can you tell me the population at least? Werewolf? Human? A combination?"

"Mostly shifters," Cal replied as Ivan shrugged.

"When you get to capitals like this, you will find very few humans inside the walls. And the ones you do are entrusted to the Alpha and his board."

"I want you three to wait out here," I said as I started removing my gear.

"What do you mean, *wait out here*?" Knox asked in surprise.

"You can't go by yourself!" Ivan exclaimed at the same time.

Cal was the only one who remained silent. He watched me as

I dropped my pack and then my swords and bow onto the ground.

"It might be her only option to go by herself," Cal said quietly. "As much as I despise the idea. We were after-all Rogue wolves."

"But we aren't now!" Knox cried.

"No, but you three walking in with a halfling is bound to cause some kind of commotion," I said.

"Very well," Ivan said in defeat. "We will be keeping a close ear and eye out for any signs you are in danger."

I nodded and patted my belt. I kept a dagger there tucked away at my back. It was hidden and out of sight, but easy to get too, should I need it.

"I hope you know what you are doing," Cal sighed.

"This is not the first time I have snuck over this wall," I replied. "It will be my first time sneaking into the castle though."

"Why were you asking about layout and such then?" Ivan said in surprise.

"You never know when maps change," I replied with a small smile and a shrug. "And it has been years since I was here, and I only met someone closer to the bridge. I never went into the heart of the city."

I turned away at their surprised faces and darted out of sight. I wanted to be up and over the wall before nightfall.

I skirted silently around two ground patrols and stopped at the base of the wall. The pearly white and gray-black stones shimmered and glowed orange and pink in the lingering light.

I quickly pulled my tangled hair back and began my ascent, the stones cool to the touch, no longer holding onto the day's warmth. At the top, I crouched and scurried across the wide expanse before dropping to climb down the other side.

Chatter from the streets floated around me as I dropped to the ground and pulled my hood up. I stayed in the shadows along the wall until I came upon a street that appeared to lead straight to the castle. My luck held as it looked to be the main street

I paused, staring down the line of shops that stood at attention on each side. The crowd of people milling around was beginning to diminish as the light continued to fade.

The air here was not as heavy with fear and tension as every other town I'd passed through. I watched guards amble up and down the streets, keeping a watchful eye.

The castle loomed overhead. Glowing and shimmering just like the perimeter wall in the dusk light. I could only imagine what it looked like under a full moon.

Five towers looked down at the streets. The tallest appeared to be in the center, surrounded by four a story or two shorter. Only the center tower had a roof, the others appeared to be used for lookout posts. The street led directly into a gate in the wall. I assumed it lead into a courtyard of some sort.

I merged with the crowd, heading for the gate. I caught a couple of curious glances as I quickly made my way through the dwindling throng. I avoided eye contact, and it took all my self-control not to run through the crowd.

As I neared the gate, I noticed the guards. There were four stationed on the ground, six directly above, and at least that many patrolling the top of each of the two towers facing me. Now for the fun part, getting into the castle.

I could feel with every fiber of my being that Kieran was behind those walls. I skirted along the shadows, careful not to draw any attention.

I rounded the corner and saw a very similar set up on this side. But with less guards and only a small side door. It seems the way I had found was actually the main road into the castle. I continued on to the opposite corner.

I could hear laughter somewhere nearby. Lots of small children running and squealing with joy. The lighthearted noise echoed through the air.

The light was gone now. I darted to the wall, pausing in the bushes. Assessing my next move. Torches were being lit up and down the castle walls and town streets.

The castle walls were much smoother than the town walls. That made scaling it directly more difficult. The castle gardener though, was not tactical. There was a tree standing proudly near where the straight wall met the curved part of the tower. And it loomed just over the top of the walkway.

I jumped up into the lower branches and began my silent climb, pausing anytime a patrol went by. It was a much longer climb than I would have liked. But I sat perched on a branch, waiting for the guards to walk past once more before dropping down on the walkway.

I avoided the patches of torchlight as I made my way across and then looked over the other side.

Children played in the courtyard below. Some played tag in the open space while the older kids sat in small clusters playing games or chatting animatedly in the torchlight around the garden.

A green house stretched along the length of the rear exterior wall and attached to the ground floor. Seems their cooks might grow some of their own supplies on the grounds.

A noise to my left had me up and dropping down into the rose bushes below. Thankfully the squealing children drowned out my fall.

I gritted my teeth against the thorn pricks and climbed as silently as I could from the vines. At least if I needed to get back out, the roses climbed up the smooth stone surface.

I wandered silently around a bush and slammed directly into someone.

"Watch it!" she cried as she patted her skirts in annoyance dusting herself off.

Her gold hair shone in the dim light, her eyes glowing a bright blue. Her pale pink gown was a stark contrast to my dark and travel-worn attire. At first glance, she seemed very much a dainty woman. Tall and slender, reveling in her titled position.

But I could also tell that she was not someone you wanted around. She would be a bad friend and an even worse foe.

"Who the hell are you?" she demanded when I did not respond.

I quickly darted back the way I went. Following the maze of flowers and bushes before finding a spot I could hide.

Her footsteps followed close behind me. She passed by my hiding spot, sniffing the air like a hound. All the pollen seemed to make it hard to track me.

"Lady Odell! My Lady, there you are!" Another woman rushed up.

She looked like a hand maid with her hair pulled back and white apron white around her dark dress.

"Is something the matter?" the maid asked.

"Come, we need to talk to the Kings-guard," Lady Odell said as she started walking swiftly away.

"We have an intruder."

part three
throne to the wolves

cal

I paced anxiously. Night had fallen, and so far no alarm had arisen. I hoped Mira had made it into the castle already.

"Would you sit down?" Ivan asked.

He sat with his back against a tree, his eyes closed. Knox sat across from him, eyes darting around at every little noise.

He fidgeted with a small pebble. We had no need to light a fire, our eyes could see almost perfectly in the dark.

"I can't until I know she is safe," I muttered.

"We may not know anything until morning," Ivan said. "Best to get some rest in case she does need us. We aren't of any use if we are exhausted."

"If only halflings could access the mind link," Knox said.

"Not helping, Knox," I growled.

He shrugged and went back to throwing the pebble from one hand to the other. The soft white seemed to glow in the darkness.

It may be Kieran's castle, but he had the best defenses of any alpha.

Mira

I left my hiding spot and crept closer to the castle. My heart hammered now with the impending pressure of the guard. Time was ticking, and it was only a matter of time before I was found.

I needed to find a quiet way inside and get away from any prying eyes.

"Hi!" a small voice said happily.

I started and looked down at the little boy. He was maybe five years old, ruffled brown hair, and light gray eyes. He wore simple clothes and held a small leather ball in one hand.

"Hello there," I said and knelt down.

He ran up to me and tugged on a lock of hair that had come loose during my fall. So much for staying out of sight.

"You have very pretty hair," he said.

"Thank you. Aren't you a little far from the other children?"

He frowned. "None of them like me. They never want to play."

My heart broke for the little guy. "My name is Mira, what's yours?"

"Merrick," he said with a small smile. "That's what the den mother named me when they found me at the castle gates when I was a baby. But everyone calls me Merry."

Orphans and abandoned children. No wonder there were so many running around the garden.

"That is a wonderful name," I said.

"Merry! Merry? Where did you run off too now?" a woman called.

"I don't wanna go back," he said, pressing his side into me.

"But it's late. I'm sure you are tired from the days events?" I asked.

He shook his head furiously. I could see tears beginning to glitter in his eyes.

"You!" a man shouted.

"That's her, the trespasser," a woman said.

I recognized Odell's voice. Four guards came barreling up with her. Their metal armor rattled and clanked together as they ran. I hoped they had more stealthy armor for quieter missions.

"Merry, you need to go back to your den mother," I whispered as I moved him to my other side away from the oncoming guards.

"No!" he cried, his tiny hands tightening around mine. His toy long forgotten.

"Merrick!" the woman who was looking for him called. "What—"

She did not have a chance to finish her question as one of the guards roughly grabbed his upper arm and wrenched him up and away from me. He cried out in pain, and my vision turned red.

I lunged forward with my dagger drawn. A quick slash to the guard's arm made him release Merrick.

He clung to me as I caught his fall.

The other woman was crying and rushing forward. I assumed she was the den mother. Two other guards stepped forward to stop her.

I dodged them, moving quicker than I thought I could, and stood in front of the den mother. I passed Merry to her despite his echoing cries and arms clinging to me.

The two closest guards pulled me roughly back as soon as he was out of my arms. The air was knocked out of my lungs as I fell to the ground and was rolled onto my stomach. A hard kick was delivered to my left ribs. I felt at least three crack as pain exploded up my side.

One guard twisted my hand and wrist in the process of relieving me of my weapon. There was a small pop, and I gritted my teeth against the heat of pain that flared and pulsed along with my heartbeat.

I hoped, for their sake, that my wrist was not broken.

"When was the last time we had a trespasser?" one guard whispered as another locked shackles around my wrists.

Despite the cool metal, my wrists burned. I breathed out a silent hiss and pressed my forehead into the hard ground, wanting desperately to break free as I pressed against the cold metal.

"Doesn't matter. Your job is to get her to the King," Odell ordered.

A guard on either side of me grabbed my arms. Squeezing as tightly as they could in an attempt to get a reaction out of me, they jerked me to my feet. I kept my jaw clamped shut as pain radiated through my shoulders. My hands tightened into fists behind my back, to the point my nails cut into my palms.

It was all I could do to distract myself from the pain around my wrists and to keep from causing even more of a scene. I did not want to scare Merrick anymore than he already was. It was enough witnessing their extremely rough treatment toward me.

Merrick and the woman I handed him too watched me with fear. I gave Merry a small smile and nod before the guards turned me away from them.

I remained silent and calm. My eyes locked with Odell's. Her triumphant smirk wavered under my stare.

The guard on my right shoved me forward, and we walked past Odell. I heard Merry start to sob. One guard led us through the courtyard, the fourth followed our group while Odell trailed behind.

My hood remained up during the evening's events. The grass gave way to stone as I was led up a staircase and then to what resembled gray polished marble as we entered the castle. Every step caused fire to burn and pulse at the injuries on my left side and wrists.

My eyes darted around, searching for an escape should the need arise. All I saw was more smooth stone, silver gilded hall furniture, and paintings on some wall, others draped in fabrics of deep blues and purples.

Up another flight of stairs we went and through a grand doorway. I lowered my head, casting more shadow from my hood. This shielded my face from view but also prevented me from seeing the small crowd that had gathered.

I could still hear them, though. A deep blue rug stretched from the door onward. It was patterned with silver moons and stars.

Murmurs filled the air. We walked across the room and then stopped before a raised platform, a strip of stone separated us from the step as we stood at the edge of the carpet.

The throne room.

I would be the evenings entertainment. How lovely.

A Halfling in court. A trespasser. An outsider. A freak. An oddity.

"Here is the trespasser, your Majesty," Odell said from my right. "She has already injured one of your guards. Pull back her hood so the King can see who disgraces his grounds!"

A hand from the left gripped my hood and my hair, then jerked back. I growled at the pain as they yanked the tie out of my hair, a few strands of hair with it.

I slammed my head back into his nose for the treatment. The scent of blood filled the air instantly, and the guard howled in surprise and pain.

"Quiet!" The guard to my right snapped. He shoved me forward.

With my hands bound, I fell onto the cool floor unable to break my fall. I hissed, and my face contorted into a grimace. Thankfully, I missed landing on the edge of the platform.

Pain exploded in my shoulder and added to the pain in my ribs as I landed. They would for sure be broken now.

I kicked out. My foot made contact with a guard's kneecap, and he collapsed behind me with a scream.

With a sharp tug, I broke the shackle chain and stood up facing the three guards. They looked terrified. One had blood streaming from his broken nose, one had a slash on his arm. The third looked worse than the others from fear alone.

Their eyes flickered from mine to my wrists. The fear in the room was thick enough I could slice through it with a knife. It was almost suffocating.

Even the audience was terrified. *As they should be.* I infiltrated their castle and took down two guards before breaking my shackles. It was my turn to be in control. It was my turn to stop being the one stepped on.

"Enough!"

I could feel the power in that order. The guards all lowered their eyes. One even knelt. Odell took a step back under the weight of that command. I straightened in defiance and turned slowly.

There on the silver throne, clad in an embroidered blue tunic, sat Kieran.

Kieran

Mira stood before me in tattered, blood-stained clothes, alive and mostly unharmed. She appeared to be unarmed, which was surprising given the stories from her journey I had heard thus far.

Blood dripped from her hands onto the pale stone floor in front of me. The glow in her eyes dulling to their normal shade. Despite her haggard appearance, she was absolutely stunning.

Power radiated from her. It was like a magnet. I could sense it and see how it affected the people around me as she roamed her eyes over each individual before returning her gaze to mine. She had tapped into her alpha side without even trying.

"You don't seem surprised to see me," she said as she crossed her arms and raised an eyebrow at me.

I caught the wince of pain at her movement, and my eyes roved over her for any signs of injuries. None were visible on the surface. Anger flooded through me to think of all of the injuries she had sustained getting here. My guards would be punished for their actions.

"Nor you that I am here," I replied.

"You will bow to his Majesty," Odell demanded as she strode over to my side, "and refer to him as Your Highness!"

Mira turned and faced Odell. Her confidence had grown tremendously since I saw her last. It made me want to reach out and wrap her in my arms.

To claim her as my queen.

Mira's eyes flashed to a glowing green as she glared at Odell. A clear challenge toward the other woman.

"Titles are just fancy words to make you feel special," Mira snapped at Odell. "They mean nothing to me."

Odell tried to form a sentence, but paused. It seems only Mira would be able to render that woman speechless. I was impressed. Quiet murmurs floated around the room at her display.

Mira was examining the metal around her wrists as if she were not in a room full of nobles and guards. As if she had not been captured. Unfazed.

With quick movements, she pried the metal off. Rubbing the irritated and bruised skin absently as she looked around the room. Her right wrist looked swollen.

I concealed my surprise as the cuffs clattered to the floor, and a murmur filled the air. Very few shifters had the strength to break a pair of shackles. Especially in human form. Especially since we used a small amount of silver and wolfsbane to create them in order to subdue prisoners. Just enough to be an irritant. And to prevent shifting.

I was more upset with the harsh treatment my guards had used against her. I could see her favoring one side slightly more than the other. What all had my guards done? And what injuries did she receive on her journey?

"Who are you?" Odell demanded after finally finding her voice once more.

"You are supposed to be a Lady, correct?" Mira asked, ignoring the question.

"I *am* a Lady, and you are to answer a question when asked!"

Mira just smiled, as if she enjoyed toying with Odell. She recrossed her arms and raised an eyebrow as if to challenge the other woman. It seemed she was subconciously playing at her role as Alpha versus Odell's position.

Which would automatically put Mira at a higher rank.

"Leave us," I said before Odell or Mira could say anything else.

"Your Majesty?" Odell asked turning to me and placing a hand on my arm.

I watched Mira's eyes zero in on the touch. Her mouth tightened and eyes narrowed in a movement that most would have missed. I could almost see the muscle in her jaw ticking, and an extra sense of annoyance washed over me. Her annoyance.

"I said leave," I demanded. "All of you."

Everyone in the throne room began to file out. After everyone was gone, the silence pressed in on us; a heavy weight that seemed to drag by slowly as her guarded eyes stared into mine.

"You have been busy since last we spoke," I said. I sat back.

She rolled her eyes. "That's all you have to say? No, *I'm glad you are still alive?* It's good to see you too, Kieran."

"You've caused quite the upset among us and the Rogues," I continued.

"How else was I supposed to make a difference?" she shouted.

Her shout, like an alpha's command, forced me further into my chair. My wolf tried to surface. Wanting to claim its mate. I cleared my throat, trying to regain control. Ignoring the waves of fury I felt rolling off her.

I needed to get away from her. Before I claimed her. Before this became something more than what it already is.

"Are you here alone?"

"No," she hissed. "My pack is a short way outside the city walls."

"I will give you and yours rooms to rest and recover," I said as I stood.

I reached out to a servant through the pack link. She came rushing in and stood beside Mira. I also reached out to a small group to find her companions and ordered them to the castle.

"I have sent for your pack. Dinner is in an hour." I turned to leave through the side door.

"That's it?" she hissed, fury rolling in her sparkling green eyes.

I matched her stare. "That's it."

Chapter twenty-three

Mira

The maid, Larissa, led me further into the castle. She was a timid little thing, maybe eighteen years old. It probably did not help that I was seething.

"Here you are m'lady," Larissa said at a door at the end of the hall. "I will bring some fresh clothes and linens. Is there anything else I can bring you?"

"Would you let me know when my pack are in their rooms?"

"Of course ma'am."

"Thank you," I said as she turned and hurried back down the hall.

I entered the room with an angry sigh and rested my forehead against the dark worn wood. That was not the reception I thought Kieran would have toward me.

He was too formal. Cold in his role as king.

I gritted my teeth and straightened. No matter. I had a job to do, and I would like to have the king's assistance. If not, oh well.

I turned and looked at the room. A large canopy bed on the left was made of the same dark wood as the door and dressed in rich blue and magenta bed clothes. A small sitting area with a loveseat and two chairs sat in front of the fireplace directly in front of me.

I stepped farther into the room and through an archway. A table with a wash basin and mirror stood just inside the passageway. A tub large enough for four people, already filled, sat in the middle of the area. Steam hovered lazily over the surface. With eager hands I stripped off my soiled garments and climbed into the tub. I sank into its warm embrace with a sigh and allowed the warmth to press against my aching muscles. I ignored my stinging wounds and closed my eyes for a moment.

A door closing startled me out of my half-sleep daze. I dunked my head beneath the surface, and when I came up and brushed my hair away from my face, I saw Larissa walking toward me.

"I see you found the tub," she said with a smile.

"I couldn't help myself," I replied with a yawn.

"I don't blame you after being on the road for so long." She set a towel on the chair nearby. "I have laid out a couple of dinner outfit options, along with replacements for what you were wearing."

"You are too kind," I replied. I rose and stepped out of the tub, and wrapped myself in the towel.

"Oh, you're wounded!"

"Old wounds, nothing to worry about," I said with an absent wave, grimacing as my wrist moved.

"I will fetch another maid to clean and rebandage them, nonetheless," she replied. "I was ordered to make sure you are well taken care of."

"Very well," I said with a small nod.

Everyone always seemed to overreact whenever they saw me bandaged and bleeding. Even if it had been a couple of days prior to the injury. Even I could not deny that my wrist and various injuries could use fresh bandages.

She motioned for me to sit on the chair. Once I was comfortably seated, she began to gently brush the tangles from my hair. When she was finished, she braided it quickly and then wrapped my hair in a towel.

A soft knock came from the bedroom and another maid entered. Her sandy blonde hair was streaked with gray and pulled back in a tight bun. She carried a small bag with her.

"Larissa asked for a healer to tend your wounds. I was the

first available. There are two new mothers in the hospital wing. I am Shey," she said with a smile.

"I am Larissa. Thank you for answering my call, Shey," Larissa said. "I'm worried about the injury on her thigh."

Larissa turned her attention to me.

"I understand you were the one found trespassing in the garden...the one who upset Lady Odell," Shey said with a chuckle. She knelt in front of me and got straight to work.

"Upsetting Lady Odell was just a plus," I replied as she began prodding at my thigh. I winced at a tender spot on the outside of my leg. They both chuckled.

"She needs to be knocked back down to her ranking," Shey said. Then her eyes widened. "Pardon me, it is not my place to speak of such things."

"Nonsense," I replied. "What do you mean?"

"She acts as if she were queen already," Larissa scoffed. "She treats everyone as if they are a speck of dirt beneath her satin shoe."

Larissa rummaged through the bag Shey brought and began to massage a salve onto my shoulders and arms. The salve smelled of lemon verbena. Then she wrapped my sprained wrist.

"Queen?" I was just able to breathe out.

"Yes, the council gave King Kieran until the end of the year to find his mate, or he has to marry Lady Odell," Shey replied. "Her father is a powerful man, and it would be a step up for his line to claim the throne."

"An awful man," Larissa interjected, shuddering. "If you think his daughter is rude, he is a hundred times worse. He thinks because they are descendants of the one of the four original lines, he should be king."

"Four original lines?" I asked, trying to maintain picture perfect calm.

"This land was built on four packs," Shey began. "King Kieran is of one line. The second died out completely after the third married the fourth and killed them all. Every last one of them. Odell's father supposedly comes from one of the first son's lines, while the third alpha married the daughter of that fourth pack."

"So two became one, one stayed as they were, and the last one was completely destroyed. Sounds like today's wars," I said flatly.

Shey sat back and stared up at me. "Except that the lines that crossed lead to the alpha we know of now as the Rogue King, or Alpha. Neither side of his blood was strong enough to destroy the King's bloodline. That is why those original packs joined together."

"Why would they want to destroy Kieran's line?" I asked.

They both shrugged.

"Some say strength was always in their favor, which is why one of the original packs married another and killed the remaining one," Larissa said. "Others say it has to do with a prophecy to join all wolves and find the true heir. Hard to say which is the truth and which is something storytellers tacked on as time wore on."

"That makes no sense," I replied.

"The prophecy says that whoever is the mate to a member of Kieran's bloodline, is the one to bring unity," Shey said.

My blood froze, and my head started to spin.

I suddenly felt the cold, wet floor beneath my cheek. Mate was pretty obvious. By the sound of it, there was no way Odell would be the one to unify the wolves. Unless it was through looking down on them all—or enslaving them.

"Miss?" Larissa asked.

I blinked and shook my head.

"Too many stories before dinner," Shey said as she and Larissa helped me stand.

"It has been awhile since I had a decent meal," I mumbled as they lead me into the bed chamber.

Rhudi

Kieran and I sat in a small sitting room when he received

confirmation that Mira's companions had been found and brought to the castle.

Gage paced in front of the fireplace.

"How long are we going to have them here?" Gage asked.

"I have no idea," Kieran sighed. "She is required to be in the Hall of Alphas in less than a month. It might be best to have them stay until the challenge."

"Did she look well?" I asked Kieran.

"Well enough for someone who has been on the road and fighting," he replied.

"Who cares how she looks?" Gage snapped. "We have a Challenger under our roof and no idea how to prepare for when she loses."

"*If,*" I growled. "If she looses. You haven't seen her fight."

Kieran glared at Gage. "Leave us, Gage. There are matters I must discuss with Rhudi alone."

"Yes your Majesty," Gage said with a small bow and hurried out of the room.

"He seems a little off," I said after a few moments.

"He has been hinting more and more lately that having Mira around is not a good idea."

"I have a feeling that isn't what you wanted to speak to me about though."

Kieran sighed and shook his head. His silence stretched between us. I waited for him to say more.

"Mira is my mate," he finally said.

I sucked in a breath. I was not expecting that bit of information.

"Who else knows of this?" I whispered. "Only Gage. I haven't even told Mira."

"You haven't told my niece that you are her mate? Why not?"

"I was afraid my people would reject her at first. And then we found out that she is the granddaughter of Lycus."

"And? The mate bond does not care which bloodline you come from," I growled. "Or are you afraid of loosing your position as king?"

Kieran glared at me. His golden eyes turning yellow with

anger. I had definitely brought his wolf to the surface. "I am not afraid of losing my position," he growled. "I am afraid of losing her to a fight that she isn't ready for."

"That is where you are wrong. If anything, her search for you has proven she is more than ready to fight by your side. Either as your queen or as an ally. But you have to tell her you are fated to her, and she to you. Let her be a part of the decision."

I paused to let my words sink in.

"It is time to stop keeping secrets from Mira," I continued. "She has to know everything."

Mira

Larissa and Shey dressed me in a deep green gown. Threads of silver sparkled when the light hit just right. I insisted on long sleeves to hide my many scars, bruises, and still healing wounds.

My hair waved lazily over my shoulders and down my back. Shey had braided a couple of tendrils and pinned them back to keep most of it out of my face.

Thankfully my boots were not heeled. I would not be able to stand the heels with the gown. The gown was already too much.

The corset was a little too tight, and my ribs protested against the confines even after Larissa loosened them when I gasped from the pain.

I donned my necklace and turned to look at Shey. Her eyes widened at the sight of me. I could not tell if it was from fear or admiration.

"You have a Tala stone? You're an Alpha!" she squeaked.

"A what?"

She pointed to my necklace.

"This is a necklace I found that my father had hidden in his belongings. I have no idea what it is."

But there was no point in denying that I was an alpha any longer. I had a small pack that I was responsible for now.

"We really were out of line with our discussion," she said bowing her head. "Please forgive our indiscretion!"

"Nonsense," I assured her. "You are free to speak as you wish in front of me. I claim no royalty nor any title."

"But—" she began.

"No, I am your equal."

She stared at me as if to make sure I was telling the truth. Then she smiled with relief.

"You are a wonder," she replied. "Let's get you down to dinner. Your pack just arrived."

I felt my own sense of relief as I followed her to the dining hall. My small group was here. I no longer felt the pressure of being alone in unfamiliar territory. The muscles in my shoulders relaxed some.

My mind absently mapped out the route while I thought over a way to approach the subject of help with Kieran.

Plum colored flowers were mixed with brighter magentas, blues, and blacks. The exotic foliage was something to admire. *Selena would have a field day in this garden*, I thought.

We paused outside of a wide, arched double door. One side was opened enough to allow passage. Laughter and the sound of cutlery clanging floated through the opening.

"Here we are," Shey said. "If you need anything, I will be a quick call away."

"Thank you," I replied. I sighed internally and strode through the door.

Silence greeted me as every eye in the room turned my way. Four vertical tables led to one horizontal. Each decorated with a simple white table cloth and navy blue accents.

I scanned my surroundings, looking for my pack.

Kieran sat at the center of the horizontal table, facing the doors. Odell sat to his left, and I had to resist the urge to frown. Cal stood off to my left, in front of Kieran's table, with Ivan, Knox, and Rhudi.

My heart swelled with relief as I made my way toward them. I ignored the whispers as I strode confidently forward. My stride steady and my chin held high.

"Is that the Challenger?"

"There's no way she challenged the Rogue Alpha."

"What is she? Or better yet who?"

"I heard she has been on the road for some time now."

"Why did she come here?"

I looked over the four of them, glad to see no injuries and that they were all cleaned up.

"Mira!" Knox called out as he hurried forward and wrapped me in a tight hug that lifted me off the ground.

"Ow," I whispered quietly as his grip pressed into my ribs. He sat me back down with a concerned look. "What hurts?" he inquired.

"Everything," I said. "I'm glad to see you all."

I put my hand on Knox's shoulder and smiled. He grinned down at me as Ivan and Cal joined our circle.

"Did anyone here hurt you?" Cal whispered, his eyes dark with concern.

I shrugged. "I infiltrated through their defenses. They were only doing their jobs." I paused and held a hand up as his eyes flashed. "I did more damage to them than they did to me."

His shoulders slumped in relief as Ivan patted my shoulder gently.

"Glad to see you arrived safely," Rhudi said.

"I'm not suprised to see you here. I'm sure you've been having us followed," I replied. "But I'm glad to see you are safe too."

He just smiled and crossed to sit on the opposite side of the table near Kieran.

"Let's take our seats," Cal said.

He lead me to the seat across from Rhudi and sat down next to me. Ivan sat to his left and Knox to Rhudi's right. Gage rushed in and took the seat between Rhudi and Kieran, his face flushed with annoyance. I exchanged a glance with Cal and he shrugged.

"We'll talk after dinner," he whispered, leaning in close so that only I could hear.

I nodded and turned my attention to Kieran as he stood.

"As many of you have heard, we have a few guests with us this evening. Please welcome, the Challenger, Mira Brianne, and her pack," Kieran projected through the hall. His eyes fixed on me.

Cheers and howls erupted around us. I turned and faced the wall, glad to have my back to everyone. My chest felt tight. I was not expecting to be thrown into the spotlight.

And who in their right mind would be excited to have a challenger in their halls? It was like supporting a theif with a death warrant. One challenger was forecasted to die either way.

"Help them with anything they may need during their stay here." He paused for more cheers. "Now, let us dine."

Countless servants burst through doors on either side of the room. Each carried a covered platter or a pitcher and promptly placed each piece on their corresponding tables. With practised precision, all the covers were removed at once, and the servants filed back out. Some lingered around the walls, keeping an eye on glasses and plates for refills.

So many cooked animals and vegetables covered the table in front of me. The aroma made my mouth water.

Everyone around me had already started to dig in. I reached for the basket of bread and caught Kieran staring at me.

My heartbeat quickened under his gaze, and I felt my cheeks flush. Heat surged through me as I held his gaze a moment longer.

I pressed my lips into a firm line, looked away, and began filling my plate. I wanted no part of a conversation with him tonight. Not after his show at my arrival.

Chapter twenty-four

Mira

After dinner, I walked back to my room with my wolves. We stopped by Cal's room so he could pick up my bag and weapons.

Once we were in my room and the door closed, a sense of relaxation wrapped around us. We were no longer directly in the line of sight.

"I hate court," Ivan grunted as he sat down on the couch.

Cal set my bag behind the couch and sat down next to him. Knox stood in front of the fireplace.

"I just hate gowns," I replied as I lifted the edge of my skirt up to the height of my knee-high boots. "I feel like I can't move."

"You get used to it after a while," Cal said absently. "Court, I mean. I have no experience with gowns."

"I don't think I could," I replied as I plopped down in the chair with a sigh.

I instantly regretted the quick movement as my body protested with a flash of burning pain. I closed my eyes and breathed through the dying flames.

"You got inside the castle pretty quickly," Knox commented in awe.

"Well, I got captured in the garden. You can blame the woman that sat by Kieran at dinner," I hissed. "She's the one who summoned the guard. Almost injured a child trying to capture me."

"Lady Odell?" Cal asked.

"You know her?" I asked, leaning forward to put my elbows on my knees, ignoring another flare of pain at my quick movement.

"Unfortunately," Cal said, running a hand through his hair. "Her father is more notorious than she is, but she can be just as dangerous as he."

I filled them in on what Shey and Larissa had spilled earlier. The more I talked, the more grim they all grew. Knox shifted uncomfortably by the fire.

"So they finally managed to find a way to worm their way into royalty," Ivan growled. "I don't like it. Something doesn't feel right."

"It's a power move," Cal said. "But it makes you wonder if it's because the family is greedy or if someone is forcing them to do it."

"I don't think anyone is forcing them," I said. "Odell has a wannabe dominance about her, like she wants to be an alpha or leader but can't command the respect or attention she desires."

"We'll keep an eye on her," Knox commented.

"I never thought I would say this, but I am glad you all are here," I said. "I don't think I could have made it this far without you."

They all looked at me. Knox grinned a large goofy, childish grin. Ivan gave me a soft smile.

"I don't think you give yourself enough credit," Cal said. "We haven't done as much as you think we have."

I frowned. "I would probably still be in that jail or dead at their hands if not for you."

"You would have found a way out," Knox said. "I know you were upset at how they treated you, but I suspect you would have gotten out of there without killing anyone."

"You are an alpha," Ivan said. "And the more we are around you and the more you fight, the stronger you grow. I know in the heat of all the fighting you may not have noticed, but some things are changing about you."

"Changing? What has changed? I know my eyes change colors," I said anxiously, leaning forward.

"Your strength and speed has increase exponentially," Cal

noted. "Your aura has changed. You've become a commanding figure, demanding others to fall in line."

I lean back in silence, processing. I had noticed the changes in my strength. I could tell I was healing a little faster. Some of the deeper wounds I had received at the beginning of the journey were already healed. Scarred, but healed.

Then it dawned on me. "I broke the shackles they put me in earlier," I said quietly. I hadn't even noticed at the time. It just seemed the natural thing to do.

All of them leaned forward.

"You broke *shackles*?" Knox asked, bewildered.

"Yep. I couldn't take wearing them. And when the guards shoved me around, something inside me snapped."

"You do realize the shackles used on wolves are a mix of iron and silver, and then infused with wolfsbane?"

"And that means?" I asked.

"That they are meant to keep wolves contained and to prevent them from shifting," Ivan replied. "Did you feel any discomfort while they were on?"

I nodded. "They burned my skin."

I looked down at the faint pink peeking out from under my left sleeve. I was surprised it wasn't worse. My ribs still throbbed, along with my sprained wrist, and my body ached from the rough treatment the guards had shown me.

"Your wolf side was reacting to the materials. As to how you were able to break the shackles, that is a rare occurrence," Cal commented.

"One more thing to make me a freak of nature," I huffed.

"No," both Ivan and Knox almost shouted, causing me to jump slightly.

"You are not a freak," Cal emphasized. "You are the best of both humans and wolves. You are trying to make a difference. Which is more than I can say of anyone else. Everyone else is just trying to survive. You are taking steps to eliminate the problem."

"Someone has too," I whispered as I leaned back and scrubbed

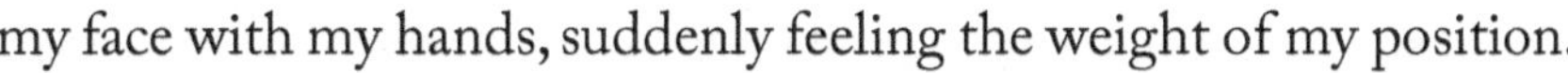

my face with my hands, suddenly feeling the weight of my position.

"But you took it on yourself," Ivan said passionately. "That is the sign of a true Alpha. An individual that is willing to knock on Death's door in order to save those they care about."

"Knocks? I am beating on the *fodido* door," I growled.

They all grinned at my vulgar expression.

"That's for sure," Knox cheered and then yawned.

"We can strategize in the morning," I said. "I think we all need a good nights sleep."

"I second that," Ivan yawned.

"Out then!" I laughed. "I need to figure out how to get out of this gown."

They chuckled as I walked them to the door.

"You know where we are if you need anything," Cal said.

"I know. And I appreciate it." I paused and stared into the hall.

Cal nodded and turned to leave.

"I don't know how any of this works," I started, "But if I survive the challenge, would you be my second in command?"

Cal's eyes widened, and he dropped to a knee before me. "You are asking me to be your Beta?" he whispered.

I nodded. "If I could make all of you my Betas, I would. But from the little I know, it seems to be a one-person role."

"I would be honored to take the role of Beta next to you," Cal murmured as he took my hand in his. "And not only on the account of you surviving. I will gladly take the position starting now, if you wish."

I gripped his hands in mine. "Then from the moment you rise, you are my Beta. We will find roles for Ivan and Knox tomorrow. And then we will try and find a solution to end this war, with or without the King's help."

Kieran

I passed Ivan and Knox on my way to see Mira. They both nodded in respect before entering their rooms. I paused when I heard voices. It was Mira and Cal. I was far enough away that they wouldn't see or hear me.

"…you are now my Beta. We will find roles for Ivan and Knox tomorrow. And then we will try and find a solution to end this war, with or without the King's help."

My heart skipped a beat. *Beta? She named Cal her Beta?*

I missed the last words exchanged, and then Cal strode into the hallway as Mira closed her door. He paused when he saw me.

"Your Majesty," Cal said with a nod. "Beta," I growled.

"So you were eavesdropping?" he said with a knowing smirk. "I thought I heard another set of feet in the hall."

"Why would you agree to be her Beta?" I asked, my hands curled into fists at my side in an attempt to contain my fury. A shudder wracked my body as my wolf attempted to surface.

"Because she needs help, and you don't seem to want to give it," Cal answered. "I know there is some connection between the two of you. Why else would she hunt this territory to find you?"

I opened my mouth to retort, but he held up a hand.

"I don't want to know the details, unless they will help save her," he said. "Her life is balancing on the sharp edge of the sword now. And I will do everything in my power to make sure Mira doesn't slip."

"You are quite forward, which I guess is why you serve the Lycus line," I hissed.

He shrugged. "My choices led me here, and the reasoning never made sense until now. I serve the one who serves the people. And that woman," he paused and pointed back toward her door. "Is risking her life for humans *and* werewolves. Despite her background and despite everything she has been put through her entire life.

"If that makes me the bad guy in your eyes for wanting to save the blood of the Alpha, then so be it. You may know my background and everything I have done to survive. But that doesn't mean you know why I made those choices and sacrifices."

I was unsure of how to reply. I thought back to meeting with Pascal and how he said no one would betray Mira. I could see the devotion in his eyes. The desperation to save and protect her. A hope for a better future.

"We will work together to protect her," I finally declared.

Cal gave me a sharp nod. "The fate of the world depends on her blood."

He strode two doors away from Mira's chambers and entered his room without another word.

I walked to Mira's door and breathed in deeply. Her scent was everywhere. She smelled of fresh rain and sage. My eyes closed as I pressed a hand into the doorframe.

I heard her rummaging around inside and despite my wolf willing me to knock on the door, I could not bring myself to do it. I turned and began the trek to my chambers. I would discuss strategy with her after she had a full night's rest and time to healed.

The pain I could feel radiating off her swirled with other emotions and energies.

Betrayal. Longing. Love.

Determination.

She was the end of one era and the beginning of the new.

Mira

After everyone left, I opened the wardrobe and rummaged around. I found a couple of tunics and pairs of trousers hidden at the bottom.

I sighed in relief and began the struggle of taking off my gown. My fingers worked at the tight knots of the corset. I stood with my back partially facing a large looking glass in an attempt to free myself from them.

After a few attempts, curses, and threats to to use my knives to cut myself out, the laces loosened, and I was able to slip out of both corset and gown.

I breathed in deeply and caught a glimpse of myself in the

glass. Black, purple, and blue splotches colored my ribs and shoulder from where I had been shoved to the floor. The bandage on my thigh was still secured in place.

I ran my fingertips over the healing claw marks on my shoulder. Their bright contrast stood out harshly against my pale skin.

I still looked mostly the same. Except for the new scars. And my eyes seemed sharper than normal. Almost feral.

It was how I felt that was different. I felt stronger. More powerful. There was a stronger connection to the wolves than I ever thought possible.

I clutched the stone around my neck. Marveling at how cold it stayed despite my grip. If finding Kieran resulted in anything, it was going to be answers.

I had a feeling all of them knew more than they were letting on. I would find out what I needed to know.

I tore my gaze from the looking glass and slipped into the black tunic I had pulled out.

And for the first time in months, I collapsed into bed without being ready to jump up and run at a moments notice.

Rhudi

Once I made it back to my room, I was able to finally relax away from the court's eyes. I sank down into a chair in front of the fire and sighed.

Mira was safe—for now. She was a little beat up, but she would heal before her challenge. Especially if Kieran told her about being her mate.

Being around each other would help her heal faster and grow stronger. I just hoped he would see how withholding that information from her would be more than detrimental.

I saw the longing in his eyes at dinner, and the attraction in hers. Their bond was one of the strongest I had ever seen.

But there was a dark feeling that I could not quite put my

finger on, too. It felt strange not having guards posted outside of Mira's door. But we all knew she could take care of herself.

We just had to be watchful and make sure nothing happened to her before the Challenge Day.

CHAPTER TWENTY-FIVE

MIRA

Long rays of sunlight splashed across my face and woke me from the deepest sleep I'd had in a very long time. My stomach growled as I stretched and sat up.

I rubbed the sleep from my eyes and crawled out of the nest I made in the center of the mattress. After splashing some water on my face, I dressed in a new black tunic and matching pants. I fitted a forest green corset over the tunic and slipped into black knee-high boots.

I went to my bag and began pulling everything out. I slipped a dagger into each boot before leaving the room.

I began my trek to the dining hall when I ran into Shey.

She wore the same type of dress as the day before, and she was carrying a covered tray.

"Miss!" She exclaimed brightly. "I was just bringing breakfast to you per your pack's orders."

I smiled at her. "Thank you, but you didn't have to do that."

"Of course I did. Now, where would you like to eat?"

"Is there a quiet place in the garden perhaps?"

Her grin widened, and she nodded furiously. "I know just the place."

She stepped around me, leading me back the way I had come.

Shey stepped out onto a balcony overlooked the side garden at the end of the hall. There was a small table with two chairs and a potted plant the color of the midnight sky. The space was only large enough to hold four people at most.

I recognized the greenhouse to my right. That meant I was on the other side of the castle from where I had climbed over the wall. I could vaguely hear muffled grunts and the clatter of wood.

"Not many people use these little alcoves, but there are a few on each floor looking out in all directions," Shey said as she set the tray down on the table and lifted the cover.

"This is perfect," I breathed as I took in the view. "Thank you."

"It's just a little hideaway spot that the servants like to use for breaks since they are so small and hidden."

"What is on the other side of this wall?" I asked.

"The training grounds," Shey replied. "I believe your pack is down there with the King for training this afternoon."

"I didn't realize I had slept so late," I said. "I will join them after I eat."

"I will come back and show you," Shey said.

"I am sure you are busy enough without having to tend to me. I just need to follow the sounds of fighting, and I'll find it."

"Very well," Shey said and flashed a genuine smile. "You can leave whatever dishes and leftovers here, and I will collect them in a bit."

"Thank you, Shey."

She bowed and left me alone on the balcony. I stood at the railing for a moment longer. I could make out a doorway in the castle wall. A building stood nearby with horses out front. I guessed it was the stables.

I turned and sat at the table. Shey had left me a plate with eggs, bread, ham, and various fruits. There was a glass of milk as well. I dug in and cleared my plate.

I sat back holding my partially full glass and scanned the sky. I breathed in deeply, relishing the fresh air and peace for a brief moment. I knew I would not have many more mornings like this.

Without wasting anymore time, I finished my glass, stood, and looked out over the railing to assessed the distance to the training ground. I saw a group of women walking and chatting nearby.

I hopped up onto the banister and jumped.

The women screamed as my feet met the earth and I crouched before them. No angry flare ups from my ribs, just a constant dull ache. *I am healing quicker than normal. Quicker even than when everything began to change after meeting Kieran.* I guess finally having a decent night of sleep helped.

"There are doors for a reason!"

I looked up through the hair that had fallen in front of my eyes to spy the one and only Lady Odell. I stood and flung my hair over my shoulder. Odell scanned me from head to toe, a look of disgust overcoming the surprise on her features.

"Are you okay?" another lady of her party asked.

"Absolutely," I replied with a smile as I turned my gaze toward the smaller brunette.

"Why would you even do such a thing?" Odell sneered.

"Why waste the time trying to find the right door to get to where I am going? If you don't remember, I only have a limited amount of days left—assuming I *don't* win this challenge."

The other women began whispering in earnest and pointing.

"And what happens if you don't win?" Odell asked.

"Everyone dies."

Her face paled at my words, and the other women gasped.

"But only time will tell," I continued with a shrug. "Now, I need to go train."

"We are headed to the training grounds as well," the brunette said. "We aren't allowed to train with the men, but we can watch."

Odell sent her a glare and swatted her with her fan.

I stepped forward and looped my arm through the brunette's, pulling her away from Odell. My protective instincts kicking in.

"Then let's go!"

I led her away from the group, listening in satisfaction as Odell huffed and started marching after us.

"My name is Autumn," the brunette said.

"It's a pleasure to meet you, I am Mira."

"You aren't from around here, are you?" she asked as we neared the gate in the wall.

"No, I am from the southernmost village in the kingdom."

"My! After all that way you have traveled, you are going to train the day after you arrive?" Autumn exclaimed.

"I unfortunately don't have the luxury of relaxing," I replied with a small smile.

"I understand. You are the Challenger. I never thought I would meet one in my time here."

"Are you from around here?"

"I am not. I am here on leave from my family for training. I am to be wed to the crown prince of Rylin."

"I hope you aren't getting your training from Lady Odell," I whispered sarcastically.

She giggled. "Goddess, no!" She was able to get out between her fits of laughter. "The King's mother has been kind enough to take me under her wing since my own mother passed before I was old enough."

"I'm sorry to hear that."

"It's okay. Some days are better than others, but even decades later I still have rough days."

"Decades?" I asked in surprise, stopping short of the training ground.

She nodded. "Shifters can live for centuries. We stop aging physically between our twenty-first and twenty-fifth birthday. After a few centuries, a wolf will begin to age again, but even at a hundred most would still consider you to be a pup."

"Then I'm an infant," I said with a laugh.

"Me too!" She giggled. "I guess in human years I would be an elder at seventy-five, but a pup among werewolves."

"That's insane," I replied as Odell bumped past me.

I glared after her and saw my pack standing near Kieran. All were in casual attire, watching the large group training with staffs in front of them. Rhudi and another man stood among them.

"Mira!" Knox called when he spotted me.

"Maybe we can have lunch together one of these days," Autumn said as I turned back to her.

I grinned. "I would like that very much. And you let me know if Odell gives you a hard time. I'll put her in her place."

"You don't call her Lady," Autumn noted.

"She's no lady in my book," I whispered as we strode closer.

Autumn smiled and went back to the group of women as I sauntered over to my pack.

"Did you get some rest?" Ivan asked as I stopped beside him.

"I can't remember the last time I slept that well," I replied. "You?"

He nodded in agreement. "I slept like the dead."

"Mira, I'd like you to meet my gamma, General Adler Korren," Kieran said after a moment's pause.

"A pleasure to meet you, General," I replied in kind.

"You may call me Korren," he said. "I have been hearing whispers of your talents all morning."

"I was telling him about how I first met you," Rhudi said.

My eyes wandered over and past him. The women that had walked with me were set up in an extravagant tent with an older couple. I could see the similarities to Kieran in their features. That must be the former king and queen.

"That fight was pure luck," I retorted. "But at least that town didn't try to detain me for helping."

Korren laughed. "Let's see what you are made of here, and what we can do to help you in your Challenge."

"Bring up Creed," Kieran said.

"Creed?" Korren asked in surprise. "You want her to fight him?"

"She can handle it," Kieran said.

"I am still here," I said sharply. "Who am I dueling?"

"Creed!" Korren called out, his voice echoing over the fighting as if it weren't there.

Silence ensued, and the largest of the fighters stepped forth from a few rows back and approached us.

Tanned skin from training all day in the sun, dark brown hair dusted with flecks of red. His muscles rippled with power with each step.

It seems size and strength helps determine rank. Creed was not as tall as Kieran or Korren. Nor quite as muscular. It was hard to tell if he would be the same size as Gage or not without the beta being nearby.

Creed was surefooted and confident as he came to a stop and bowed his head toward Kieran.

"Creed is my second in command," Korren replied. "And our best fighter, besides myself, the beta and Kieran."

I raised an eye toward Kieran. "How often does the King lose a duel?" I asked.

"Never," replied Korren.

I clamped my lips together to keep my laughter bottled. "Something wrong?" Cal asked with a smirk.

"Nope, I'll save it for after the fight."

I reached behind Kieran and grasped one of the staffs.

"No other weapons," Korren said. "We don't want to draw blood here."

Knox held out his hand for my staff as I reached for my concealed knives. I pulled them out of my boots and traded them for the staff.

As I stepped forward, the front line of warriors stepped back and fanned out to allow us room. I paused and twirled the staff, testing the weight.

"Creed," I greeted with a respectful nod.

He just grunted at me with a frown, then dropped into his fighting stance.

"This is an evaluation," Korren called. "We test every initiate on their capabilities."

Cal and Ivan shared a look. Ivan crossed his arms and pursed his lips. Knox glanced at the two of them then back at me, sending me a small encouraging smile.

Rhudi looked calm, but he shifted uncomfortably on his feet. Nervous energy radiated off him.

Kieran was the only one who seemed calm.

This would be interesting.

rhudi

I was surprised Kieran brought up Creed to duel Mira. I could tell her pack was also wary.

Creed was notorious for his ruthless fighting style and seemingly unending strength and stamina. Being the right hand man to the General meant he was loyal to those he served. He went into every fight with the mindset of it being his last.

Kieran stood still, his eyes locked on Mira as she assessed her new opponent. I could tell he was confident in her abilities, but also wanted to test her.

I turned back to the fighters. Mira tested the weight of the staff she held while keeping her focus on Creed. He was already in his fighting stance, while she was more relaxed.

"Begin," Korren called.

Creed launched forward with a strong downward strike. Mira spun out of the way, landing in a crouch. Her left hand rested on the ground, her right positioned behind her.

As she looked up, her glowing eyes met Creed's gaze, and his steps faltered in surprise. Gasps echoed through the air.

The glowing green of Mira's eyes had brightened considerably since the first time I saw her fight—brighter than any other alpha I ever met.

She launched herself into the air, bringing down a light, quick strike. Creed easily block it, but Mira wasn't finished. She used the pause of Creed's block to sweep her leg out.

Creed jumped to avoid it, but missed her following movement

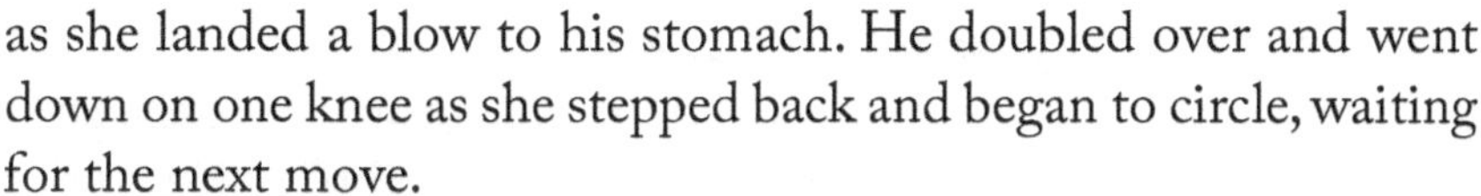

as she landed a blow to his stomach. He doubled over and went down on one knee as she stepped back and began to circle, waiting for the next move.

He looked up and grinned.

"Korren?" Cal whispered. "How often does anyone get a hit on Creed?"

"Not often," Korren replied in awe, watching her movements intently.

At that moment, Creed attacked with a growl. His staff came down hard and heavy. The sound of splintering wood cracked through the air.

Mira

My staff splintered in half when Creed attacked.

I had to launch myself backward to avoid being hit, but I kept a broken piece of my weapon in each hand.

His attack didn't let up, though. He advanced, swinging low.

I jumped and brought a double jab toward his left, making him end his move short to block, locking us together. He was grinning, amusement twinkled in his brown eyes.

My heart pounded in my chest and sweat beaded on my forehead. I adjusted my grip on the pieces of my staff and leaned into our tangled weapons. Both of us were breathing heavy.

Creed also leaned in, using his strength to try and overpower me. I used that to my advantage. I feigned falling backwards, throwing Creed off balance.

Then I pushed forward, jumping up and kicking him in the stomach with both feet. He flew backwards, flipped and landed in a crouch. I landed with a soft bend in my knees.

Murmurs filled the air as Creed and I studied each other. Each of us contemplating our next move. Wondering how to get the upper hand.

"Draw," Korren called.

Creed stood up straight and gave me a small bow. I mirrored the movement back toward him. Korren and Kieran approached me.

"I must say I am impressed," Korren said, rubbing his chin.

Creed joined us. "My duel opponents rarely get a hit on me. Thank you for the challenge."

He reached his hand out and gripped my forearm beneath my elbow. He grinned at my surprise.

"It's a warrior's shake," he explained. "I look forward to working with you in the coming days."

A warrior. Despite what I am, they were accepting me. My eyes stung with unshed tears.

"That was a bold move, your Majesty," Odell said as she strolled over and placed her hand on Kieran's arm.

Kieran shifted, and her hand fell to her side. She quickly hid her frown as her gaze flitted around the group.

"She is a notable warrior and challenger. Mira needed a challenge," Kieran replied.

"Mira!" Autumn exclaimed. "You will have to do some trainings with the rest of the ladies."

I smiled. At least *she* liked me. If only I could wipe that righteous smirk off Odell's face.

"Creed didn't even go all out," Odell retorted.

I raised my eyebrows. "Do you want to duel me?"

She blanched, and Autumn covered her own snicker behind her fan. She obviously did not believe my skills could match his.

"I… I am not dressed for dueling today," Odell rushed as she smoothed the skirt of her gown.

"Ah, well, I guess you better go change. And then I can give you a demonstration firsthand," I retorted.

I caught the gleam in Kieran's eye and the amusement on my pack's faces.

"Perhaps another day," Odell muttered.

"Tomorrow, then," I pressed, feeling a shift in power. "I expect you to be ready."

She blinked at me in surprise, taking the smallest step backward. The other men around me shifted uncomfortably.

"Very well," she agreed quietly with a small nod.

"Good."

"Ready for more training today?" Korren asked me.

I nodded. "There's no time to waste."

part four

Reign before the storm

Chapter twenty-six

Kieran

It took all of my control to keep my expression neutral as Mira released her aura over the unexpecting Lady Odell. I shifted as my wolf attempted to surface, awakening in the presence of our mate bond.

I could feel her power press against my skin. It made me shiver, while those that were weaker shifted uncomfortably. It was difficult to tell if she knew exactly what she was doing or not.

Mira followed Korren and Creed further into the center of trainees. I followed them with my eyes as Cal came up behind me. Lady Odell had turned and quickly made her way back under the canopy.

Korren was introducing Mira to the other officers present. Each one gave her a warrior's handshake and an open grin.

"They adore her," Cal murmured as he observed their interactions.

"She is their first bit of hope in a long time," I replied. "They feel like there is finally a chance for peace and unity."

"Let's hope they still like her when they find out who she's related too," Rhudi murmured.

"Her actions speak louder than her lineage," Cal snarled.

I raised an eyebrow and stared from one to the other.

Rhudi raised his hands in surrender. "Yes, but I am sure even the King had reservations when he found out."

My jaw tightened, and my gaze hardened. I did have initial reservations when I first found out Mira is the granddaughter of my worst enemy.

"She is nothing like the Rogue Alpha," I growled in warning. "She has never hesitated to protect the weak instead of attacking them. She is not after the power. From what I have heard and witnessed first-hand, she has the gifts of an Alpha, but she won't be a commanding figure until she has to be.

Mira

After meeting the other officers, Creed and Korren resumed training. They worked with me directly, pausing only when another officer approached with a question or comment.

Despite the initial reaction of meeting Creed, his personality was the opposite of his fighter persona. He was a giant softy.

Confident and knowledgeable, he guided me through various training forms that were specific to shifters. One group trained with various weapons, another dueled with hand-to-hand combat. Others broke off, shifting to duel in their wolf forms.

Korren was impressed with how quickly I caught on to their fighting styles. And for the first time in a long time, I felt the challenge of a good dueling partner.

A part of me felt like I finally belonged. If it weren't for the looming Challenge, I might have encouraged that inkling.

"That's it for the day," Korren called out. "We will resume again tomorrow."

My muscles ached, and my body felt the exertion from the training. I was sticky with sweat. Cal approached me and held out a water skin. I nodded my head in thanks and took a long drink.

"You keep getting better and better," Cal said while I caught my breath. "You will be a big topic among the warriors in the coming days."

"Only if it's about my fighting and nothing else," I said.

Cal raised his eyebrows in surprise before bursting into laughter. "I don't know how to respond to that," he gasped.

I grinned at his outburst. I glanced over the training field and out into the landscape beyond the castle. The sun would be setting in the next few hours.

"Mira," Rhudi called as he jogged over.

I turned and looked at him. "Rhudi," I replied.

"His Majesty has requested a private dining table with you and your pack this evening. I believe there are some topics he would like to discuss."

"Who am I to turn down an invitation from His Majesty," I said snarkily. "I must go prepare myself for the lovely offer."

Cal snorted and walked away, hands up in surrender and laughter shaking his shoulders.

"Everything okay?" Rhudi asked.

"Why wouldn't it be?"

"I know how eager you were to find him, but now you seem as though you want nothing to do with him."

"Well, when he greets me as just another of his subjects and none of the warmth he had before, I believe you too would have the same attitude."

"I'm sure he has his reasons," Rhudi began. "Perhaps just hear him out?"

"I doubt he will want to converse with me in private," I replied.

Rhudi gripped my shoulder, and I met his gaze. There was an emotion there I couldn't quite decipher. He gave me a little squeeze and nodded.

"Go relax some before your meal," he finally said. "I'll come and bring you to dinner myself."

"Thanks, Rhudi."

I trudge behind my pack as we made our way to the castle. I made sure to use a set of stairs this time to spite Odell, who followed behind with her group of ladies and the King's circle.

Once inside the castle, they went one way and we another.

We trailed up a couple flights of stairs before filing down the hall to our rooms.

"See you all at dinner," Knox said as he stepped into his room.

The rest of us muttered our replies, and one after the other stepped into their quarters until I was alone.

I strode to the end of the hall and found an identical alcove to the one I had eaten breakfast in earlier. I stepped onto the balcony and looked out over the grounds. I could hear children playing in the garden below. A gentle breeze swept through my hair.

"I wish Remus and Selena could see this," I murmured aloud.

I turned and went back to my rooms. To my surprise, another bath was waiting for me. Steam filling the washroom with warmth and the scent of sage and mild mint.

I slipped out of my soiled training clothes and sank into the warm water. Fresh herbs floated on the surface and clung to my wet skin.

I sank deeper, plunging my head beneath the surface; holding my breath for as long as I could; attempting to clear every thought from my mind. I noticed the water ripple above me, a thump echoing off the side of the tub, and I emerged with a gasp.

Larissa's screech made me jump. I laughed as I wiped the water from my eyes and attempted to brush my soggy hair out of my face. She had one hand pressed to her breast, and I could hear her accelerated heartbeat. Her cheeks flushed with surprise and a towel was gripped firmly in the hand at her side.

"My Lady," she exclaimed. "I did not realize you were back already."

"I haven't been back long," I replied, my laughter quieting. "I did not mean to startle you."

"No need to apologize," she said with a chuckle as she calmed. "I think you would have startled even the most seasoned warrior with hiding in a washtub."

"I just needed to clear my head before having dinner with the King," I said as I turned and leaned against the side of the tub.

"I heard that you and your pack are dining privately with him tonight," she murmured.

I felt her hands begin to work through my hair and I closed my eyes as she kneaded my scalp.

My thoughts drifted back in time to when Selena first washed my hair.

Chapter twenty-seven

Mira

Eleven years old

It was the night they brought me into their home.

Snow fell in large fluffy flakes, floating lazily through the air like cotton buds, but the ground was not quite cold enough for it to stick. Selena walked with her arm wrapped tightly around my shoulders, transferring her warmth and strength into me.

"What is your name, child?" she asked me.

"M-M-Mira Br-Brianne," I spit out through clattering teeth, trembling with cold and fear.

"You are safe, my dear. No one will ever hurt you again," Remus said from my other side, just outside of arm's reach.

He caught my eye, and it was like he knew what I was feeling. He gave me a small smile before turning to face forward. I was wary of him. Of all men.

I stared down at my bare feet. From afar, caked blood and dirt made it look as though I wore shoes. Up close anyone could see the state of my feet, along with the bruises and scrapes my father had given me.

The cold helped numb the physical pain. It did nothing to quiet my mind. My right cheek stung just below my eye, and I could feel the blood freezing to my skin. My father had backhanded me as a final farewell.

I shivered beneath my tattered dress, and Selena pulled me tighter, rubbing a hand up and down my right arm to generate warmth. Tears stung my eyes, and I blinked furiously against the cold air to keep them at bay.

"Not much farther, love," she whispered in my ear. "Not much farther."

We arrived to a gray stone house surrounded by a wooden fence. It was larger than my father's family home that only had one room. A warm glow lit up the lower windows toward the right side. I could make out the monochrome shapes of various plants that decorated the front yard.

"Welcome home, Mira," Remus said as he held open the gate for us.

"Let's get you cleaned up and fed, child," Selena cooed.

She led me up the cobblestone walkway and through the front door. Warmth greeted me, slowly sinking into my bones. She sat me down by the fire and busied herself with preparing a bath.

I looked around. The kitchen and living area were completely separated from the other rooms. There was a divider with clothes and towels thrown over it—a small washroom, I assumed.

A door behind me opened, and Remus came back out. A ladder to the right allowed for access to a loft.

Remus strolled over to me and held out a soft bundle.

I flinched involuntarily and cast my eyes down. But not before I saw the sadness and anger flicker over his features.

He slowly sat and placed the bundle between us.

"I know it might not mean anything now, but I will never harm you like your father did." His voice broke.

I looked up to see him staring at the fire. He had brought me a blanket. I picked it up with trembling hands and wrapped it around my shoulders, reveling in its warmth and comforting weight.

"Th-thank you," I managed to whisper.

He smiled warmly at me, stood, and moved to a chest by the counter. He pulled out a loaf of bread and some other items.

Selena bustled out from behind the divider and picked up two of the four pails that sat near the fire. She disappeared again, and I heard the splashing of water into a tub.

Remus brought a cauldron to the fireplace and hung it up, stirring the contents. He went back to the counter and then returned with a plate, which he sat in the same spot as the blanket.

"This will tide you over until the stew is warmed up. You won't have to ever worry about food again," Remus said as Selena came back and switched out the pails.

More splashing a few moments later as I reached for the plate. A thick slice of bread sat in the center. I broke off a piece and ate it. I closed my eyes and felt my shoulders sag as the morsel melted in my mouth. It was a mixture between a pastry and bread.

"Selena's secret recipe," Remus chuckled as he watched me inhale the food.

As I ate and the cold subsided from my body, the aches and pains began to stab at me.

"Alright, the bath is ready," Selena said. She threw a bundle of cloth over one arm and looked expectantly at me.

I popped the last piece of bread into my mouth and stood, letting the blanket pool on the floor at my feet. I winced with my movements but did not stop as I stepped lightly over to Selena, and she led me behind the divider.

A looking glass stood atop a chest of drawers with a wash basin on top, and a tub sat in the corner, filled a little over halfway with steaming water.

"I will go refill the water pails," Remus said. "Holler if you two need anything."

I heard the front door open and then close.

"Let's get you cleaned and patched up, yes?" Selena asked.

I nodded and began to untie the laces at my sides. While I undressed, Selena opened one of the drawers and pulled out a brush, a handful of glass jars, and a wooden box that looked full of rolled fabric.

"Bandages, salve, and herbs," she said with a wink when she saw me watching her.

She turned and helped me lift the tattered pieces of my thin dress over my head. Her gasp echoed harshly in my ears as the dress whispered to the floor.

"My poor child!"

I knew what she could see. The bruises, new and old, painted across my body. Old scars drawn in here and there. My skin stretched tightly over my bones from starvation. I stared down at my feet.

"He will pay for this," she vowed as she gently rested a hand on my shoulder.

"No he won't," I muttered as I stepped into the tub. "No one cares what he did."

I tried to control my winces as I sank down and leaned back in the warm, comforting water.

"We live in a world where most can't see the strength of a woman. Or the power she possesses. But you, Mira, can change that. You can make him pay."

"How?"

"By thriving and letting him know that despite everything, he didn't break you."

I looked up at her and saw the tears sparkling in her eyes. Warmth bloomed in my chest. I felt a bond begin between us. I set my jaw and nodded.

"You are going to change the world," she said proudly as she began the pour water over my hair. "One way or another."

I closed my eyes as she began to knead my scalp and work the knots out of the tangled mess on my head. I focused on the feeling of her tending to me, humming softly as she worked. The smell of the herbs in the water and oils.

For the first time in my life, I felt safe. Loved even.

mira

I opened my eyes as Larissa rung the excess water from my hair and wrapped all of it in a towel on top of my head.

"Meditating?" she asked.

"Remembering," I countered. "I was remembering the first time someone washed my hair, and how everything changed then. And now everything is changing again while someone else washes my hair."

"Was it your mother?"

"Not by blood," I replied. "She and her husband took me in when I was eleven. I owe them everything. I was told my birth mother died having me."

"I'm sorry," she whispered.

"I always wondered if I look anything like her. I know for a fact I looked nothing like my birth father."

"Is he still alive?"

"Kieran killed him last time I saw him."

She dropped something, and I turned to look at her. My eyes peeking out over the edge of the tub.

"His Majesty killed your father? That means the two of you know each other?"

"I wouldn't say *know*," I said tightly.

I stood, and she helped wrap me in a robe.

"He rescued me when my father left me for dead," I said as I sat down before the vanity. "I thought after I was healed enough to go home, I would never see him again. Then he showed up one day, witnessed the treatment my father gave me, and on the day Kieran left, my father was found in the center of town. With his head torn off."

"That's quite a story," she murmured as she unwrapped my hair and began to brush and style it. She pulled it back into a low braid before wrapping it all loosely and pinning it.

"They say the strongest alphas are the ones who have been through the most trials."

"Perhaps," I finalized.

Larissa smiled at me in the looking glass before heading out of the room.

I followed.

Laid out on the bed was a pale green dress trimmed and embroidered with a deep, dark green.

"Did His Majesty have all these made for me?" I asked, nodding toward the dress.

"He did," Larissa replied. "I think he wanted to make sure you felt like you fit in."

I snorted. "I can guarantee you that dressing me up like a doll does *not* make me feel like I fit in."

Kieran

I paced the private dining room anxiously, glancing every so often out of the large windows that span one wall.

Gage sat at the table, reading a stack of documents. His brows kept furrowing the longer he read.

"What's got you all worked up?" I asked.

He glared at me over the top of a sheet before sighing and setting it down. "Just reading the accounts of all the destruction. Now that we can safely count numbers and regroup."

"And how do we stand? I have already read through everything, but I want your input."

"I hate to say it, but casualties went down after Mira started fighting back. At least until Lycus ordered the destruction of that one town," Gage replied with a sigh.

"But that doesn't help the two other territories that Mira wasn't in. Their casualties are almost double. But the mess Mira has left behind. Her actions are beginning to blur the line between humans and shifters. Lots of complaints and fear has arisen because of it."

My eyes narrowed as I glared at him. My wolf bristled. "Sounds like you're blaming Mira for all of this," I said coldly.

I watched him chew the inside of his cheek while he contemplated his answer. I crosssed my arms as my anger rose.

"She is a part of it, but I don't blame her fully," he finally said.

"But you do blame her."

He just shrugged and went back to reading. I watched him. He had become different since this all started. Normally, he was the one keeping me calm, keeping me on track. Now he was the one easily aggravated and on edge.

And he seemed to get worse the closer Mira got. Now he was drawn as tight as the bow she carried with her.

"Your Majesty, the Challenger and her pack are on their way," a guard said from the doorway.

I nodded my thanks and turned to the windows. I wrung my hands together as I felt a rise in anxiety. It took me a moment to realize that some of that anxiety was Mira's.

It was strange hearing everyone calling her *Challenger*. It had been more than a century since the last alpha challenge. Despite all of the time that had past since then, no one ever used the title. Until now. She was making a change in the shifter community. In everything.

I heard their footsteps as they neared.

"Time to put that away," I said coldly. "Our guests have arrived."

Mira

I was led into a much smaller dining room than the more formal one from the night before. Cal, Ivan, Knox, and Rhudi were all ushered in behind me.

"Welcome," Kieran said from the opposite side of the table. "I'm glad you could join us."

I smiled tightly and gave a small nod. The air felt stuffy.

"Of course," I replied. "From what I am told, we have important matters to discuss."

"Yes, but first let's start the first course," Gage said in an overly enthusiastic manner. "I am starving."

I noticed Kieran raise an eyebrow toward him in question. Tension flooded the air.

Rhudi, Knox, and Ivan sauntered forward and sat in the three seats facing the door, their backs to the windows. Kieran took the head of the table on the left, Gage the right.

That left the two seats with backs to the door. One of which Cal was already pulling out and sitting in.

I was left to sit in the chair on Kieran's right with Rhudi directly across from me. My shoulders tightened as my anxiety and stress increased tenfold. The tightness in my chest had nothing to do with the corset Larissa had laced me into.

I took a calming breath and scanned the room as I took my seat. More blue and silver.

"If werewolves can't wear silver, why do you use it?" I blurted out the question without thinking.

"In jewelry and other materials that come in direct contact with our flesh, we use steel," Kieran said with a smirk. "For decor, it is to honor the Moon Goddess, or the one who granted our first ancestors the ability to shift."

"I was just curious since most royalty I've heard of, gild everything in gold," I replied as I picked up my wine glass and took a sip. "Having a muted night sky to look upon instead of the sun was a pleasant surprise."

"I never thought of it that way," Kieran said thoughtfully as a group of servants strolled in carrying covered dishes.

One was set in front of each person, and as one, each cover was lifted to reveal a bowl of soup. I picked up a spoon and stirred the contents—vegetable by the look and smell.

Gage dug in before the servers even left the room, slurping loudly. How could someone of his high rank have worse manners than myself?

I gripped my spoon tightly and shot him a glare.

"You may be the King's Beta," I snapped. "But you should at least show some table manners and not eat like a child."

He paused mid-bite and stared at me in surprise. I raised an eyebrow in challenge, and he put his spoon down and sat back.

"My apologies," he mumbled as he wiped his mouth with a cloth.

I nodded and turned back to my bowl. I caught the amused smile Knox and Ivan shared as they took a quiet spoonful of their soup.

We all ate in silence for a few moments.

Gage's spoon clattered into his empty bowl, and he sat back, his eyes lingering briefly on each member at the table before landing on me.

"It has come to my attention that you have named Cal your Beta," he said in a formal tone.

I did not like the formal tone he used. It sounded as though he was either talking down to me or mocking me. I narrowed my eyes.

"I have," I confirmed. "Why does it matter at this very moment?"

"Because it has to be properly documented," Gage snapped at me, leaning forward to put his elbows on the table. "Don't you know anything yet?"

My vision turned red.

"I only want it documented if I win the fight with the Rogue Alpha," I spat back. "If it has to be documented, there is no point in documenting something, just to go back and undocument it when it changes in twenty-something days."

"Gage!" Kieran barked.

"As for what I know or don't know," I continued. "I only know what everyone at this table shares with me—bits and pieces of information about a world that I have but one foot in. So, if you want to play the game of who has the most knowledge, congratulations. You win. But if you want to determine who has more will power, I will run you into the ground before you finish your next comment."

I took a long gulp of my wine, trying to calm my fury.

My hands shook as I set my empty glass on the table. Everything in me wanted to storm out the room, but I needed answers—and yes, information.

"Peace," Kieran said wearily. "I wanted this to be a quiet, informative dinner. There is much we have to tell you."

"We thought it would be better in person," Rhudi interjected.

"We?" I asked ignoring the glare Gage kept leveled at me.

More servers arrived, and the second course was set down. I looked at the tempting array of meat, potatoes, and bread, but I found my appetite decreasing as the evening wore on.

My wine was refilled and a glass of water was brought in for everyone.

"I thought it best that you heard it from me," Rhudi started. "But Kieran also wanted to be a part of it."

I played with the potatoes on my plate. Waiting.

"The Alpha you challenged," Kieran began. "His name is Dornan Lycus. Or simply Lycus as he prefers to be called. He has been Alpha for centuries, and has been working on this overtaking for awhile."

"He is also my father," Rhudi said calmly.

I almost spit out the piece of bread I managed to make myself chew. My eyes flitted back and forth between Rhudi and Kieran.

"Then how does the two of you being here together work?" I managed to finally say.

"Lycus thinks I am spying for him, but I am giving Kieran information straight from Lycus himself."

"So you're a what—a double spy?"

"Essentially, but I firmly want to end my father's rule. It is time his quest for power ends."

"Couldn't you just take his place and end things?" I asked. "If he is an Alpha, wouldn't leadership pass down to the first born?"

Rhudi sighed. "It's not that simple. At least not in this case."

I raised my eyebrows waiting for an answer. Gage drummed his fingers on the table impatiently. I wanted to cut them off.

"I am not the first born. I am a twin. My sister was born ten minutes before I was."

"Then where is she? Why am I the only one willing to fight this Alpha?"

"Lycus banished her years ago when she refused to follow in his footsteps. I never wanted to be an Alpha and refused training. That's where you come in."

"Only the blood of Lycus... can destroy Lycus," Kieran said softly.

My heart stopped. "No."

"You are the granddaughter of Lycus," Rhudi confirmed, "and my niece."

I looked around the table. "All of you knew," I said.

Eyes and cutlery dropped. I closed my eyes and tried to control my breathing. I placed my hands on the table. My appetite completely gone, and I struggled against the nausea rising in my chest.

"All of you knew that my grandfather wants to kill me. My uncle doesn't even want to claim that he is of the same blood as me. And apparently my mother might still be alive?"

"Mira," Kieran started, placing his hand on mine.

The sparks that danced on my skin only added fuel to the fire. I jerked away, jumped to my feet. My chair toppled backwards with an echoing clatter. My body trembled with rage and hurt.

"No!" I shouted. "I have spent my entire life trying to get my own blood to see my worth. Trying to be better. All for what? A chance to save others from a fate similar to mine? So they can say someone saved them, when I didn't have that luxury?"

I stared down at them as I stepped away from the table. My hands shook in the skirt of my dress. Only Gage was brave enough to meet my gaze. My chest felt as though a vice were tightening around me.

"You all want me to save you. But where were you when I needed saving?"

I turned and sprinted from the room before they saw my tears.

CHAPTER TWENTY-NINE

Mira

I had no idea where I was going. And once I had calmed down enough that I had stopped crying, I paused and looked around. I stood in the middle of yet another hallway filled with even more doors. My hair had fallen in my sprint to get away, so I unbraided the mess and contemplated everything I had learned.

I had one more piece of the puzzle, and I did not like how the picture was turning out. I kept walking, lost in thought.

"Watch it you wretch!" Odell spat at me as I almost bumped into her.

My eyes snapped up to hers as she raised a hand toward me. Quicker than I thought I could, I grabbed her wrist and slammed her, chest-first, into the wall, her arm twisted painfully behind her.

"You will not raise a hand to me outside the dueling field," I growled. "Especially not when we have a duel tomorrow."

"Wait until my father hears about this!" she whined as I released her. Her wrist was already bruised from my grip.

I shrugged. "I'll give him the same treatment you give to me," I replied coldly. "We will finish this tomorrow."

I turned and continued on my way, eventually finding myself in a library. The smell of papers, old and new filled the air. I could smell the leather used to bind the books and alcohol from drying ink. I ran my fingers gently along the spines as I meandered up and down the aisles.

The shelves were made of a gray wood, adorned decoratively at the top with a scrolling moon and floral motif. I looked up. The library was at least three stories tall, shelves lining every wall. A balcony separated each level for easy access.

The ceiling was made of glass, and I stared at the stars above.

"Can I help you dear?"

I jumped and stared at the elderly man before me.

He smiled. His pale eyes crinkled at the corners. "I did not mean to startle you."

"I'm sorry. I got turned around," I replied, "and found myself here."

"More than a few troubled souls find solace in the library," he said knowingly. "The quiet helps sooth what sound cannot."

"Something led me here," I replied with a small sigh.

"Follow me."

I looked up to see him disappear around the end of a bookcase. I darted forward. His white hair was pulled back, and he wore deep purple robes.

"We don't get many challengers," he began, "let alone, halflings, anymore. Perhaps the answers you need aren't ones that people can tell you. Or ones you can fight for."

"Everything I've been told hasn't been the full story."

"Exactly. You need to make your own story. But first you have to know why you are here."

"Do you know why?" I asked.

"Only you can know that answer."

He pulled a large, brown leather book off a middle shelf, followed by a red one about half the size. He held the two as his gaze skimmed over a few others.

"These will get you started," he said, turning and handing me the volumes. "If you end up with more questions than answers, just let me know, and I will help find more material that may help."

The books were heavy in my hands. I stared down at them.

"Thank you..." I started.

"Rian," he grinned. "You may call me Rian."

"I appreciate it, Rian. I'm Mira."

"I know who *you* are," he said as he pointed to his ears. "I may be stuck in here, but I hear everything. There are chairs and desks scattered about. Make yourself at home, and let me know if you need anything. No one will bother you here."

I nodded as he turned and walked slowly away, disappearing back among the shelves. I walked in the opposite direction until I came across a small seating area.

Two oversized, patched purple chairs sat near a small fireplace against the wall. The fire was contained behind a glass enclosure of various colors. The glass prevented any smoke or sparks from entering the library, while still providing light and warmth.

I sat down in one of the chairs, slipped off my boots, and tucked my feet underneath me. I opened the smaller of the two books first.

The Blood of Change was written in beautiful calligraphy on the first page. I opened to the first page of the second, *Four Roots*.

The second felt like a history book, but I guess in a way both would be. I closed *Four Roots* and opened the smaller one again.

I dived into the pages, searching for the answers that would guide me. Or any piece that would fit the puzzle.

KIERAN

We all sat in stunned silence after Mira ran out. Even Gage's usual annoyance toward her turned to worry.

"I'll go after her," Knox said, pushing his chair back.

"Wait," Cal said. "Mira's whole world just got turned upside down. She probably needs a few moments to herself to get her thoughts straight and then she will return if she wants too."

Rhudi was watching me. I was trying to sort through the overflow of Mira's emotions. Betrayal, grief, sadness, loneliness, anger.

I stood up and started pacing as a distraction. I felt a sudden

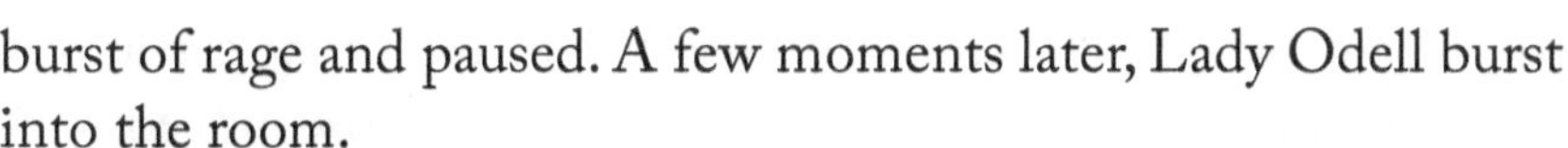

burst of rage and paused. A few moments later, Lady Odell burst into the room.

"Your Majesty! That Challenger of yours has to get her temper under control," she shouted.

"What happened?" Gage asked.

"She threw me up against a wall."

She held up her wrist, and I could see the purple marks as if someone had grabbed her. That explained the rage I felt.

"And?" I asked, crossing my arms over my chest.

"What are you going to do about it?" she asked me in surprise.

"I'm not going to do anything. If Mira did that, then you provoked her. You're lucky she didn't do anything worse."

"But—" she began.

"No," I said. "If you want something done, you have a duel against her tomorrow."

She huffed and stomped out of the room.

I pinched the bridge of my nose and sighed. Then I blinked in surprise. I could not feel Mira. It was as if her entire presence vanished.

"Mira won't be returning," I found myself saying. "Not tonight."

Mira

I must have dosed off while I was reading. I woke up covered in a light blanket, and the library was beginning to glow orange. I looked up, watching the sky begin to lighten.

The books Rian had lent me were stacked on the side table, a small piece of parchment stuck in the pages of *Four Roots* where I must have fallen asleep.

I needed to get back to my room and change for training. I picked up my boots and paused. I looked down at the two books, picked up *Four Roots*, and trudged silently through the maze of books.

I stepped out into the hallway quicker than I thought possible, and it was as if I was thrown out of one world and back into another.

The contrast between the library and the rest of the castle was night and day. I could hear the chirping birds and the movements of maids and servants as they started their chores for the day.

I held my boots in one hand and the book to my chest as I worked on finding my way back to my room.

After getting turned around a couple of times, I finally made it back. I threw my boots by the wardrobe and set the book on my bed.

I pulled out another pair of black trousers and black tunic. This time with a brown corset and matching boots. I dressed, leaving my hair wild around my shoulders, and left my room again.

This time, I wandered right into the kitchens. Maids and servants scurried around as if they had sat in coals.

"You there!" a brash woman called to me.

I looked at her. She was curvier than the others, with blonde hair and brown eyes. If anyone got too close, they earned a sharp *whack* with the ladle she was waving around like a sword.

"Who are you, and why are you in my kitchen?" she demanded.

"I'm Mira, and I guess I got turned around," I replied.

"Mira?"

"The Challenger," I added.

Her whole face lit up, and she sauntered over to me. She placed both hands on my shoulders, one still wielding that ladle. I gave her a small smile, wondering if I would recieve a *whack* for being here.

"It is an honor, my dear," she exclaimed. "I'm Marjoram, or Marj for short."

She stared at me and then in one move pulled me into a hug. It was one of those hugs only a mother could give. And it made me miss Selena even more.

I found myself melting into the woman's embrace. She gave me an extra squeeze of reassurance and stepped back.

"Thank you," I whispered.

"I may be just a cook, but I know when someone is hurting," she replied. "Now, it's too early for breakfast, but, come, sit, and I'll pull something special together for you."

She lead me to the counter near where she was working and pulled out a stool for me.

"Everything has been abuzz with much more activity since you arrived," Marj said. "Lots of preparations are being made."

"What kind of preparations?"

"Why for the ball in your honor," she exclaimed excitedly.

"We haven't had a ball in sometime, and the King wants to show that you have his support and the support of the neighboring kingdoms."

I sat back and pursed my lips. "The King failed to mention that to me."

"I'm sure he was just waiting for you to settle in some and get a feel for the castle.

She set a plate in front of me with fresh muffins and an assortment of fruit. As I picked at the fruit, she tended to various other pots over a large stove.

I broke open a muffin and watched the steam rise. "How long have you been working in the castle?" I asked.

"I remember when the King was still a babe, so I have been here for a very long time," she said with a laugh. "Of course, I took over the position as head cook when my mother passed, and the tradition will continue when my eldest daughter is old enough."

"Have things always been this stressful with the Rogue Alpha?"

"Aye," she said as she set more muffins before me along with a plate of bacon. "We are a little better off than the other kingdoms because the King comes from one of the four original bloodlines. Other than the Rogue Alpha, no one truly tops him in strength."

I snorted, and she raised an eyebrow at me.

"And if I told you that I had bested him in a sparring match, would that still put him in a strong position?"

Her expression of surprise morphed into cheerful laughter. The workers around cut us strange glances.

"I would pay to witness that!" Marj chortled.

"Well, depending on how my duel with Lady Odell goes, I might be dueling His Majesty by this evening as well."

"That woman needs a swift beating," she said as her laughter faded. "No one has ever had a stern hand with her. She is a decent fighter though, so don't let her act fool you."

"She won't fool me. I called her bluff the second she had the guards manhandle me before the King."

"I knew I was going to like you," she said with a grin.

I finished my muffins and bacon while she finished up some of the dishes. I knew it was getting closer to time for everyone to start their day.

"Thank you, for offering comfort this morning," I said as I stood and stacked my plates.

Marj began to shoo my hands away from their work.

"Anytime, my dear. I will always have a stool open for you if you want to visit."

She gave me another hug before I left.

I found the front entrance of the castle and made my way to the training grounds. The sun was just beginning to peek over the horizon.

I picked up a staff and began my exercises. Loosing myself in the familiar movements and muscle strain.

Creed and Korren were the first to show up. Surprising me from my concentration.

"Early riser, huh?" Korren asked.

I whipped around in a defensive stance and eyed the two of them.

"Couldn't sleep," I said.

I stood upright and leaned on my staff, rubbing my forehead. I felt the start of a headache.

"It happens to the best of us," Creed said knowingly.

"Let's run through a few drills then before the others get here. Some one-on-one practice might do you more good than the whole group training," Korren said.

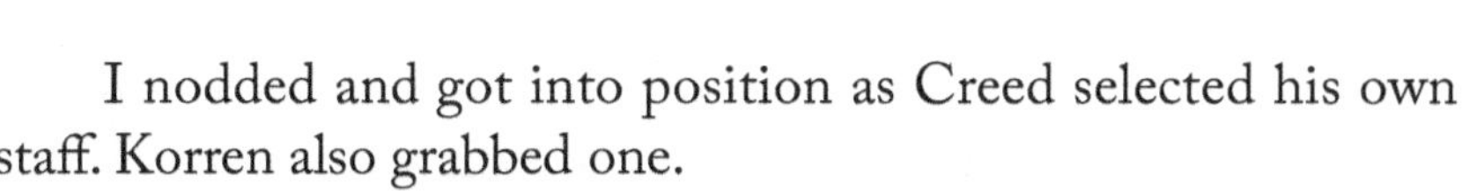

I nodded and got into position as Creed selected his own staff. Korren also grabbed one.

"Let's begin," Creed said.

Creed advanced, taking the upper hand. I countered, keeping an even distance between us.

"A Challenge won't be like any duel you've had," Korren called out over the clashing of our blows. "Each person is there for one of two things: either to be killed or to kill."

"Winner takes all," Creed grunted as he lunged.

I dodged, aiming a swing at his shoulder. He dodged, and in one fluid move I spun and had him on the ground, my staff positioned above his throat.

"Good, Mira. We'll have to get some training in against Creed when he's shifted," Korren said. "Let's go again."

I went through the movements, analyzing all the possible ways for Creed to advance. He rolled over and leapt to his feet, staff held with both hands.

Korren decided to join the fray as the first trickle of warriors began to arrive. I ducked his swing and rolled backwards, my eyes flickering between my opponents.

They advanced as one. Creed swinging high as Korren went low. Time slowed as I lunged forward. I avoided Korren's blow and blocked Creed's.

Korren recovered and advanced from behind. My senses sharpened, and I felt a slight change in the air. Something within me stirred, and my skin tingled from head to toe.

I advanced on Creed, ducking and then jumping over two quick jabs from Korren. I leapt and brought my staff down on his with a sharp crack.

He stumbled back with a piece in each hand, staring at me with a shocked smile. Murmurs filled the air around us—and then applause.

I saw my pack with Rhudi and Kieran at the front of the group.

"Tomorrow, we'll get Creed to shift, and we will try to find a challenge for you," Korren said with a pat on my shoulder.

I laughed lightly. "I guess we will wait and see how today's duel against Odell goes."

"I have no doubt you will show her exactly why not to cross you," Creed whispered with a nod. He strode away from us just as Odell, sandwiched between two of her ladies, arrive. Odell wore an outfit similar to mine, black trousers and boots with a pink tunic and black corset, her hair braided into a tight plait down her back.

"Let's get this over with," I sighed.

cal

Watching Mira training with Korren and Creed when we arrived was a relief. It meant she was safe.

After being dismissed from dinner, I went looking for her with Rhudi, Knox, and Ivan. We searched well into the night without finding any trace of her. As if she had disappeared or left the castle altogether.

I stopped on the edge of the training field, observing as Mira took on the top two fighters of Kieran's army with ease.

"I never would have thought she was not full shifter," Ivan commented. "She fights as if she were full-blooded."

I nodded, wincing when the crack of a breaking staff echoed around us. Mira stood over Creed, determination etched into the planes of her face.

Applause from the onlookers sounded as Lady Odell and her group of ladies made their way to Kieran.

Mira

I strode over to Cal, pushing down the conflicting emotions from the night before.

"Morning," I greeted.

Cal and Ivan nodded back at me as Knox sauntered over and threw an arm around my shoulders.

"We were worried about you," Knox whispered. "We searched for hours. Where were you?"

"I'm alright. I just needed time to process everything," I replied.

"We understand," Ivan murmured.

I stood with them in silence as Korren began giving orders to the warriors and telling them the events of the morning. Autumn caught my eye and gave me an energetic wave. She was also dressed in training gear.

"I guess it's time to show Odell who she keeps pissing off," I muttered.

"Mira," Korren called to me.

I strode forward, shoulders back and head held high. I had a role to uphold. A job.

"And Lady Odell," Korren continued, "will be dueling first thing this morning."

A clear space was left to us. Korren and Creed stood the closest.

"This is a simple hand to hand duel," Korren's voice boomed. "First to five hits or knock downs wins."

"Simple enough," I agreed with a nod.

"Agreed," Odell seconded.

I readied my stance, mirroring Odell's movements. She lunged. I blocked her first few blows, testing her. She was quick in her attacks, I'll give her that. Then she landed a punch to my shoulder. A sloppy one, but she still got first hit. I will let her have this little victory. It would be all she got.

"One for Odell," Korren called.

She grinned and did a small twirl. As she spun back to face me, I made my move. A quick double jab to her stomach had her bent over, wheezing.

"Two for Mira," Creed shouted.

Odell glared at me and lunged. I side stepped, grabbed her by the waist and flung her to the ground.

"Three," Creed called out.

Odell recovered and came at me. She landed an open palmed hit to my sternum, and I slid backwards. She was on top of me in an instance with another punch to the stomach and a kick to my side. I went down with a gasp, pain flaring from the points of contact.

"Four, Odell," Korren scored.

"You can't beat me," Odell murmured as she circled. "An unwanted Halfling could never win against a full-shifter."

My vision turned red. How could she know? I rose into a partial crouch. Watching. Waiting. Trembling as the tingling sensation along my skin returned.

"No one wants you, and they never will," she taunted.

I lunged. A swift kick to one side had her off balance, followed by a heavy hit to her chest that sent her flying backwards a few feet. I followed, landing on top of her with a fist to the nose. The crack of bone and cartilage was almost as loud as her scream. I kept going, feeling the skin on my knuckles split and scream with pain at each blow I gave to her.

All Odell could do was attempt to block my assault.

It took both Korren and Creed to pull me off. One held each arm and pulled me away from the bruised and bleeding Odell.

Two ladies in waiting rushed to her aid, trying to slow the bleeding from her broken nose.

"Your hand needs bandaged too," Korren muttered.

They were struggling to keep me at bay. I wanted to rip her blonde head right off.

"Let go of me," I hissed.

I jerked myself free and turned away from the field. I marched away from the blubbering mess Odell had become.

"You will pay for this, you bitch!" she screamed after me.

"You deserved what you got," I called back over my shoulder.

As I walked, I tore a sleeve off my top. I entered the tree line and slunk out of sight. I leaned against a tree and examined my hand. My knuckles were swollen and bloody, bruising already beginning to creep up the back of my hand.

I ripped my torn sleeve into strips, used one to clean what I could and the other to bind my hand.

My body still hummed with rage, and I turned to walk farther into the trees. I breathed deeply in an attempt to calm my racing heart. My vision still tinted red.

Remus would be disappointed in me. I had lost control. I won the duel, but at what price?

I sensed Kieran before I heard him. He moved silently behind me, but I could hear his steady heartbeat.

"You shouldn't be out here," I said, stopping and turning to face him.

"Neither should you," he replied.

We stared at each other. His eyes roamed down my right arm, narrowing at the hatching of scars and my bandaged hand.

"I still need to talk to you since our conversation came to an abrupt end last night."

"What did you expect when you drop all that information on me?" I challenged, throwing my hands up in irritation. "I keep finding out more information from people who don't know me, than the ones that do."

"I'm sorry. I was trying to protect you," he countered.

"From what? Myself? Or just from the information getting to the wrong person?"

"All of the above."

"Then before I lose my mind again," I breathed out. "What do you need to talk to me about?"

"The first thing I wanted to tell you that we will be hosting an event ten days before the challenge."

"I know about the fancy ball and all the other leaders that are coming in."

Kieran stared at me in surprise.

"How? I wanted to be the one to tell you as a show of support."

"Marj. I spent some time in the kitchen early this morning when I couldn't sleep," I said dismissively.

"Ah, well, then the tailor will be visiting you in the next day or so to finalize your gown."

"Are you enjoying dressing me up like a doll? These dresses are not me!"

"Unfortunately, life at court is different than the life of an assassin," he snapped.

I turned and took a few steps away before turning back to him. My anger coming in full force again. I curled and uncurled my fists, using the pain in my knuckles to focus.

"Is there anything else you want to inform me of while you have my attention?" I asked. "Because if you don't tell me now, you might not get the chance too."

"Yes," he said.

He crossed his arms over his chest and stared at a spot in the trees above my head. I waited, crossing my arms across my chest in annoyance and taking a deep breath to calm myself.

"I have been debating telling you ever since I met you..."

I raised my eyebrows, encouraging him to continue. He took two steps forward and paused an arm's length from me.

"Another difference between humans and shifters is how we choose our partners. Shifters have a fated mate that they may or may not find in their extended lifetime—essentially their other half."

He ran a hand through his hair and met my gaze.

"It wasn't just that I thought you were a part of my pack that drew me to you that night," he said. "*You* are my fated mate."

My mind went completely blank, and my jaw went slack. The attraction, the sparks every time he touched me. The reason I had to find him. I knew very little about the concept of fated mates, but it all suddenly made sense. Everything.

"What... does that mean?" I whispered hoarsely.

"I refuse to reject you, because it would weaken both of our wolf sides."

"But you don't *want* me," I choked out, feeling a horrible ache begin in my chest that had nothing to do with healing injuries.

The pain in my chest reminded me of that dream I had of him stabbing me.

"It's not that," he said reaching out to me.

I stepped back, my injured hand pressed over my heart. I took a shallow breath. If he touched me I would lose the last amount of composure I had managed to scrape together.

"Then what?" I asked, strength clawing its way back in my voice.

"To protect you from the backlash of my kingdom and the others."

I shook my head, refusing to let my tears fall. Refusing to believe him. Hoping that he at least felt a fraction of the pain he was causing me.

"You only want to protect yourself. Because a part of you doesn't want to be associated with or tied to your enemy. You don't want anyone else to find out that I am the heir of Lycus."

"Mira," Kieran began.

"You have your warrior, Kieran. I'll follow through with the challenge, but I hope that whatever happens, you survive the aftermath."

"What are you talking about?"

"It's none of your concern now. Shouldn't you be tending to your future queen?" I threw over my shoulder as I turned and strode away.

Rhudi

I remained on the training field with the others after Mira stormed off.

"Why do you think Kieran followed her?" Knox asked.

"I have a hunch, but we'll have to wait and see," I replied.

Cal gave me the side eye. I had a feeling he knew what was going on. Knox shrugged and dove into a nearby group of trainees.

The woman that Mira arrived at training with the day before approached us.

"Is Mira okay?" she asked. "I know Odell can really get under your skin, but that looked personal."

"I'm not sure," Cal replied, giving her a small smile. "She has a lot going on right now."

"I hope I can help in some way at least," she said hopefully.

Movement caught my attention and I turned toward the forest. Kieran came strolling back out. Alone.

I frowned. "Wait here with Cal. We might need your help with Mira after all."

Her brow furrowed in worry as I turned and made my way toward the king. As I neared Kieran I could see the tension in his shoulders and the sharpness to his movements.

"What happened?" I demanded quietly.

He met my gaze, causing me to pause mid-step. I could see the pain he held back.

"I told her like you wanted," he said.

"That's not all you did, or she would have came back out here with you," I hissed.

"I tried to explain why I couldn't," he pleaded, his eyes filled with pain.

"Don't tell me you rejected her," I growled, struggling to keep my voice low.

"I didn't," he said looking over my shoulder. "I told her that I refused to reject her."

"But not claiming your fated is almost as bad!"

"I don't know what you want me to do, Rhudi," Kieran said. "I am trying to do what is best for everyone."

"I doubt she sees it that way," I said as I brushed past him and sprinted into the forest.

Mira

Once I was alone again, the tears came. There was no stopping them this time. Despite being named an alpha and feeling welcomed by most of the people I had met, at that moment I felt more alone than ever. Empty. I leaned against a giant tree and slid to the ground. I curled in on myself, shutting out the world around me.

Maybe I should just march right up to Lycus with my head on a platter. It would simplify a lot of things. If only Selena and Remus were here. They would be able to guide me. They would know what to do.

I was so caught up in my thoughts that I let out a startled shout when I felt arms wrap around me.

"It'll be alright," Rhudi said. "Shhh."

I sobbed harder. "Why are you here?"

"Because we are family, and family takes care of each other." He pulled back and lifted my face up.

"I'm just sorry it was never the right time to tell you," he said as he wiped my tears away.

"You knew that Kieran was my fated, didn't you?"

"I did. He told me when I first arrived."

"He kept it silent this long. He should have just remained silent," I sighed.

"Why?" Rhudi asked.

"I would have been better off not knowing."

"Even if you win the challenge?"

I smiled sadly, and the realization dawned on his face. "You don't think you will win. Do you?"

"What is there to win? If I win, I will be the new Rogue Alpha with a pack of three that belongs... nowhere. If Lycus wins, then the whole human race is in peril. And the more I hear about Lycus, the less I believe I stand a chance."

I could feel Rhudi's eyes on me as I stared at the dirt, tracing circles with my fingers.

"I don't know what to say to that," he finally said.

"Have I finally stumped you, Uncle?" I asked with a humorless chuckle.

"Perhaps," he replied. "But, you must believe in yourself."

I snorted. "There's nothing to believe in. As everyone has determined, I am an unwanted orphan who should have stayed home and died defending what she knew."

"No, you're not," he said. "You have a group of people that care very much about you. Emotions are much stronger among shifters, and we tend to shut them down before expressing them."

"That explains why I feel like I'm going crazy," I joked, rubbing my temples.

"Well, you just found out you're half-shifter. You have a good excuse for going a little nuts," he laughed.

I rolled my eyes and wiped away a stray tear.

"Let's get back. There are some people who are worried about you."

CHAPTER THIRTY-ONE

MIRA

Twenty days.

That was the ever-shrinking number that lived in the back of my mind. Repeating over and over, pounding within my skull. I had a permanent headache from it.

Twenty days until I met Lycus for the first and last time. The day I either live to make a difference or die trying.

The last few days had been a blur. Rhudi left the day after my duel with Odell to report back to Lycus. Creed and Korren started training me privately very early in the mornings before the normal training schedules.

I avoided the King every chance I could.

Odell was still sporting two black eyes at least, while my beat-up hand had already healed.

"Are you ready?" Autumn asked.

I blinked and turned my attention back to her. My mind had wandered off again.

"I'm sorry," I sighed.

She smiled. "Stop apologizing. I know you have a lot on your mind. I was asking if you were ready to go see our gowns for the ball. The tailor is on his way."

"Yes, let's go before I get lost again."

She laughed and looped her arm through mine. If I was not training, researching, or trying to sleep, I spent any free time I had with Autumn. When my mind wasn't wandering, she helped me feel normal.

Autumn had become the closest I'd ever had to a friend. And despite the internal struggle of whether or not I should be getting close to anyone in these last days, she was there for me.

"Where are the guys today?" she asked.

"Knox and Ivan are helping out with training, and Cal is meeting with the King," I replied.

Cal was more than willing to take over all communication with Kieran after I told him that I no longer wished to speak with His Majesty. Unless I absolutely had too.

"Ah," she said thoughtfully.

I was thankful she was not one to pry.

I followed her from the garden and to a common room near her bed chamber. A small man was setting up one gown on display with an even younger man, while two women set up the second.

"They are gorgeous," Autumn exclaimed as she ran up to the bronze and gold gown the women were setting up.

The small man grinned and bowed. His red hair was pulled back at the nape of his neck, and he was dressed almost as well as the nobles I had seen parading around the castle.

"Welcome," he said. "I am Finius, the royal tailor. And these are my assistants, Anya and Mary. And this is my apprentice, Ezra."

"A pleasure to meet you all," I replied with a nod of my head.

"The pleasure is ours," Finius exclaimed. "It is not everyday that we get to dress both a future queen of a neighboring territory and a Challenger."

His excitement was palpable. I watched him look Autumn up and down with a small smile before turning back to me.

He frowned.

"What's wrong?" I asked, suddenly self-conscious.

I looked down at the outfit I had changed into after training this morning. A green brocade dress that, with the help of Larissa, I had altered. I cut a slit up the front and trimmed the length so that in the back it hit mid-calf and in the front, just about my knees. I work black pants and boots with a black leather corset on top. I refused to wear the slip underneath because that would make the dress stiff and bulky. The alterations made it easier for me to move around and access my weapons if needed, while also making me at least presentable at court.

We were currently altering two more of the simpler gowns to match this new style.

"Nothing is wrong, I'm just surprised at this take on my design," Finius replied. He walked around me, observing the design.

"Anya, sketch this out. We will design more that fit the Challenger's warrior aesthetic," he declared with a grin. He crossed to a trunk and pull out a stack of pages. "Which means, we will have a few more alterations to your ball gown than I originally anticipated, but," he began scribbling on one of the sheets, "I love new ideas and challenges!"

Autumn came over, wrapped an arm around my shoulders, and gave me a squeeze.

"You are making a statement!" she squealed.

I smiled tightly, not entirely convinced. I just knew I preferred function over fashion.

"Let's get you two in your gowns so we can catalog the final adjustments," Finius said with a clap of his hands.

Anya and Mary set up a divider and lead Autumn behind it. While they helped undress Autumn, Ezra began to dismantle the bronze and gold gown. He carefully untied the black ribbons and set aside the various layers. Once the base of the gown was revealed, he lifted it off the display and took it to Anya, who stood beside the divider.

The pair went back and forth, meticulously reconstructing the gown onto Autumn. As they worked, two servants entered the room, rolling a large, covered frame which they uncovered and opened it. Inside was the largest looking glass I had ever seen. Two panels looked out at me, doubling my reflection.

The frame itself was taller than I. The servants set it up and then set a small wooden box a few feet in front of it.

"Are you ready, my dear?" Finius called. He had a small notebook, a bunch of pins, and a measuring tape thrown over his shoulder.

"Just about," one of the assistants called.

"While I am assessing Autumn, they will get you dressed in your gown," he said to me with a smile.

I finally turned my attention to the second display. Mine was the color of an angry sea—deep blue-green that almost looked black in some places. Barely-there silver lace covered the bodice, chest, and arms. The embroidery on the skirt reminded me of tree roots.

"I do hope you like it," he said.

"It is a beautiful piece," I replied.

"Finius, I believe you have outdone yourself with these," Autumn exclaimed as she stepped out from behind the divider.

We all watched as she did an elegant spin, her skirts flaring out around her. She practically glowed. Shades of crimson and maroon flashed with her movements, adding even more depth to the decadent outfit.

"*Bap bap bap*, I am not finished yet!" Finius declared as he led her to the small wooden box and allowed her to step up on it.

"Your turn Lady Mira," Mary said, motioning for me to step behind the divider.

I went away from view, and she began to unlace my corset while Anya helped with my boots.

They followed the same routine as with Autumn. I was undressed, and then layer by layer I was engulfed in a sea of fabric.

All of the layers were heavy and bulky. There were at least three skirt layers. The silver lace clung to my arms and throat effectively disguising my scars.

Anya pulled my hair back into a loose braid and pinned it up. "This has been our favorite project to date," she said as she looked me up and down in awe.

"It's gorgeous," I said.

"Mira, are you dressed yet?" Ezra called.

I put on a small smile and walked out from behind the divider. Both he and Finius' jaws dropped.

"Goddess," Autumn murmured.

"I have no words," Finius said. "Let's get you up on the box."

I strode over to the looking glasses and stepped up onto the box. I stared at my reflection. I hardly recognized myself.

Finius and Ezra began tugging at my skirts. "Is it too bulky for her?" Ezra whispered.

"Exactly what I was thinking, my boy," Finius replied.

Ezra lifted the top skirt while Finius reached under and ripped out the scratchy fabric that made the dress poofy.

I instantly felt freer as the fabric fell around me. The top layer smoothed down, instantly making me feel less bulky and my figure appear slimmer.

"We don't need that. We'll pin this here," he mumbled.

They worked on pinning and pulling at the skirt until Finius was happy with the final outline.

"You will be my masterpiece," Finius said as he helped me step down. "I am excited for these fixes."

"Thank you," I said.

Autumn came back out as Anya and Mary packed away her gown for transport.

"I cannot wait for this ball! One to see my mate, and two for everyone to see you in your gown," she exclaimed.

"It will be an interesting evening, I am sure," I commented.

Mary and Anya helped me change as Ezra and Finius began to pack up.

"I look forward to working on this new collection as well," Anya told me as she carefully folded up my gown and packed it into a trunk.

"You are going to make huge changes," Finius commented, grasping my hands in his. "We all believe in you."

I squeezed his hands, holding back tears. "Thank you."

Chapter thirty-two

Kieran

Distance. That is all that I felt since leaving Mira in the forest days ago. And numbness.

Every so often I would feel pangs of sorrow and pain. Sharp enough that it felt as though I were being stabbed in the heart.

I only saw her in passing, and she refused to make eye contact with me.

"How are you holding up?" Cal asked.

"It has been chaotic," I replied.

Any time I tried to meet with her, she sent Cal in her place. I knew she was busy, but I wanted a chance to talk to her again. To try and make her understand.

"Lady Odell seems to be in mood," he commented.

I rolled my eyes. "Ever since she dueled Mira, she's been taking her anger out on anyone she can. It's been a major pain. And now her family is coming into the picture. I'm not excited about the prospect with Odell in such a temper."

"I figured it was only a matter of time before Oberon joined the fray. Especially since you are required by law to marry his daughter by the end of the year now—unless, of course, you choose your own mate before then."

"Not just Oberon," I growled, my wolf bristling at his words.

Cal raised an eyebrow in question.

"Her brother is coming with them."

mira

Nineteen days

The sun had just started to rise as I made my way to the kitchens. The brief moments I spent here before training reminded me of the downtimes with Selena.

"Good morning, my dear!" Marj greeted me with a tight hug.

This had become our routine. She even had a basket ready with breakfast for me to take out to everyone. I just hated that she altered her schedule to accommodate me, but any time I tried to bring it up, she would wave her hands in dismissal.

"Good morning!" I returned.

"Were you able to get some sleep? I feel you have been looking haggard." She grasped my chin and gave me a thorough look.

"A little," I replied.

"Too much reading again?"

I just nodded and pinched the bridge of my nose. My head felt like it was splitting open. Headaches had become a daily occurrence, along with other aches and pains from exhaustion and training. I refused to stop though. There was not enough time to stop.

"Learn anything new that might help?"

"I don't know," I sighed. "Everything Rian keeps giving me is on the history of Halflings, Challenges, and the four bloodlines."

I paused as Marj handed me an extra muffin. I could smell the fresh berries she had used to make them, the tartness made my mouth water.

"I appreciate the history, don't get me wrong, but how is a child from two shifters, without their own ability to shift, going to help me? And why are they still called Halflings when both parents are shifters?"

"My father always likes to give multiple potential answers to multiple questions all at once," Marj said thoughtfully. "As he told me when I was a pup: *All of the important answers are those below the surface, you just have to dive a little deeper for them.*"

I sat, chewing her words as I did the muffin.

"Any luck with pack link research?" she asked.

I shook my head. "I found something that basically said that among Halflings it is rare for such a link to develope, but if it does, the link is always strongest with their family members."

"Not even their mate?" she asked in surprise.

I shrugged. "Not much mention of mates and Halflings in the same sentence. It seems no one wanted to be associated with them."

I felt a sharp sting at my words, and my heart skipped a beat, but it was true. Nothing in my reading mentioned Halflings having mates. After they were used for study, they were executed.

"That's a shame," she said with a frown. "You're my favorite Halfling."

"I'm your *only* Halfling," I laughed.

She shrugged and laughed. "Still my favorite."

I finished my muffin and sighed, enjoying the last bit of calm before the chaos returned.

She put a hand on my shoulder. "Everything will be okay," she reassured me.

I smiled, stood, and gave her another hug. The more time I spent with her, the more it felt as though she could feel what I did.

"Time to get this to the boys. You know what happens when they get hungry."

She made a face of mock terror. "Just keep them away from my kitchen and they can have all the muffins they want!"

I laughed. "Deal!"

I picked up the basket and strolled out of the kitchen, making my way to the training grounds.

"Finally!" Creed exclaimed as I neared the group. "I'm starving."

"Patience," I said as I set the basket down and everyone dived in.

Cal, Ivan, Knox, Creed, and Korren—my impromptu training group. As they devoured the muffins, I grabbed a second while I still had a chance.

"How's research going?" Korren asked.

I shrugged. "A bunch of information, but nothing that I can see that would help."

"Only time will tell," Cal replied around a mouthful of muffin.

I raised an amused eyebrow at him, and he grinned.

"Hurry and finish up breakfast," Korren said. "We have a lot to cover."

A few moments later, Ivan, Knox, and Creed had shifted and were charging toward me. No weapons. We had moved toward doing mock challenges, which did not allow for them.

Without weapons, I was out of my element. I had to learn to use my surroundings to gain the advantage. I blinked against the blurriness in my eyes and focused on the duel.

Cal and Korren stood off to the side, observing.

I rolled under Creed as he lunged for me, grabbing one of his legs to throw off his balance. Ivan was right behind him, nipping at my heels.

I twisted, sending Creed to the ground and rolling on top of him, avoiding Ivan's teeth. Blinding pain shot through my head, turning my vision white. It spread from my head to every muscle in my body, as if someone poured scalding water over me.

Knox slammed into my side, knocking both of us to the ground. His teeth grazed my throat, and I froze with a whimper.

"That's enough," Korren called out.

Knox moved and sat beside me as I remained splayed out on the ground waiting out the waves of heat in my muscles and for my vision to return.

"Mira, are you okay?" Cal asked.

I sat up and pressed my fingertips to my temples, closing my eyes against the pain.

A heavy hand sat on my shoulder, and I blinked up at Korren. Cal knelt in front of me.

"No more practice today," Korren said. "You need to rest." I shook my head. "There's no time for rest."

"You can't keep this up," Ivan seconded. "Go rest," Creed said.

I knew they would not let me finish out the rest of the day. I nodded as Knox helped me stand.

cal

I watched the fight leave Mira's eyes as Knox helped her up. Her body sagged with exhaustion. Her face pale.

"I will send for Autumn to check on you in a few hours," I said. "Get some sleep. You can't fight if you are not well."

She nodded as Knox and Ivan helped her off the field and back to the castle. They passed the trickle of early trainees on their way.

"I'm worried about her," Korren said. "She's been pushing herself too hard."

Kieran and Gage appeared nearby, watching. "Is Mira alright?" Kieran asked.

"She's exhausted," I replied.

"I was just saying she's pushing herself too hard," Korren continued.

"She can't make a difference if she runs herself into the ground," Kieran said, concerned.

"She has nothing left to lose," I said flatly.

Mira

Knox and Ivan left me alone in my room. A new stack of books sat on the table by the armchair with a folded piece of parchment on top.

227

I stared at it as I unbraided my hair and kicked off my boots, then I changed into a sleeping tunic and curled into bed. I closed my eyes, trying to will the pain behind my lids away.

A soft knock echoed through the room. Larissa stepped inside with a tray and closed the door softly.

"I was informed that you were not feeling well," she whispered.

"Just tired, and my head is bothering me," I replied.

"I have just the thing to help you relax."

She sat her tray on the table by the bed and handed me a cup of warm tea. I wrinkled my nose at the herbal concoction.

"It will help you sleep and alleviate any aches and pains," she said with a small smile. "And you can use this to help block out any light."

She placed a loop of fabric in my lap. I sighed and gulped down the tea as fast as I could.

"Thank you," I said, handing the cup back to her.

She smiled. "Get your strength back. I'm on your side Alpha Mira."

Tears clouded my already blurry eyes as she smoothed my hair and left me alone.

I placed the fabric loop over my eyes and nestled deeper into my pillows. Sleep quickly pulled me into its embrace.

Chapter thirty-three

Mira

Nine days

Two days until the celebratory ball. I sat, curled up on the sofa in my room in front of the fire. A large, red bound book sat in my lap. I rubbed my temples and stared into the flames.

Guests had started arriving a couple of days ago from all over. Anyone who knew of my existence and wanted to make a show of standing with me against Lycus was in the castle.

Training had been minimized to observing and reading since my episode on the training field. I still had a lingering migraine that refused to go away, but the waves of muscle pain had decreased. Every now and then I would get a flare up.

Larissa and Cal compared it to what they felt when they had their first shift. I blamed it on spending too much time around shifters, stress, and overexertion.

I just wanted this Challenge over with.

My eyes swept from the flames to the stack of parchment on the small desk under the window. Crisp new sheets sat beneath a bunch of crumpled balls, an ink well, and my journal.

My attempts to say goodbye.

I had a feeling that this would be my last fight, and I would not get the chance to tell Remus and Selena. That they would not know the sacrifice I made for them.

Cal came in without knocking, and I look up at him. "I wanted to inform you that Lady Odell's family has arrived," he said flatly.

I sighed and stood, closing my book. "Just now?"

He nodded.

"Has her temper improved since I have been cooped up in here?"

"Slightly. She has stopped harassing the servants and other ladies," Cal replied, a slight twitch tugging at the corner of his mouth.

I pulled my robe closer around me.

"How are you feeling?"

I looked into his eyes and smiled sadly. "Weak," I said honestly, letting my shoulders sag. "I feel like there is more I should be doing to prepare, but I can't muster the energy for it."

"Kieran is worried about you. We all are."

"His Majesty has an odd way of showing his concern," I snapped. "I'm sure part of this, whatever *this* is, is because of our last encounter."

"He is your mate, isn't he?"

Cal never held anything back. I nodded, feeling pressure start in my chest again.

"He basically said he didn't want me but that he would not formally reject me," I finally said aloud.

I had not wanted to say the words aloud. To bring that pain back again. I wrapped my arms around myself, feeling as though I were cracking open.

"I came all this way," I muttered, "for that."

Cal crossed the room in quick strides and wrapped his arms around me. His strength helped hold me together in that moment.

"There's no other pain like the loss of one's mate," he whispered.

My tears fell as he squeezed me tighter.

Kieran

I paced the ballroom, watching as servants set up the decorations for the ball. Gage stood nearby, conversing with the planner.

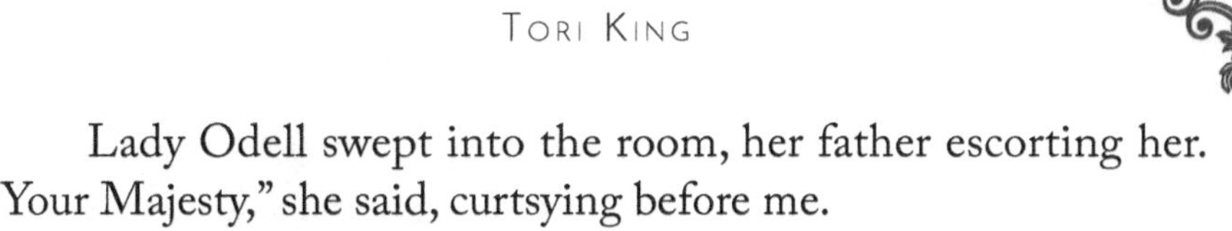

Lady Odell swept into the room, her father escorting her. "Your Majesty," she said, curtsying before me.

Her father bowed formally.

"Welcome, Lord Oberon Creighton. It is a pleasure to have you and your family here," I replied with a small nod.

They both rose and grinned at me.

"The pleasure is ours," Oberon exclaimed. "We have been looking forward to this event since we received the invitation. I am personally looking forward to becoming acquainted with your Challenger."

My eyes narrowed slightly. "She has been limiting exposure to guests until the ball," I replied cautiously. "Too much training has left her weary."

"I can imagine," Oberon said with a mock flourish. "I heard about the duel against my dear daughter and was surprised that Odell even let her get close. She must really have some talent."

I knew he was attempting to goad me. I looked up as Rhudi and Cal wandered in, whispering to themselves.

"Gage, keep an eye on the events here," I called over my shoulder. I turned back to the Creighton's. "If you'll excuse me."

I stepped around them and strode to meet Cal and Rhudi.

"Your Majesty," they chorused.

"How is she?" I whispered. They turned, and I followed them from the ballroom.

"The same," Cal said flatly. "And you thought *not rejecting* her wouldn't be bad."

My step faltered at his words. "Yes, I know."

He continued as Rhudi shot me a look. "She regrets making the journey here because of what you told her."

I came to a stop. Feeling her pain well up inside me again. Pain that was caused by me. I closed my eyes and sighed. There were somethings I knew I could never make right.

"How did your meeting with Lycus go?" I asked Rhudi, pushing the conversation forward.

Rhudi shrugged. "He is growing more antsy as the days go by. But he is excited to get this Challenge over with so he can continue his take over. Keeps asking me to tell him about Mira."

"And what did you tell him?" Cal asked, instantly defensive.

"That I don't know much. Just that she showed up one day and started fighting against the rogues."

Cal nodded thoughtfully. "Which still gives us the upper hand."

"How?" I asked.

"If he doesn't know she is of his blood, he will get cocky and think that he can win this fight with no preparation, right?"

Rhudi nodded. "He has done nothing to prepare for the Challenge."

"That may be, but that still doesn't take into the account Mira's condition right now," I replied.

"If you had accepted her," Rhudi growled. "There wouldn't be an issue. She would still be strong and able to prepare."

"She can still win," I argued back.

"She isn't planning on winning," Cal said softly.

My heart stopped. We both turned to look at him.

"Even if Lycus dies on that field, I believe she will as well."

mira

Seven days

Seven days until my last breath. Seven hours until I have to face all the people that have come to gawk at me.

I pulled my knees up to my chest, causing the scalding water around me to ripple. Purple rose petals and sage leaves floated on the surface around me.

I had awoken this morning to a red sky and with a hollow feeling in my stomach.

I was healed. No visible bruises were left on my skin, no open wounds. Only scars remained. But it was the invisible ones that burned.

They crept along my skin with razors, stabbing at any moment of peace. Reminding me that not everything was well.

That a part of me was shattered. Was missing.

I closed my eyes and tried to focus. Larissa directed two servants in the main room on where to set up my gown and accessories for the evening.

"I'm sorry but you cannot come in here," I heard her exclaim. "My Lady is preparing for the ball."

"I just want to see her alone for a moment."

My eyes flew open and my heart pounded at Kieran's words. He was at the door, and he wanted to see me.

"I'm sorry, your Majesty. I cannot let you in."

The door closed with a snap, and I focused on the heavy footsteps as Kieran walked away. Larissa's quick steps came up behind me.

"Thank you," I said, looking over my shoulder at her.

"Of course," she replied. "You said you didn't want to see him."

"What would I do without you?" I murmured.

"You would have no idea how to prepare for this event," she cawed proudly.

I laughed and splashed water at her as she knelt and began to wash my hair.

Rhudi

I adjusted my jacket once more and stared at Mira's pack. All three were dressed in black pants, various shades of green tunics, and deep gray jackets.

My own jacket was a pale gray in comparison.

"You all clean up nicely," Kieran said as he and Gage strolled into the hall. "Are we ready for the evening?"

"As ready as we'll ever be," Knox grumbled, pulling at the scarf around his throat.

Ivan smacked the back of his head and whispered something in his ear. They all seemed uneasy.

"Cal, you will wait behind to escort Mira to the ball room as planned," Gage instructed.

"Actually, I will be escorting my niece," I cut in. "I offered, seeing as she might not get another chance for a familial escort."

"Very well," Gage replied tightly. "The sun is beginning to set, it is time for Your Majesty to make his entrance and mingle before dinner is served."

"Lead the way," Kieran said.

I watched them go down the hall and stopped Cal when the others were out of earshot.

"Anything I need to be aware of?" I whispered.

"There's something in the air," he whispered back. "None of us can explain it, but there are emotions rolling off Mira that we haven't felt before."

"You're feeling her emotions?"

He nodded. "Just flickers. She has strong emotional control, but some blaze in, and it's those that keep flaring up. She's on edge."

I sighed. "We all are. Just keep an eye out. It is our job to protect her."

"It is," Cal seconded as he turned and followed the path to the ballroom.

Music floated softly through the air as I turned and walked in the opposite direction. I strode up two flights of steps, up to the floor Mira's room was on.

Finius threw open the door and stepped out as I approached. He grinned with tears in his eyes. He looked me up and down.

"You are the escort?" he asked.

I nodded.

His brow furrowed as he studied me. "You'll do," he said after a moment. He turned back to face inside the room as giggles erupted from inside.

"Is she ready?" I asked.

Finius grinned and stepped aside dramatically. Two ladies and a young man stepped out. "Lady Mira has been my greatest creation," Finius exclaimed. "Come on out, dear!"

The maid I frequently saw with Mira stepped out and paused.

"Promise not to laugh," Mira said from inside.

"I would never," I said lightly, a small chuckle rising. She stepped into the hallway and my jaw dropped.

Kieran

Mingling at balls was always the worst. I listened to some nobles drone on about their complaints. Waiting with bated breath for the guest of honor.

Gage stood just behind me, as was tradition. I had lost sight of Cal, Ivan, and Knox after we entered the room, but knew they were nearby and watching.

Autumn and her betrothed came up to me next.

"King Kieran!" King Rhodri greeted, clasping my arm just below the elbow.

"King Rhodri, Lady Autumn, so glad you two could make it this evening," I said with a smile.

Rhodri was an old friend, and we got along well. And I had heard that Autumn had become good friends with Mira.

"Your Majesty," Autumn said with a curtsy. "Any news on the arrival of Lady Mira?"

"She should be here any moment," I replied with a nod. "Being the guest of honor, she deserves a grand entrance."

As if summoned by my words, the trumpets rang out and silence fell over the room. Everyone turned to look at the door. The herald looked down the staircase at us and smiled.

"Ladies and gentlemen," the herald called out. "The King would like to extend his gratitude for gathering this evening and showing your support."

Applause rang out, and I bowed my head to those smiling nearby.

The herald's grin widened. "It is my great honor, to present to you, the Challenger, Lady Mira Brianne!"

Deafening applause and howls rang out. Rhudi stepped through the door first, then turned and offered his hand.

My breath caught as the light glittered off the silver material of her sleeve. I watched in awe as Rhudi led Mira to the edge of the top step. A small smile sat on her lips.

Her hair was swept back, but not in typical court fashion. It was still wild and fit her personality as the untamed curls fell down her back and framed her face.

Finius had outdone himself on her gown. She looked like the daughter of the Moon Goddess herself.

The front of her skirt was a little shorter, I could see the tops of her laced boots.

My heart threatened to burst from my chest as I watched Mira look out over the room. Her eyes met mine for a brief moment before passing to Autumn next to me.

Rhudi watched her proudly as the applause and cheers kept going. He finally guided her down the stairs where she was swarmed by a crowd of people. She glided as she walked, a carefully hidden slit in her dress allowed for ease of movement, should she need it.

"Doesn't she look stunning," Autumn exclaimed to Rhodri. "Finius will have to start designing more warrior fitting clothing for shifters now. He has gone above and beyond."

"Introduce me to your friend, my love," he said warmly.

Autumn grinned and wove her way through the crowd. I watched them sidle up to Mira and Rhudi.

Ivan, Knox, and Cal had materialized and were standing close to Mira, ready to intervene if anything seemed suspicious. Autumn threw her arms around Mira's neck with an excited squeal.

"Your Majesty," a feminine voice called.

I turned and looked into Lady Creighton's brown eyes. Her blonde hair was pulled back tightly. She clung tightly to her son's arm. Both of them watching me with their matching eyes.

"Lady Creighton, so nice to see you. And you as well, Silas," I greeted.

"Majesty," Silas responded.

"This is quite the event," Lady Creighton continued. "Odell has been talking about it non-stop since we arrived, and her letters mentioned hardly anything else."

"It's not everyday we have someone challenge the Rogue Alpha," I replied stiffly. "I wanted to show Mira that she has my support as well as those who decided to attend."

"You always liked playing to the people," Silas said with a smirk.

His mother playfully swatted at him with a laugh and led him away.

I sighed. It was going to be a long night.

Mira

"Your Majesty," I said with a curtsy to the man on Autumn's arm. "It is a pleasure to finally meet you."

He took my arm in a warrior's greeting. "And you as well," Rhodri said with a smile. His dark hair was trimmed short. His jacket matched the copper tones in Autumn's gown.

"You look lovely," I told her as someone grabbed my hand and squeezed before walking away.

She grinned and blushed. "As do you, Lady Mira. If I didn't know you were a warrior, you would have made me believe you were a princess."

I chuckled. Another hand grasped mine, squeezed, and let go. I felt like a trophy on display. My stomach fluttered. I casually let my hands fall to my sides.

Finius had disguised a slit in the fabric, much like what I had done with the other gowns. I pressed lightly against my upper thigh, feeling the knife I had secured there. A wave of calm rushed over me as the metal pressed into my skin.

"We will see you on the dance floor later?" Autumn asked as a bell rang.

I nodded. Rhudi offered me his arm and guided me through the throng to the dining hall.

A strong hand grabbed mine and squeezed tightly, pulling me to a stop. My eyes met a pair of brown ones. Brownish-red hair fell into them. High cheekbones accentuated his face.

"Is there a problem?" Cal asked, stepping forward.

"No, I just wanted to look into the eyes of the Challenger before she got swept off her feet by the evening," the wolf said.

He glanced at Cal, and then back at me, his hand still wrapped uncomfortably tight around mine. It felt as though he were searching for something.

I stood awkwardly under his gaze as guests strolled past. I was also terrified. I squeezed Rhudi's elbow after a moment.

"Alright, Silas, that's enough," Rhudi said.

Cal stepped forward and clamped a hand down on Silas' wrist. He let go.

"You've lost your fight, haven't you?" he asked with a smirk.

I snorted. "I don't know who you are and what this is about, but I assure you there is plenty of fight left in me."

Cal let go of Silas as he shrugged and went into the dining hall. I nodded with a tight smile.

"Let's eat," I said. "I'm starving."

Once again, we were at the head table. However, I sat facing the crowd this time. I noticed a table against the back wall. It was hidden behind the open door and overflowing with boxes.

I frowned. *Gifts for the sacrifice*, I assumed.

Kieran sat a few seats down from us next to Odell. Silas and an older couple sat across from them.

I leaned closer to Cal.

"Are those Odell's relatives?" I whispered.

He nodded behind his goblet.

I took a sip of my wine and frowned. "That explains Silas' behavior," I muttered.

I stabbed a piece of meat and popped it into my mouth. I had a sickening feeling while I ate. It also did not help that my headache had returned with a vengeance.

My stomach churned.

"Are you alright?" Ivan asked. He and Rhudi sat across from me and Knox to my right.

I nodded and finished my plate. I picked up my goblet and downed the rest of it. Knox raised an eyebrow at me.

"The veggies tasted off," I whispered to him.

"They tasted fine to me," he said with a puzzled expression.

I shrugged. "We all know I'm losing my mind. Why not sense of taste too?"

"Maybe you *did* catch something," Knox suggested. "It is not uncommon for shifters to get sick."

A servant reached between us and filled my goblet. I recognized Shey and smiled at her.

"I wouldn't be surprised," I countered, taking another sip as our main dish plates were cleared away and dessert was served.

A chocolate pastry with fresh berries was set in front of me. Marj had out done herself preparing everything. I took a bite and frowned. It was much more bitter than I would have thought for a dessert.

The fruit helped, but I was quickly losing my appetite. My head throbbed, and I placed my cutlery down on my half-eaten dessert with a small groan.

"It's very filling, isn't it?" Rhudi asked.

I just nodded and rubbed my stomach. Something was not right, but I did not want to worry them.

I ignored my wine and took a couple of small sips of water, my hand shaking slightly as I brought the glass to my lips.

As people finished their desserts, they found their way back into the ballroom.

"Ready to dance?" Knox asked excitedly.

"Only if you take the lead," I replied with a smile.

"Deal." He stood and held out his hand to me. I followed, swaying just so.

"Mira?" Cal asked.

"I guess I had too much wine," I laughed.

They smiled at me as I placed my hand in Knox's, and we went into the ball room. My head throbbed in time with the music.

This was not a wine dizziness, though. Something was wrong and I would have to quickly find my way back to my room the first chance I could.

Knox was a surprisingly good dancer. I, on the other hand, had a hard time keeping my eyes focused through the dizzying fog in my head that kept increasing. I stumbled and laughed.

"Go find a better partner," I chuckled as I patted his arm. "I need to clear my head before returning to the dance floor."

Knox bowed his head to me with a grin.

"Just let me know when you are ready," he said.

I grinned and watched him weave his way through the dancing couples. I made my way to the nearest wall. Smiling and nodding at anyone who looked at me.

I leaned my back against the wall, feeling my forehead break-out in sweat.

Merda! Was something put in my food or drink?

Nausea rolled through me, and I turned and made my way as calmly as I could out of the room and into the hallway. Some couples lingered outside the door, and I strode past them.

I held one hand to my stomach as I quickly made my way through the halls. My fingers were starting to go numb, and my vision was blurry.

I stopped, breathing heavy. I leaned with my freehand braced against the stone wall. I could see another grand staircase in a smaller formal area.

All that mattered at the moment was that no one else was around.

I heaved. Bile scorched my throat and mouth as my stomach emptied.

I moaned and wiped my mouth with the back of my hand. I opened my eyes and everything spun. I closed them and breathed as calmly as I could, sweat covered my body.

I heaved again.

"Aw, poor Challenger," Odell sneered.

I turned and looked at her. A russet-colored wolf sat just behind her.

"Looks like you found out what happens when a shifter ingests wolfsbane."

mira

I stared at her fuzzy form. "You did this," I stated.

She grinned. I watched as she paced back and forth. The wolf kept its eyes locked on me.

"After our duel, I knew I couldn't beat you hand to hand," she said. "And with you around, Kieran won't marry me. I've seen the way he watches you."

"You know the rules about harming a Challenger," I croaked.

"The only ones that would care are Kieran and your sad band of dogs that follow you around. Soon enough, none of them will be able to stop me."

I swayed and took a shaky step toward her.

"You think that becoming Queen will make a difference?" I asked. "You will have no power under Kieran."

Her grin changed. "You don't get it. I marry Kieran and my family becomes rulers. My mate and I will rule."

Realization dawned on me. "You plan to kill him. You and your mate."

She frowned. "You're smarter than you look. But yes, Gage and I will rule this land and make sure only the strong survive."

I clenched my fists. It all made sense now. "That won't happen if you're dead," I snarled.

My stomach churned, and I swallowed the bile that rose in my throat. Her laughter rung in my ears.

"Kill her," she ordered the wolf.

It lunged for me. I lurched to the side as its claws raked across my left arm. I fumbled for the knife at my thigh but my fingers were too numb to respond.

My heart raced as as the wolf rounded on me again.

"You won't make it out of here alive," Odell taunted. "You should have stayed where you belong."

I turned and sprinted toward her. Her eyes widened in surprise.

The wolf, realizing my move, slammed into me. It's teeth sunk into my left thigh, and I screamed. I kicked with my right leg, landing a blow to its shoulder.

The wolf skidded backward, and I stared into its eyes. His eyes. "Silas," I hissed.

"My brother is notorious for his fighting skills. More so even than my father," Odell explained.

"I guess grudges run deep in your family," I grunted as I stood.

"We fight for what is rightfully ours."

Silas lunged for me. I collapsed again, barely keeping his snapping jaws from my throat.

Voices echoed in the opposite hallway and Silas looked up, ready to eliminate the problem. He lunged forward.

I followed his movement, finally grasping my knife and plunging it into his shoulder.

He roared and flung me backwards. I flew through the air and landed on the staircase, my head cracking against the stone steps. Black spots erupted across my vision.

Silas lunged for me, his teeth sinking deep into my shoulder and throat. My scream echoed in time with Odell's laugher.

Cal! I screamed in my head.

Silas retracted some of the pressure only to clamp back down. Fangs pierced deeper.

Mira? Mira! Where are you?

Cal's voice echoed in my head, laced with concern. The mind link. Tears streamed down my face as I replayed everything to Cal.

"No," Merry screamed. "Mira!"

"No," I whispered as Silas and I looked up.

Merry and the den mother stood in the opposite hallway, staring in horror.

I am on my way! Stay with us! Don't you dare let go!

Silas and Odell took off as Merry and the den mother rushed to my side.

"Mira!" Cal roared from the hall.

"I mind linked the King," the den mother said as Cal dropped to his knees beside me.

Their voices were drowned out by a deafening roar that shook the castle.

cal

I knew who had roared. I stared down at Mira, my mind in overdrive. Bruises already marred her pale skin. Blood poured out of the wounds on her neck and shoulder.

Ivan, Knox. Find Silas, Gage, and Odell. I ordered through our pack link. *Make sure they get locked up. And find someone to send for Remus and Selena. They need to be here.*

I began ripping strips of fabric off Mira's skirt as quickly as possible and wrapped up as many of her wounds as I could.

"Did you see what happened?" I asked Flora, the den mother.

"Just the end where he..." she gulped, tears filling her eyes, "he did that to her throat."

I nodded. "Help me bind what we can so we can get her to the infirmary."

Her hands shook as she tore off strips and began pressing the cloth into wounds.

"Where are they? What happened?" Kieran roared as he stormed into the area.

"I am already on it," I said without looking at him. "I'll tell you everything when she is in the infirmary."

He made a choking sound when he saw her. Horror filled his eyes.

"I never should have said what I did the last time we spoke," he groaned. "I should have just accepted her."

"It's not too late," I said sharply.

"Has anyone seen Rhudi?" Kieran asked.

"He took off with Ivan and Knox," I replied.

"Alright, I think that's the best we can do," Flora whispered. She stood and pulled the little boy against her.

Kieran took her spot and gently picked Mira up. He took off down the hall at a dead sprint.

"I have already let the doctors know," he called over his shoulder.

Guards followed behind us as I followed close on his heels.

We reached the infirmary in record time. Three doctors and just as many nurses were waiting at the entrance for us.

They ushered us in and took Mira from Kieran. They took her into a separate room and Kieran went to follow. Another nurse stopped him.

"Please, Your Majesty. Let us work," the nurse said quickly. He nodded and sank into a chair outside the door.

Kieran

Cal paced in front of me as I sat. "What the hell happened?" I hissed. "And how did you know she was in danger?"

"She mind linked me," Cal said.

"She what?"

"Mira was able to mind link me."

He relayed what happened and the events she had played for him through the link.

"Any updates from your men?" I asked after he was finished.

"Korren and Creed have just locked Silas and Gage up," Cal replied. He paused and looked up as a flash of red came running down the hall.

"Cal, what are you doing here?" the woman asked.

"Mira was injured," he replied.

"Your Majesty," she said in surprise when she saw me.

"You are the best," Cal continued. "You have to help her. She's also been poisoned with wolfsbane."

I stared at the woman. Green eyes. Pale skin. Red hair. Lillia. Her eyes widened, and her face paled as she looked to Cal, who nodded. She darted to the door and looked in.

"Mira!" she cried.

We followed, but only to the doorway. Watching as she and the others scrambled with bandages, both clean and bloodied.

Lillia's eyes scanned over the injuries, assessing the damage with concern.

"We need to try *vivifica*," she said.

"She's a Halfling," another said. "We don't know what will happen."

"It will work." I cut in. "If it will save her, use it!"

"And who are you to her to tell us to use it, Your Majesty?" Lillia asked with fire in her eyes.

"Her mate," Cal and I chorused.

"Then both of you out. We need space to work," she ordered. "You, grab our newest vials of *vivifica*. We need the strongest batch."

Cal and I sat in the hall side by side.

"How do you know Lillia?" I asked, curious at the familiarity. "She's my mother."

I gaped at him in surprise. He stared back calmly, his eyes filled with worry.

"Not by blood," he corrected. "Lillia is mated to my father. My birth mother was killed when I was young, and Lillia raised me."

"No wonder you are so protective of Mira," I finally said.

He nodded. "I didn't believe it at first when the rumors started to spread. And then when I first saw her. She's the spitting image of our mother."

A scream rang out from the room and my blood chilled. Cal

closed his eyes as even more nurses ran in. The herbal stench of *vivifica* filled the air, followed by another scream.

Lillia stepped out, her gown soaked in blood. She glanced at Cal and then at me. Tears filled her eyes and worry was etched into her face.

"Kieran, I don't know what you did, but if you are her mate, it's not helping any. Mira's wounds should be starting to heal by now," Lillia said shakily. "Especially with you nearby."

I felt Cal's eyes on me as my heart plummeted. They all knew that my not accepting her as my mate was the cause of this.

"Damnit," I growled.

I pushed past her and into the room. Mira lay on the cot, her dress ripped open so her wounds could be tended too. A bandage was wrapped around her thigh, blood seeping through already.

It was her throat and right shoulder that made the blood rush in my ears and my heart stop. Nurses alternated between pouring *vivifica* straight into the wound, attempting to stitch, and applying pressure to stop the bleeding.

There was so much blood.

Her skin was too pale and sweat gleamed on her skin. Without thinking I strode forward and knelt down on her left, pressing my lips to her temple.

"Your Majesty!" someone said, grabbing my arm to pull me away.

My growl echoed through the room.

"Leave him," Lillia commanded.

I took a deep breath and placed my lips near Mira's ear. "I accept and claim you as my Mate," I whispered.

My canines elongated and I sunk them into her neck, just below her jaw. Marking her as mine.

She whimpered as I pulled back and Lillia rushed forward, ushering me out of the way.

She lifted Mira's head and poured a dose of vivifica into her mouth.

I looked up to see Cal standing in the doorway. Hope glittered in his eyes. All of the nurses stared in shock at me.

"Wait outside," Lillia ordered. "We have work to do in order to make sure Mira makes it through the night."

I turned and walked from the room, feeling my connection to Mira growing. A subtle fire burned in my veins that I recognized from the medicine.

Her pain was now my pain. Her emotions. I could feel her heartbeat in my veins, beating in time with my own.

And if she died, I would not be long behind.

Mira

Fire. Inside and out.

My head throbbed in time to the flickering flames in my veins. The last time I had felt this pain was in the cabin.

The cabin.

Kieran.

Vivifica.

My eyes flew open.

The stench of alcohol and that burning, herbal remedy saturated the air around me. Rhudi was passed out in a chair on the far side of the room. Kieran in the chair beside the bed. His hands rested on the bed near where my right one lay limp.

Something had changed. I was too weak to put all the pieces together, but there was a change.

Remus and Selena stood at the window, whispering quietly and staring outside. My heart swelled. Ivan and Knox sat on the floor near Rhudi.

Ivan met my gaze and then looked up at the ceiling, as if in prayer. He looked back at me with a relieved smile.

Welcome back, Ivan whispered in my mind.

I blinked and smiled in relief that I had not imagined the connection to my pack.

A woman with red hair and green eyes stared back at me from the foot of the bed. Relief softened her features as I met her gaze.

It felt like I was staring into a looking glass, but at an older version of myself.

"You're awake," she said as tears filled her eyes.

to be continued in:

Bloodlines

book 2 of

The Alpha King

tori king

Tori King started writing as a way to bring life and background to her illustrations. She would draw and paint various characters throughout her school years, even acquiring freelance projects. Tori graduated with a degree in graphic design and minor in painting.

Tori returned to writing as an escape when COVID hit. It became easier for her to write instead of other creative outlets. She worked little by little while also working on freelance illustrations. With her first novel, An Alpha's Blood, Tori dives headfirst into the fantasy realm.

When Tori is not writing, she can be found illustrating, reading, listening to music and going to concerts, watching movies, playing video games, at Pilates or spending time with friends and family. She resides in Tennessee with her husband and two cats, Loki and Mew.

Connect with Tori on Instagram at:
tori.king_creative.art

ALSO AVAILABLE FROM

wordcrafts press

Furious
by Aaron Shaver

The Scavengers
by Mike Parker

Gretchen and the Bear
Carrie Ann Noble

Shadows of the Past
Luther Salyers

www.wordcrafts.net

www.ingramcontent.com/pod-product-compliance
Lightning Source LLC
Chambersburg PA
CBHW061345310726
48974CB00001B/206